PHANTOM LOVERS
Two Novellas

Pushkin Medal Winner
Achala Moulik

NIYOGI
BOOKS

Published by
NIYOGI BOOKS
Block D, Building No. 77,
Okhla Industrial Area, Phase-I,
New Delhi-110 020, INDIA
Tel: 91-11-26816301, 26818960
Email: niyogibooks@gmail.com
Website: www.niyogibooksindia.com

Text © Achala Moulik

Editor: K.E. Priyamvada
Design: Nadeem Ahmed
Cover Design: Ramdas Lal

ISBN: 978-81-964053-3-5
Publication: 2023

Printed at Niyogi Offset Pvt. Ltd., New Delhi, India

Contents

I With Fate Conspire   4-149

II Wait!   150-382

Acknowledgements   383

I

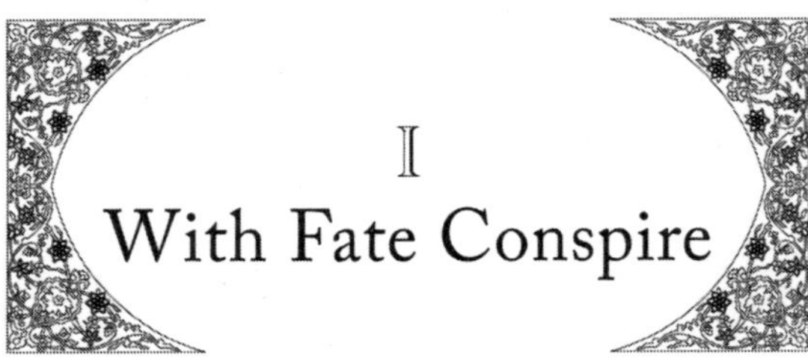

With Fate Conspire

To the memory of
Aloka Moulik,
who inspired this story

***

'Ah love! Could thou and I with Fate conspire,
To grasp this sorry Scheme of Things entire!
Would not we shatter it to bits–and then
Re-mould it nearer to the Heart's Desire!'
—Quatrain 73 of the *Rubaiyat of Omar Khayyam*

***

Author's Note

In his dance drama *Shapmochan (Effacing the Curse)*, Rabindranath Tagore narrated how two celestial lovers, Madhusri and Sourasen, were banished from heaven by a god's decree due to a musical lapse. They were sent to earth, where 'pain is inflicted and pain is received'. Born as mortals and separated by the god's curse they are reunited by the power of human love. In this present story, two mortals—Julian and Radha—find love on earth, but are separated by a bloody Mutiny that shook India and made foes of erstwhile friends, and enemies of lovers. They meet again beyond the boundaries of life and death and across strange frontiers of time.

With Fate Conspire

Julian Ruthven and Radha Chowdhury: *Calcutta, 1855* — 9

Idyll of the First Spring — 34

The Indian Mutiny: *1857* — 39

Between Two Worlds: *Delhi, 1858* — 48

When You and I behind the Veil are Passed… — 53

The First Day of Spring: *London, March, 1961* — 58

Vernal Days — 68

Rough Winds do Shake the Darling Buds of May — 85

In Search of Laura and Petrarca — 91

Torrents of Spring — 104

End of an Era — 113

Mirage — 119

Ah my Beloved, Fill the Cup that Clears Today of Past Regrets and Future Fears — 127

Things Fall Apart — 133

And in thy Joyous Errand Reach the Spot Where I Made one Turn Down an Empty Glass — 138

Tryst by a Sacred River—Once More — 139

Julian Ruthven and
Radha Chowdhury
Calcutta, 1855

The Scottish Ruthven family had struck roots in India in the mid-1700s when Alexander Ruthven, a penurious, barely educated youth, had come to work as a clerk in the notorious East India Company. Like many Scotsmen he had fled the vengeance of the British-Hanoverian King, George II, who had massacred Scottish rebels at the Battle of Culloden. Ironically, the battle that had destroyed his family had paved the way for young Alexander to pursue a splendid career in grand larceny and betrayals. Another battle—Plassey—brought him into contact with a young Muslim woman who was a cousin of Siraj-ud-Daulah, the Nawab of Bengal. To secure protection from the East India Company, she offered Ruthven marriage and funds to become an independent merchant. He accepted her offer, took her guidance in regal skulduggery, begot on her five Scottish-Indian progeny, and ran through *nautch* girls and European adventuresses. In a decade he had become a 'Nabob' with a mansion in Calcutta's Alipur Road, a villa at

Garden Reach, and acquired a *jagir* (revenue from an estate) in Rajasthan, by training a Rajput chief's army.

Alexander had a son, Charles Edward, by his Scottish wife; the son was the father's opposite. Charles won his spurs while serving under Wellington in Spain and at Waterloo. Thereafter he married Lady Eleanor, daughter of an Earl. He did not wish to be associated with his infamous father. But when Alexander Ruthven died, leaving a vast fortune, Charles Edward's mother Georgina prevailed upon him to go to India and claim his inheritance. Eleanor and he arrived in Calcutta in 1828.

Charles Edward came to continue his father's numerous commercial ventures, started a joint stock company and purchased an Indiaman ship for trading between India and Britain. But these activities soon wearied him as he was drawn to the intellectual ambience around him.

The Indian Renaissance had begun flowering on the banks of the Ganges. Under the guidance and encouragement of Warren Hastings, Governor General of Bengal, Sir William Jones, Nathaniel Halhed and Charles Wilkins began exploring and reviving the forgotten grandeur of Indian civilization. The newly established Asiatic Society became the repository of ancient texts and documents. They made momentous civilizational discoveries about India, which became known to European scholars. In the 1820s the Governor-General of India, Lord William Bentinck, sought to introduce social reforms.

He was aided by the Bengali merchant-prince Dwarkanath Tagore and social reformer Raja Ram Mohan Roy. This renaissance would reach its spiritual apogee with Ramakrishna Paramahamsa, the reformist missionary Vivekanand, and the creative polymath Rabindranth Tagore. The Chowdhury family of Mayurganj were part of this cultural and political awakening.

Paradoxically, accompanying this British-inspired Indian renaissance was a swift expansion of the British-Indian Empire. There were Indian collaborators—educated youths who were trained for the civil service with British counterparts at Haileybury. Rajas and Nawabs surrendered their pride for plump privy purses. In return they were permitted to impoverish their subjects. Fed on Indian raw material, enriched by revenues from Indian princes, landlords and peasants, the Industrial Revolution gained momentum in Britain. By 1857 Britain's empire extended from London to Hong Kong, an empire as grand as Rome's had been.

Pax Britannica bestowed a semblance of law and order to India. Three great universities were established in Presidency towns, where young Indians studied science, medicine and engineering along with Western literature and philosophy. While visionary Orientalists like Sir William Jones made Indian civilization known to Europe, the West simultaneously opened its doors to Indians for mutual enrichment. In time, dedicated Britons framed the Indian Penal Code, Evidence Act, Codes of Civil and Criminal Procedures and laws on revenue and administration. They established the Archaeological Survey of India, the Indian Museum and the Imperial Library.

The Ruthvens and Chowdhurys established their renaissance relations in the early 19th century. Charles and Brajesh became friends and formed the 'Indian Renaissance circle' comprising Lord Bentinck, Raja Ram Mohan Roy, Prince Dwarakanth Tagore, Ishwar Chandra Vidyasagar, Henry Derozio and Bankim Chandra Chatterjee. Brajesh Chowdhury tried to forget that Charles Ruthven's father had seized lands from his father at Mayurganj during the Sanyasi Rebellion in the 1770s.

Their sons—Dilip and Julian—studied together at Oxford University. Dilip was one of the first Indians to study at this hallowed institution. Their fathers' friendship strengthened their bonds. When revolutions erupted all over Europe in 1848, the two young men discussed the implications for India.

'Britain supports Italians, Greeks, and Hungarians in their demand for freedom,' Dilip protested to Julian. 'Would they be sympathetic if Indians demanded freedom from British rule?'

'No! The East India Company is despoiling India—peasants and princes alike. The decadent rajas and nawabs have accepted British rule. And India has no leaders like Cavour or Kossuth.'

'Will we be forever under foreign rule?' Dilip asked him impatiently.

Lowering his voice, Julian said, 'India needs an army of trained rebels and a leader to throw off the foreign yoke. But for that Indians must enter the modern age through education and science.' He smiled at his friend. 'Who knows? One day men like you could lead a revolt.'

'Are you an agent provocateur, Julian?' Dilip asked sharply.

Julian laughed. 'No, I have been inspired by the events of this year in Europe. I enjoyed seeing the autocrats of Europe challenged by revolutionaries.'

After completing their studies, Julian Ruthven and Dilip Chowdhury returned to India in 1855. Both vowed to work for the modernization of India. Dilip's sister, Radha Chowdhury had also accompanied him on educational trips to England.

Julian's brush with authorities began on the India-bound ship *H.M.S Bentinck* when he rebuked a missionary. 'If you wish to succeed in India, Reverend Saheb, you would do well to remember that you are dealing with a civilization of grandeur and complexity, a race that is fierce in their devotions and unpredictable in their actions.. Do not offend their souls if you wish to win them for Christ.'

Charles Edward Ruthven tried to make a merchant prince out of his heir—to no avail. Julian had caught the contagion of the European Enlightenment and the Indian Renaissance. After graduating from Oxford, he had refused to go on the customary Grand European Tour, or roister in country houses, or attend the Season in London, or conduct discreet affairs as befits young aristocrats. Instead, he applied for the post of a civil servant in the East India Company. Charles Edward was furious. Why should a young man of assured wealth and position wish to work as a civil servant in the notorious Company Bahadur? Reports of Julian's fascination for Indian civilization and irreverent observations on British rule disquieted the newly knighted Sir Charles Ruthven.

At Ruthven House in Alipur Road, there were a few days of what Julian called 'social fripperies' and discreet enquiries about Julian's plans by prospective in-laws who came to meet the wayward heir to a handsome fortune. Sir Charles Ruthven and Lady Eleanor encouraged these meetings in the hope that their restless son would settle down with a demure English maiden to a life expected of an upper-class Englishman in India.

'I should have been born earlier,' Julian announced at a dinner party at Ruthven House. 'How I would have loved to study Sanskrit with Sir William Jones at Krishnanagar! To translate the *Vedas* and Kalidasa and become a famed Orientalist!' Normally, such declarations would have invited a stony silence but no one reacted because Sir Charles was a member of the Governor-General's Council and his devotion to Julian was well known. Julian's sister smiled in support of her brother's foibles. The conversation was resumed on British policy and Lord Canning's efforts to deal with dissent among the native princes.

'India cannot be ruled by collaboration of the Company Bahadur with decadent rajas and nawabs,' Julian observed. 'We need the cooperation of the people.'

A senior East India Company official asked angrily, 'People? The ignorant, superstitious hordes?'

'Your attitude, sir, will invite a revolt,' Julian retorted.

The dinner proceeded with portents of gloom.

Soon after, Julian took charge in Bishnupur sub-division, not far from the city of Nabadwip, where the mystic and reformer Shri Chaitanya had preached the brotherhood of man four centuries before the French Revolution.

Across the eternal river Ganga was the Chowdhury estate of Mayurganj, where the family had lived for centuries. They claimed descent from the seven Brahmins of Kannauj who had come to Bengal at the invitation of a Pala king in the eighth century. Their ancestors had witnessed the vicissitudes of Indian history—the rule of the imperial Guptas, silver age of Sanskrit literature, revival of Hindu monotheism by Shankaracharya to counter the Buddhist challenge to Brahminism. Accompanying this was burgeoning trade with East Asia. Ships with merchandise and messages of Hinduism and Buddhism sailed from Tamralipta to Thailand, Cambodia, Laos, Vietnam, T'ang China, Korea and Japan, where temples were built to honour new divinities.

But the splendid world of Indica Magna was nearing its end. Galloping horses and sword brandishing invaders from Central Asia reached Bengal in the 13th century. Bhaktiar Khilji invaded the fertile kingdom of Lakshman Sena, who fled to eastern Bengal, where the network of rivers halted the Muslim advance. But other armies soon followed. Eventually, the Bengal Sultanate became a powerful force. During the reign of Emperor Akbar in the 16th century, Bengal was the richest province of the Mughal Empire. As the Mughal Empire disintegrated, Murshid Ali Khan established a powerful kingdom, which prospered until the Bengali Hindus joined hands with Robert Clive to depose Nawab Siraj-ud-Daula to end Muslim rule in Bengal. They did not know they had mounted a tiger which would build an empire that would humble and impoverish India for two centuries.

Alexander Ruthven belonged to the galaxy of commercial buccaneers who had plundered India. From being an impoverished fugitive from British justice, he became a 'semi-Oriental potentate'. His son Charles Edward was caught in a dilemma between his inheritance and his desire for reforms. Charles' son Julian deplored British rule. He was appalled by the situation in rural Bengal. He toured his bailiwick extensively, observing the conduct of the *mustagirs,* revenue officials, who went from one village to another to collect taxes. Julian stopped in each village to inspect its fields, irrigation, and yield of crops.

Summoning the peasants, he sat in the village square under spreading banyan trees and coaxed them to talk. A Magistrate Saheb who behaved like this was a phenomenon, particularly one with the name of Ruthven. They recalled tales of another flame-haired Ruthven who had despoiled Bishnupur 80 years ago. Intrigued and sceptical, they sat around Julian, wondering what motive lay behind his benevolence.

'The *mustagir* collects too much rent from you,' Julian declared, hoping to provoke them.

Paan-blackened teeth were bared in smiles and grizzled old heads were scratched. But they did not confirm the allegation. The Magistrate Saheb was a remote boon, whereas the *mustagir* was a ubiquitous curse.

Then an angry young man spoke. 'Yes, Saheb, our thin shoulders carry the fat bailiff, the fatter *zamindar*, and then the Company's weight. Do you wonder why we are bent and bow-legged?'

The words were said in mocking jest but Julian Ruthven felt anger tighten his chest. He replied, 'In the final analysis the Company is perpetrating this through Cornwallis's nefarious Permanent Settlement.'

Astonished and emboldened, one farmer said, 'Look at our lands! We hardly have enough water for our little canals. If we cut a tiny one from the river, the *mustagir* raises the rent. With the enhanced amount he builds another house and the *zamindar* goes to Calcutta to squander on fancy women. Every drop of our blood and sweat enriches them.'

'Why do you not go to the mofussil court in appeal?' Julian asked.

'Cursed destiny!' cried another farmer, slapping his forehead as if fate was etched on that furrowed brow. 'We cannot get redressal in any court! What do we know of laws? And who will listen? One farmer in a neighbouring village went in appeal against enhanced taxes before the mofussil court. The *mustagir* and his thugs came at night and burned the farmer's hut and grains. No, Magistrate Saheb, there is no justice for Indians in British courts!'

With deepening gloom Julian gazed around the village scene. Clusters of thatched huts stood huddled together. Clumps of bamboo, mango, and jackfruit grew around them. The fields were fallow, awaiting rain. Villagers ate coarse rice with green chillies and salt. There was no surplus money to buy seeds, or implements or clothes. Even the seed-grains were eaten in a lean year.

'A century of Company rule,' mused an angry Julian, 'has impoverished this once-rich province. And we alien marauders heap scorn on the hapless people!'

He often accepted the villagers' hospitality and stayed in the villages at night—to see cattle return in the 'cow-dust hour', the dust from their hooves mingling with wood-smoke, casting a pall over trees and fields. Laden with water pots, women hurried home, naked little boys in tow. The brief dusk dissolved into night, a time for peace—or was it oblivion from an endless and accursed fate? As a flute piped in the darkness in immemorial echo of Lord Krishna, a thin reedy voice invoked the god in tender homage, with a song by Saint Chaitanya. Gazing at the star-embroidered sky, Julian planned future action.

Julian set himself on a collision course with the local *zamindar* and his acolytes. Scrutinizing land records and assessment of crops and finding the taxes exorbitant, he ordered revision and then remission. 'Assessment of yield of grains should determine the quantum of taxes. The *zamindar* and *mustagir* cannot impoverish tillers of the land.'

Julian's opposition to the Company's arbitrary methods and exorbitant taxation infuriated the Company officials at Writers Building in Calcutta. Many British officials depended on *zamindar*s for their luxuries. The powerful officials decided to teach the rebellious Julian Ruthven a lesson; they transferred Julian from Bishnupur to parched Purulia. Julian took leave in protest.

His lineage protected him from dismissal, so he had to be cajoled into submission. But submission was not on the rebellious Julian's agenda. He intended to fight for justice. Sir Charles and Lady Eleanor felt pride for Julian's idealism and concern for his insubordination.

He was temporarily diverted from this crusade by the attraction of the Chowdhury mansion where the gifted family lived. 'There is a Renaissance atmosphere here,' Julian confided to his sister Isabel. 'Everything is discussed here from land reforms to Franz Lizst. Everyone is charged with ideas and sentiments.'

'Like Cavendish House?' Isabel asked archly. She knew the real reason for his going there often.

Julian responded, 'Indeed! Dilip and I discuss the revolutions of 1848 and political ideas which will one day change the world.'

The young men went further. They wondered when India would aspire for freedom, as Italy, Poland and Serbia were doing. Greece had already expelled Ottoman rule.

Dilip was particularly agitated over this. 'How are we different from these people? Have we not experienced the same chaos and upheavals, invasions and plunder? Have we not the same proud past? Why should we be ruled by another nation?'

Julian was disquieted by Dilip's impatience. 'The liberal traditions of England will prepare India for her liberation. Everything, even freedom, needs preparation.'

Dilip spoke angrily. 'A revolution is like the Ganges in full spate. There is no preparation. It sweeps everything from its path.'

Discussions were followed by stimulating dinners, where the luminaries of Calcutta graced Brajesh Chowdhury's generous table. Here the aristocratic Governor-General conversed with the patrician Tagores and Roys. Erudition and wit enlivened the evenings. Julian listened, exhilarated. 'We are present at the creation of a new age,' he told Dilip.

'To be alive in this dawn is very heaven,' Dilip murmured.

After dinner the guests strolled in the lamplit gardens or sat on the terrace while music emanated from a room within the house. Julian waited on the terrace to see the real reason for his frequent visits.

Nineteen-year-old Radha Chowdhury had left the seclusion of the *antar-mahal* (ladies' apartments), to appear before the world.

Julian had seen Radha as a sad child weaving jasmine garlands for her dying mother, as a shy girl discovering England with wonder-filled eyes. And now she was a comely young woman who sang *ragas*, played Chopin *études* on the piano, laughed behind latticed windows, and whose dancing eyes quickened his heartbeat. After returning from Oxford, he saw her at the Chowdhurys' roof garden one spring morning when she was reciting the hymn to the Sun God:

> *Seven mares draw you, oh Lord,*
> *In your chariot, oh Sun divine,*
> *Oh radiant one, with hair aflame,*
> *Radiant above the world of men.*

'Beware, fair maiden,' he had said. 'The Sun God often comes down to seduce his devotees. Remember the story of Kunti?'

Radha had turned to see Julian watching her with a smile. Sunlight glinted on his auburn hair and sparkled in his sky-coloured eyes.

'Why, you look like the Sun God,' she murmured, and then blushed at her audacity.

Glancing at her graceful figure and clouds of black hair, Julian replied, 'I have no chariot or seven horses to take you into the kingdom of clouds.'

Smiling, Radha replied, 'You are an accomplished flirt.'

He caught one slender brown hand. 'I have come to your father's house many times hoping to see the disembodied being who sings and laughs. Now that I have seen you, I wonder how I shall return to earth.'

Radha laughed. 'Why, but in your chariot, Mr Ruthven!'

'Come then in my *pakshiraj*,' Julian replied. 'It waits outside.'

Radha leaned over the balustrade. 'Will your splendid *pakshiraj* fly over clouds and take me to see strange new lands?'

Julian had regarded her intently. She was different from the married women he flirted with at Government House parties, the calculating members of the 'fishing fleet,' and Isabel's simpering debutante friends.

They met often after that, but always in the company of others. Radha accompanied her brother Dilip and Julian when they sailed on the Chowdhury's barge, or rode with them to the Botanical Garden, or met at each other's houses. No one seemed to notice their mutual enchantment until a reception at the Chowdhury mansion.

One autumn evening in 1856, the baroque-styled Chowdhury mansion at Belgachia was illumined by a thousand lamps to celebrate Diwali, the festival of lights. Nature contributed to the splendour by offering a profusion of flowers whose fragrance blended with the cool breeze. Inside the opulent reception hall, carpets had been rolled away from veined marble floors for dancing. At one corner a band of Anglo-Indian musicians played Strauss waltzes. In the adjoining hall, a sumptuous feast had been laid. Barefooted turbaned attendants brought delicacies on silver trays for the elite guests. They were members of the landed gentry of Bengal, officials of the East India Company, military officers, rich entrepreneurs of many races: Armenian, Jewish, British, Dutch, Portuguese, and Indians. Renowned scholars from Europe and their Indian counterparts conversed in the terraced garden.

Lord Canning had condescended to come. He felt comfortable with this gracious 'Hindu gentleman' of distinguished lineage, who believed in the benefits of British rule. Members of Government House stood stiffly in silence, listening to the Governor-General.

Brajesh Chowdhury was progressive, but he would not permit Radha to participate in the dancing. No male hands must touch her until marriage. So, an impatient Radha stood on the gallery above, watching satin crinolines swaying to the cadence of waltzes.

'How unfair,' she protested to her governess, Miss Delphinia Evans. 'Why am I not permitted to dance?'

'Silly, if you ask me,' Miss Evans retorted. 'I don't hold with such rigid Hindu customs.'

Wistfully Radha watched Julian resplendent in evening attire. She thought to herself, 'Let me pretend for one night. Let me imagine myself in his arms.' She closed her eyes and began to turn and whirl in tune to the music. Minutes passed. The music rose to a crescendo and stopped. Radha too stopped and opened her eyes to find Julian Ruthven standing before her. Breathless, she glanced around nervously. Miss Evans had vanished.

He bowed, stretched out both hands and asked quietly, 'May I have the honour?'

Radha gazed at the bronzed face and the eyes that regarded her tenderly. 'I dare not,' she whispered. 'Father…has forbidden me.'

'We shall see,' he replied. Taking her hand, he led her down the curving staircase and entered the hall where a waltz was in progress.

An astounded audience watched in silence as Julian led her to the floor and began guiding her over the marble floor to the tune of '*Tales from the Vienna Woods*'. They danced, eyes resting on each other, exhilarated by a mutual discovery. When the music stopped, Julian bowed, released a breathless Radha, and murmured, 'You see, we dared'.

Disregarding the astonishment of the guests, Julian Ruthven led Radha Chowdhury to the terrace. Vigilant eyes watched their progress, but no one summoned courage to admonish the defiant Julian and the radiant Radha. Undeterred by Brajesh Chowdhury's disapproval and his parents' anxiety, Julian continued to see Radha at the Chowdhury mansion, or at the Maidan where they kept their assignations on the pretence of horse-riding or at the Ruthven villa at Garden Reach, where Dilip Chowdhury and Isabel Ruthven acted as chaperones. Dilip and Isabel were also drawn together by similar ideals. Julian and Radha sat conversing for hours by the riverside, while fisherfolk sang *bhatiali* or river songs. It seemed as if Fate conspired to make them happy, as if they were part of the timeless scene and a fragment of eternity. There were no thoughts of the past or the future—but only of the blissful moment.

'We must make plans for the future,' Julian told Radha.

Plans had already been made by the Ruthvens and Chowdhurys to thwart their defiant progeny. Julian was posted as magistrate to a dreary district on the Bihar border. On receiving the official order, he burst into the library where his parents waited for the storm to break.

'This is absurd!' Julian exploded.

Sir Charles heard a past echo of his father banishing his half-Muslim son for misdemeanour. And Charles was now doing the same to his son, not in anger but out of concern.

'There are rumours of an uprising…they want an able officer there. Lord Canning has recommended your name,' Sir Charles replied sternly.

'Nonsense!' Julian stormed. 'His Lordship cares tuppence for me! I go as a part of a conspiracy to separate me from the young lady I wish to marry!'

Charles Ruthven rose in anger but Lady Eleanor stood between husband and son.

'Please,' she whispered to Charles. 'Please let me explain'. Turning to a furious Julian, she said gently, 'Darling, listen to me. You cannot marry Radha. She is a high-born Hindu and would be ostracized by her people if she married you. You too would be an outcaste in your world.'

'Damn her people and damn mine!' Julian shouted. 'We have no need of anyone but ourselves!'

Timidly, Lady Eleanor took his hand and murmured, 'Radha has been betrothed to a *zamindar* and will be married shortly.'

Snatching his hand from hers, Julian regarded his parents with blazing eyes, then flew down the stairs to the portico where his chestnut horse was impatiently pawing the ground. Barefooted, dressed in shirtsleeves and breeches, he mounted his horse and galloped towards Belgachia, stopping at a Kali temple to obtain *sindoor* (vermilion powder). As he strode through the main door of the Chowdhury mansion, household retainers stared at him in bewilderment. He asked them the whereabouts of Radha.

One retainer muttered, 'She is sitting by the river-side temple, Julian Saheb'.

Julian walked swiftly towards the river bank where Radha sat weeping with head bent over her knees. Hearing footsteps over crackling twigs, she raised her head and saw him.

Grim faced, he asked harshly, 'Is it true? Are you marrying some *zamindar*? How can you do such a thing?'

'I have no choice but to obey Father!' she cried.

'Your life is your own! We will build our own paradise. I shall protect you with my life's blood. Are you afraid, Radha?'

'I am afraid of the unknown,' she whispered. 'I am afraid of what they could do to us.'

Julian drew her close. 'Radha, you will not marry the *zamindar* or anyone else. Do you understand? You will marry me!' He brought out the tiny jar of vermilion powder. Swiftly, before she could move, he inscribed a *bindi* on her forehead and drew a red line in the parting of her hair.

Trembling, Radha whispered, 'Do you know what you've done?'

Julian nodded. 'I have done what a Hindu husband does—puts vermilion on his wife's forehead. You are bound to me now by the sacred vermilion of the Kali temple. The sun, sky, river, wind and earth are witnesses to our betrothal. Tell your family that they cannot break our bonds. I shall come soon to take you away.'

'They might separate us even now.'

'Tell them that if they try, I shall kill them in cold blood. The Ruthvens have done such deeds in the past.' Now they both laughed and walked back to the house. 'We must escape before they make another ruse,' Julian said.

Radha replied, 'I cannot offend my father. Can we not get his blessings?'

The storm that greeted Julian's proposal to marry Radha matched the *kalbaisakhi* storm raging outside. Brajesh Chowdhury declared it was pure madness. The Ruthvens had already pronounced such a union ruinous to Julian's career.

'Radha will marry a man of impeccable lineage chosen for her,' Brajesh declared with finality. 'Julian, forget Radha and marry a woman of your own world.'

Though in a dire predicament, Dilip Chowdhury decided to help his sister and his friend. He informed them that Brajesh was leaving for Calcutta to arrange Radha's wedding at their Belgachia mansion. 'Leave when he is away. I cannot hold things together much longer.'

Julian sent a telegram to his district office that he would be arriving in four days to take charge. He stayed for a day in a mud and thatch-roofed house of a trusted revenue clerk and returned when Brajesh Chowdhury left for Calcutta.

That morning dark clouds rushed in from the Bay of Bengal, bringing rain and wind to swell the river and drench the parched earth. The wind tore thatched roofs of huts from bamboo frames and flung them across the leaden sky. Mangoes and jackfruits were hurled to the ground. The high iron gates of the Chowdury estate swayed in the frenzied wind. Secret preparations began for the wedding. No *dhols* were beaten, no conch-shells were blown, and no chatelaine performed the welcoming ceremony of *arati* with oil lamps and flowers. Dilip received Julian in the ornate hall. 'Everything is in readiness at the temple,' he said.

A stormy dusk encircled the temple of Lord Shiva. A Brahmin priest lit a 108 lamps before the shrine of Shiva the Creator and his consort Durga. Jasmines and hibiscus were heaped on a gold plate and the ceremonial fire burnt with sandalwood logs, wafting fragrant smoke around the temple.

Julian Ruthven entered, dressed in *dhoti* and shirt. Radha was dressed in a bridal sari and jewellery made in anticipation of a different wedding. Her long hair was braided with jasmine buds. They sat across each other while the priest murmured incantations and threw ladles of butter onto the ceremonial fire. Dilip sat beside his sister, to perform *kanyadaan* (giving away the bride). From his shirt pocket Julian drew out an emerald solitaire he had ordered earlier and slid it on the ring finger of Radha's left hand. The solitaire was supported by two gold letters—J and R. The chanting of Vedic *mantras* was accompanied by the roaring wind. The priest was surprised to hear Julian fluently repeating the Sanskrit *shlokas*, which invoked the five elements to bear witness. Their union was sealed when they walked seven times around the sacred fire. Only Yama, the lord of death, could sever their bond in this life.

As thunder boomed outside, the troubled priest muttered, 'This is the auspicious *godhuli lagna,* the cow-dust hour. There should be no storms.'

Looking at the tempest with foreboding, Dilip said, 'Julian and Radha, the *bajra* (houseboat) is ready to take you. Retainers have packed clothes and other necessities in the boat.' Dilip paused and told Julian in an unsteady voice, 'Take care of my sister. She has been a joy to all of us.' Looking sombrely at Dilip, Julian murmured, 'I will never fail her'.

Radha bent down to do *pronam* (touching the feet in homage) to her older brother. The two men embraced each other. Then Dilip bade them farewell.

The couple entered the brightly lit *bajra* swaying by the bank. Radha's old nurse, Mukta, followed; two retainers drew up the plank. A pensive Dilip stood on the shore. Radha and Julian watched Dilip and the temple vanish in darkness. The once benign river tore at the fertile banks. A monsoon storm shortly hit the *bajra*, which began swaying. The table was laid, candles were lit; food cooked in the nearby kitchen was served in the main cabin. Julian and Radha sat opposite each other, happy but pensive, as they toyed with the food. Mukta watched them from a distance, staring at the tall flame-haired Angrez saheb. She wondered how her 'little mother' was going to live with the foreigner. The bride and bridegroom went to the jasmine-scented lamplit cabin. They lay awake on the flower decked bed as the *bajra* rolled and pitched on the churning water. The howling wind drew them close. When the violet light of a monsoon dawn broke, they saw the barge sailing on the broad sweep of the river Ganga, towards the district headquarters where Julian was posted.

A cluster of Indian officials and British soldiers waited on the banks of the riverside town to receive the new District Magistrate. They were unprepared for the sight of a comely, jewelled, sari-clad Indian woman, whom he helped to alight from the barge. In silence they brought the carriage forward, which Julian and Radha boarded. The puzzled army officer, soldiers and clerks followed on horse-back to the district headquarters.

The European populace consisting of the commanding officer of a native regiment, garrison and civil engineers, district surgeon, and the district police officer and their wives were curious about the new magistrate and his Indian wife. The men soon overcame their reservation in admiration of Radha's grace and poise. If they had expected a gorgeous nautch girl they were surprised to find a refined woman who transformed the district magistrate's austere bungalow into a comfortable home, with furniture, curtains and porcelain gifted by Dilip.

The women were less enthusiastic, seeing in Radha Ruthven a threat to their own position. If their menfolk felt prey to 'these exotic, native women,' what would happen to those young hopefuls who came in the 'fishing fleet' to marry British soldiers, traders and administrators?

Julian assiduously performed his duties as district magistrate. Radha felt lonely; she did not enjoy the society of the memsahibs, who did not conceal their resentment. Nor could she seek the company of Indian women from the landed class, who regarded her as a renegade. But the lovers remained cocooned in their private idyll as they lived rapturous days in the dreary district.

Julian liked the rambling river-side bungalow with its gardens. Galloping his horse on the last stretch of the road from District Office to home, he would gently wave away the guards and enter to watch Radha lighting *puja* lamps. Sensing his presence, she would turn and enter into his outstretched arms until Mukta announced the serving of tea. While he read dispatches and wrote orders, she read or played the sitar on the terrace. Sometimes they discussed Sanskrit literature; Kalidasa's *Meghdoot* and Banabhatta's *Kadambari,* with its tangled tales of passion, death, and reincarnation.

'An ancestor came from Kannauj in the eighth century. He knew Pundit Banabhatta who is revered as semi-divine in our family,' Radha told Julian who agreed.

'Indeed, there is no one his equal in medieval European literature—except Dante.'

After dinner they sat in the garden, watching clouds fly over the river as thunder boomed and rattled windows. They discovered one another with joy and wonder. Each moment was a celebration of life.

'Will it be always like this?' Radha asked Julian one night.

'I hope not. Let us soon become a sedate couple and move into old age—lest the gods become jealous of our happiness.'

Idyll of the First Spring

In early 1857, Jeremy Latimer, a cousin posted in the East India Company Army, came to visit the Ruthvens in Calcutta. He spoke about his military adventures in Punjab.

'Taught the Sikh fellows the meaning of obedience,' he said, slicing a papaya with needless force. Isabel noted that Latimer enjoyed cutting everything.

'Caught a rebel Sikh. Do you know what I did, Julian old chap?'

Julian looked away at the garden.

Not discouraged, Major Latimer sat back with a sigh of pleasure. 'Cut him in half from skull to crotch as I rode past on my stallion.' His laugh was malevolent. 'Better than pig sticking, if you ask me.'

A stunned silence followed. Julian muttered icily, 'You are a fiend'.

Isabel's cheeks paled under the tan. Radha stared at the bowl of jasmines. 'I see blood on the flowers,' she murmured.

Undeterred, Latimer resumed, 'This Sikh had fought against us with the Afghans. I recognized him at once. I ordered him to be tied to the mouth of cannons and watched him fly. What a scattering of offal there was!'

Radha closed her eyes in horror.

Julian rose, flushed with rage. 'That was vile of you! I am amazed you confess to it. And that too before Radha and Isabel!'

'Ha!' Latimer exclaimed, his hungry eyes on Isabel. 'Ruthven women are resilient, Julian old chap. They can cope with blood, like our grandmother Georgina.'

Julian's jaws tightened. 'You will atone for this with blood. What is so terrible is that your hatred of Indians will destroy us.'

Radha rose and ran down the shallow flight of steps to the lawn and the lotus pond, where a washer-woman was singing.

> *'What a vision of sweetness*
> *did I see in my lord Krishna*
> *as I fetched water from the Jamuna*
> *What kindness was there*
> *in my dark lord.'*

Radha sat beside her, trying to control rasping sobs.

The alarmed woman glanced at her. 'Why do you weep, *bahu-ma*?' she asked.

Fearfully, Radha whispered, 'What a terrible vision I see before our sacred Jamuna!'

A few days later, Julian, Radha, and Isabel set off for Lucknow—ostensibly for a brief holiday—but in fact Julian had been ordered by the Governor-General to see what was happening in Avadh, where Nawab Wajid Ali Shah was playing inscrutable games.

A Company official showed them around the city. 'Lucknow has become a city of luxury, of glittering palaces and parks where exotic animals are caged. The river Gomati is illumined by barges at night and every day is a festival with processions by day and fireworks by night. The bordellos are the most exotic in the world. Every vice can be sampled in return for high payment. The Nawabs of Avadh have been servile before the Company. The present Nawab has paid them high taxes and lends himself to extortion by unscrupulous Residents.'

'We hear so much about the present Nawab, Wajid Ali. What is he like?' Julian asked.

Smiling, the Company official asked, 'Would you like to meet him?'

Julian assented.

The Nawab was all courtesy to Julian and showered the two women with extravagant Persian couplets. Then he summoned his boon companions—fiddlers, buffoons and dancers. The Nawab executed a few dance steps and sang in an untrained voice. Radha and Isabel smiled and clapped but were immediately sobered by Julian's grim expression. When the audience was over, the Nawab summoned a retainer, who brought him a parcel.

For you, Ruthven saheb. I understand you know Farsi. This is a manuscript copy of Firdausi's *Shah Namah.* It was brought from Persia by Badshah Humayun.'

Julian gazed at the brittle pages of exquisite calligraphy but shook his head. 'How can I take this, Your Majesty? This is priceless.'

Wajid Ali sighed and shook his head. 'It will soon be stolen by greedy Company officers.' He paused, glanced around and whispered, 'This Resident fellow, Jackson, is an insatiable thief. Please take it, Ruthven saheb. When Avadh is swallowed up in the Company's domain, remember me, Wajid Ali, whose only sin was love of poetry and music.' The Nawab wiped away his tears with a plump, bejewelled hand. Julian bowed and accepted the Nastaliq manuscript.

The three Ruthvens went for a sail on a gilded barge that night.

'Avadh,' Radha mused sadly, 'the ancient Ayodhya of the *Ramayana,* the glory of Muslim culture, how sadly has it fallen!'

Julian spoke bitterly. 'Avadh is ready for dissolution. Wajid Ali lives on borrowed time. Sleeman has sent a report to the Governor General. Sati, infanticide, slave trade—everything is going on here. The Company extorts from the Nawab, who in turn bleeds his peasantry.'

'Is there no remedy?' Radha asked anxiously.

'Some things have no remedies. Avadh is ready for the final dance of death. Lord Canning's men will soon be here.'

From Lucknow they went to Deogarh. Julian wanted Radha to see where his grandfather Alexander Ruthven had received a *jagir* from the Raja, in return for training the latter's army. He had built a Scottish-style castle where his progeny by his first wife, Shirin Begum, now lived. Afraz Ruthven, the Muslim grandson of Alexander Ruthven, met his English cousins with a mocking courtesy that barely concealed antagonism. After a lavish dinner he took them to see the view from the ramparts. A high wind sang around the towers of Deogarh as the group stood surveying the grey-pink hills in coral twilight. Below was a garden where Alexander's Begum and their progeny were buried. Staring below and shivering, Radha murmured, 'Why do I feel a sense of impending peril?'

Julian held her hand and said gently, 'This wild and melancholy place is not conducive for a genial holiday. Let us return to our house on the bend of the Ganges.'

The Indian Mutiny
1857

An air of deceptive calm hung over the Bengal Presidency in April 1857. Julian Ruthven felt the vibrations rumble like distant drums. But he refused to acknowledge the implications. Once they visited their families in Calcutta. The Ruthvens had reconciled themselves to Julian's marriage to Radha. The Chowdhurys concealed their apprehensions about Radha's future. They discussed the disbandment of the 34th Native Infantry, which was intended to discourage other regiments that nursed plans of mutiny.

Dilip regarded his British brother-in-law gravely. 'It is not a mutiny when a people rise against their oppressors. It is a rebellion like that of France in 1789 and England in 1642.'

The *punkha* (fan) bearers slowed their movement and attendants paused in their serving of sherbet. They were keen to glean news and pass it on.

'My dear Dilip,' Julian said sternly, 'when soldiers revolt it is mutiny. When people rise, it is revolution. People as such have not risen. Mangal Pandey and his comrades were soldiers.'

'It will be a rebellion,' a brooding Dilip murmured, staring at the stark landscape outside.

Julian glanced at Dilip with concern. 'Take care not to get involved. It would be a pity if the efforts of your family over a century to modernise India were to be destroyed through your indiscretion. What you say before me will not endanger you, but take care how you express opinions before those who can cause harm.' He paused and added sombrely, 'The price of rebellion is reprisals—to see one's home burnt, one's village erased, one's life cut short. It happened to the Ruthvens after Culloden.'

Dilip smiled sardonically. 'You should then have sympathy for rebels.'

Julian sighed. 'Sympathy should not provoke recklessness.'

'Are there no laws then for the ruled? Or does Pax Britannica stop at Garden Reach? British liberalism and justice is a mirage. But these myths have taken root in our hearts. How will we pluck them out?'

'Do not pluck them out,' Brajesh Chowdhury replied. 'British rule has brought law and order, education and science to this land after seven centuries of Muslim invasions. Don't follow the banner of a decadent Mughal ruler and his motley crowd!'

'I shall join those who seek to free India from the injustices and dishonour of foreign rule,' Dilip retorted.

In the ensuing silence Radha glanced anxiously at her husband and brother, then lifted her eyes to the sky in a silent prayer.

The mutiny of *sipahis* or soldiers of the East India Company began at Barrackpur in Bengal; then it spread across the Gangetic plain with a fury and swiftness that the British Raj never expected. British garrisons at Lucknow and Kanpur were besieged. The titular Mughal emperor awaited the rebel army to arrive in Delhi. British officers, merchants, and their families were killed by the Indians, while Indian mutineers were savagely slaughtered by the British. It was a fearful and turbulent time. Amidst this there were also episodes of kindness and compassion.

Whenever the district officers discussed the mutiny, Julian used the authority of a district magistrate to quell plans of retaliation. 'The mutiny is a military matter and therefore the responsibility of the army. The sepoys have been disgruntled for some time. Company officers have set poor examples of discipline and decorum when they opposed Lord Bentinck's and Lord Dalhousie's efforts to curtail their extravagance. Impecunious boys from Britain coming to India start behaving like nabobs, getting into debts and asking money lenders to reimburse their escapades. But they impose rigorous discipline on the sepoys. Let the army deal with the rebels. We civilians are not involved.'

The commander of the local garrison declared, 'Mutiny is illegal and has to be punished.'

Julian replied coldly, 'Certainly, with military procedure. There have been mutinies in British history. King Charles I was beheaded by his soldiers.'

May passed. The scorching heat interspersed with the cooling nor'westers; hailstorms temporarily moistened the baked earth. Julian went on inspections to nearby sub divisions, afraid to leave his pregnant wife alone. The district officials were on alert as northern India prepared for more violence. It came in early June, first as a whisper and then like a scream of outrage. Julian could not believe the account of the Kanpur massacres.

'It cannot be!' he exclaimed, staring at the commanding officer of the garrison, who was preparing to leave for Lucknow, where East India Company soldiers were urgently required.

The commanding officer said heavily, 'I am afraid it is, sir. We have first-hand reports'. He paused before continuing, 'We are organizing reinforcements to relieve besieged British people in Lucknow. British forces are outnumbered by the native forces. The bulk of the Company army is held up in the Punjab. Civilians have taken up arms in Kanpur. There are hardly any Europeans between Calcutta and Meerut.' The commanding officer looked at Julian with a challenge in his eyes. 'Will you join us, sir?'

Julian Ruthven spoke brusquely. 'I am a civilian magistrate. I am not part of the East Indian Company army.'

The commanding officer rose, hat in hand. 'That is for you to decide.'

Julian inclined his head to acknowledge the officer's salute. Julian sat at his desk for a long time. He did not call for his horse; he walked home through the hot coral-hued dusk, stopping to gaze at the river where fragile fishing boats floated towards the Bay of Bengal. Women drew water in brass pitchers and children frolicked in the cool water. Standing there, he wondered why Indians—who had endured so much suffering and plunder, who accepting their fates, passed from existence to eternity without a cry—why had they now erupted into violence?

Anger simmered within him. 'My parents, Raja Ram Mohan Roy, and Lord Bentinck had sought to better the life of Indians. I returned here to work for India. Am I expected now to take up arms against the people whom I came to serve?' Sadly, Julian walked towards his bungalow surrounded by a cluster of scarlet gulmohur trees. He saw Radha supervising laying of tea in the garden.

Since the mutiny began Radha had noticed his abstraction. An imperceptible veil had fallen between them. Unable to sleep that night, Julian went into the garden and stared at the hot starlit darkness. Hesitantly, Radha joined him. Staring at the river, he said, 'What happened in Meerut and Lucknow has nothing to do with us. Do you understand, Radha?'

'No,' she replied miserably. 'It has everything to do with us. We married because our families were friends, because our fathers believed in a better future for India. But now my people have called war on your people.'

'We married because we cherished the same ideals.The action of a few sepoys and rajas do not alter this. Our bonds transcend all that!'

'I am so afraid for us!' she cried, flinging her arms around him.

Julian drew her close. 'We must not be afraid. We must not allow external events to destroy our happiness. This upheaval will pass. We will have sons and daughters who will embody all that is best in both our civilizations! They will forge a new imperium—as the Romans did—in North Africa, West Asia, and Europe! We will work for and believe in that!'

Julian went through the rituals of his work, hearing civil and criminal cases, receiving petitions and issuing orders and judgements on these matters.

The Superintendent of Police commented openly: 'The detachment of the District Magistrate is shocking. His sympathy is with his wife's people'. But the district surgeon and engineer agreed with Julian that a sepoy's uprising was not a cause for reprisal against hapless Indian civilians. Learning of these comments, Radha stayed at home, afraid to go into town where hostile memsahebs glared at her—'a native woman who has bewitched one of our finest young men'.

What she had secretly feared had now actualized. She, the Indian wife, had become a liability to the English magistrate husband.

In mid-July 1857 Julian heard the news of the massacre of British women and children in Kanpur. It was reported that his sister Isabel, who was visiting friends there, might have been one of those killed. He returned home early that day and told Radha the news. He did not look at her as he said, 'I can no longer remain detached. Isabel may have been killed. I must join the Bengal Army as reinforcements are needed at Lucknow and Allahabad.'

Radha spoke in agitation. 'You said you were not involved, that this was a military matter…that…' When her voice broke, he said gently, 'So I did, my love. But things have changed. Don't you understand? I cannot remain detached when my sister…' Now Julian's voice broke. 'I must avenge her …death.'

Neither slept that night. They lay still and separate, listening to the rain lashing the bamboo groves and mango trees and replenishing the drying river. Windows rattled in other rooms but no one closed them. Radha rose, and opening the balcony door, went out to stare at the deluge, fearing what lay ahead. Julian followed and stood in silence nearby. She turned and looked at him in despair.

'What will happen to me if you…die?' Radha cried out. 'I will die too—and with me our unborn child. Please don't go, my love and life, I entreat you! Revenge cannot bring back those who are gone!'

'Sometimes, we have to think of the departed to set their souls at rest.'

Radha stared at him bewildered; this grim faced brooding man was not the cheerful and strong Julian Ruthven she had known all her life. 'The sun-god of my life has drifted away,' she thought in desolation. 'I must leave now, before our love dies.' Radha Ruthven felt that the world she had cherished was being destroyed in one night. Or had it been destroyed on the sacred river where innocent blood had been spilt?

'Radha,' Julian said quietly, 'I must leave soon. I had come to serve Indians and now I have to fight them.' He paused. 'I feel I am being severed in half!'

He caressed her wet cheeks and held her close for a long time. Releasing herself, she removed a golden chain from her neck and put it around his neck. Smiling sadly, he said, 'We never exchanged garlands on our wedding day, did we?'

With tears brimming in her lambent eyes, Radha shook her head. 'My mother gave me this chain before her death. Wear it, so that from heaven Mother will watch over you in the battlefield.'

They sat together until a pre-dawn light dispelled the stormy darkness. Then leading her into the house, Julian murmured, 'Let us start packing now. I shall take you to your father's home, where you will be safe. When the battles are over, I shall resign, and we shall start a new life somewhere with our child. Wait for our reunion.'

Radha nodded and murmured, 'If not now—then in another life.'

He frowned, puzzled at her words. But living in his private hell, he brushed away her words and began arranging documents in preparation for departure. Watching him she thought, 'I shall not be a burden to my husband. I shall set him free to return to his world. Our perfect life is over.'

When Julian went on tour of a *taluk* nearby, Radha left their home in a rented carriage. He returned home two days later. The strange stillness of the house told him that something had changed irrevocably. Fearfully, the chief orderly gave him a sealed letter from Radha.

I am going where you will not find me. It is better this way. The fragile world we lived in has been shattered by an episode on the river at Kanpur—that same river which had been the spring of our lives. You are free now to do what you want. One day, when the blood and tears are washed clean by the same river, remember me with love.

Between Two Worlds
Delhi, 1858

I, Julian Ruthven, was devastated when I found Radha had gone. After threats and rebukes, I got the orderlies to tell me what had transpired in my absence, of how Radha had packed a few clothes and books, of how she had persuaded our major domo to arrange a carriage and guards to take her away.

Between preparations for joining the army, I lived in terror that some disaster would befall her. I felt immensely relieved when I received a letter from her father's *Munshi*, informing me that Radha-devi had arrived in Calcutta, sunburnt and exhausted by the journey. There was no reproach nor offer of further correspondence. But the last line sent an arrow through my heart. 'Mr Brajesh Chowdhury wishes to inform Mr Julian Ruthven that Radha-devi will now remain in her own world.' But she was the bridge between two worlds—hers and mine. I felt as if the wellspring of my life had dried.

In September 1857 a combined assault of four columns arrived in Delhi. Brigadier General Nicholson commanded the 75th Regiment, the 1st Bengal Fusiliers, and the 2nd Punjab Infantry to storm the bridge near the Kashmir Bastion and escalade its face.

Reluctantly I joined the 75th regiment. Nicholson was known to be a fiend. Other infantry regiments and fusiliers followed. Both the Indian and British armies waited throughout the hot humid night, firing and shelling and splitting the darkness with constant flashes. As rain fell intermittently the fragrance of jasmines rivalled the odour of gunpowder. Nicholson's column moved relentlessly forward, capturing the Mori bastion, the Kabul Gate, and the Burn bastion. There the British army met the stoical determination of Indian sepoys who were prepared to die rather than permit a British advance. Burnt by the sun, bruised by injuries, I saw no way to push forward. My soldiers were falling like pins before the firing by the sepoys. But Nicholson ordered them forward regardless of casualties.

At this point an Indian officer emerged from the darkness of the ramparts and stood before the massive figure of the British general. 'So, we meet again, Nicholson,' he said. "Do you remember the *zamindar* of Mayurganj whom you insulted for speaking the truth? I am his son—come to avenge the insult.'

The British general peered at the lean patrician face contorted by rage and muttered, 'Lord protect me!'

The Indian officer took aim from the Enfield rifle on his shoulder and shot the fearsome John Nicholson. Then he began running towards the river bank. I recognised the Indian rebel officer—Dilip.

Shocked but not sad, for I had heard of Nicholson's savagery, I dragged the general's body and laid it under a banyan tree. Leaving my soldiers, I began running in pursuit of Dilip, who went to a burnt house whose terrace sloped down to the river. He turned on hearing me approach. Both of us stared at each other.

'Julian,' he cried, raising his rifle. 'Do not come closer!'

I shouted back, 'Dilip! I had hoped better sense would prevail. You can be arrested as a rebel and inciter of mutiny.'

Dilip smiled sardonically at me. 'My British brother-in-law, will you hand me over to your sham justice?'

I stepped closer, torn between anger and pain. 'Don't mock our justice. We do not massacre women and children.'

'Neither do we. In fact…' he hesitated before continuing, 'I left Isabel in Allahabad with her friends before the Kanpur episode.'

'You saw Isabel…after the Delhi riots?' I cried out, running to him.

Dilip nodded. 'I fetched her from Kanpur and left her at Allahabad.'

'Then she is safe!' I exclaimed in relief.

'Yes, I learnt Isabel has reached Calcutta.'

In anguish and relief, I clasped his hand. 'How can I ever thank you, Dilip?' I paused. 'Leave now, dear brother. Go away before you are caught or killed. Return to Calcutta! No one will know what happened here tonight. We will be friends again. We shared a splendid world.'

'Slaves share nothing with their masters!' Dilip replied bitterly. 'We *were* friends. Now we are foes. I saved *your sister* from danger—risking my life.' He paused, eyes blazing. 'And you abandoned *my sister* because she became a burden to you when the revolt began.'

'That is absolutely false! I continually told Radha that the mutiny should not come between us. But she left when I was away! Believe me!' My hands tightened on his. 'Return to Calcutta soon!' I paused. 'If anything…happens to me…take care of my wife and our child yet to be born. Promise me!'

'I promise,' Dilip replied sombrely. Then he ran towards the river and told the waiting boatmen to row faster towards his secret destination.

Several days later I vehemently protested against the barbaric executions of Indian rebels ordered by General Hodson. I never imagined that so called civilized men could display the cruelty that I witnessed at the siege of Delhi.

It was then that I regretted joining the East India Company army. What legitimacy did this alien army have in India? For a century my compatriots plundered the long-suffering people of this ancient land. And after despoiling them, the rulers heaped scorn on a people whose civilization is older than ours. Snatching their resources, Britain had fuelled her Industrial Revolution. With Indian mercenaries, Britain suppressed revolts and conquered other lands. India became poor, food production declined, village schools, *pathshalas*, and *madrasas* were closed. Only the affluent Indian collaborators learnt English, leading to a sudden decline in literacy. The British Raj nurtured an Indian buffer class which would assist them to rule India.

My story was different. I was inspired by great Britons like Sir Thomas Munro, Governor of Madras, who died while assisting people in a cholera infested town. And Sir William Jones who revealed the greatness of Indian civilization to the West and who worked till his last hour translating Sanskrit texts. They had so identified themselves with India that they called this land their home. I too consider India my home.

Why then did I join this army? Was it a false sense of duty, or a spurious sense of honour? Has my lineage, rather than my loyalty, dictated my decision? The tragedy of my predicament is that the Indians whom I came to serve call me an oppressor. My dilemma alienated me from the British Raj that thinks I am a traitor.

When You and I behind
the Veil are Passed...*

Perhaps it was fitting that the bullet which pierced my chest was fired from the carbine of a red-necked British subaltern of the East India Company.

In that moment of intolerable pain, I heard you, Radha, cry out in pain. Standing in the garden of the Mayurganj mansion you looked upwards at the sky, seeking an explanation for the piercing pain. Heavy with our unborn child, you sat under our Shefali tree and wept brokenly. When dusk fell you walked slowly towards the mansion.

For some time, I was suspended between the turrets of the Red Fort and the star-strewn sky. This strange sensation divested me of terrestrial burdens. The vagaries of time puzzled me as did the unimagined scene spreading into infinity. What was this Infinity, I wondered? We had experienced joys of the phenomenal world, refusing to travel

---

* Quatrain 47 of the *Rubaiyat of Omar Khayyam*

to the Infinite. This new ambience bewildered me. Then another reality emerged from the abyss of darkness. The trivia of daily rituals, pursuit of success and recognition, the quest for power and glory seemed redundant in this new realm. In this realm knowledge and answers flowed into my consciousness. And spinning in an ocean of stars, I found an illuminating peace.

Slowly, images of the journey which brought me here assembled themselves. These launched me on a voyage where earthly emotions dissolved into comprehension of our terrestrial existence.

Now shorn of vanity, I told you, Radha, it had been within my power to avert the events that changed our two destinies had I refused to join the Company army. I allowed our plans to drift. Believing Time stands still is the folly of youth.

I began sending you messages which were carried by wind and clouds. We recalled our halcyon days. With new wisdom we discussed freedom, violence and peace.

Your response came across the barriers of time and space. 'Yes,' you whispered, 'I remember our days adorned with dreams! My pain dissolves in thoughts of what-might-have-been. We two travellers met on a caravan trail and found an affinity not many find.'

I quoted Khayyam. 'The stars are setting and the Caravan starts for the Dawn of Nothing.'

You smiled and replied, 'Khayyam was old by then. Dawn is always a beginning.'

Sometimes we communicated without words. I saw you retreating to the world we had shared. Watching you brought me serenity. The detachment that had eluded me in the other life came easily to this place of liberation—or *moksha* as you Hindus call it. Moksha brought knowledge of the universe. I did not ask you to leave behind the planet—now stained with blood, drenched by flood and tears, scorched by fire—to the unimaginable splendour of Elysium or *nirvana*, because our son had yet to be born.

Our son was soon born into this world. Do you remember our desire to raise children who would have apricot-hued skin, auburn hair, 'blue eyes put in by smudgy hands', of how they would embody the best of our divergent civilizations? I watched our son with a detached joy. I saw you strolling by the riverside, cradling him in your arms, and gazing at the horizon. When I did not return after the Mutiny, you thought that I had abandoned you because divided loyalties were a painful burden. When my parents informed you of my fate, you fell very ill. Anxious about our son, they took him to England. He was named Marcus. Desolate and weary, you went to live at an ashram in Saint Chaitanya's Nabadwip. There you meditated on life and eternity.

As you loosened your terrestrial chains, the distance between us shrank. I could feel your palpable presence. I realized that our minds are not imprisoned in our physical entities; a gossamer veil separates different realities. Terrestrial identities were replaced by celestial ones. Indeed, it is as if we had never been separated.

One day I heard your merry laughter; their waves came nearer and encircled me. Out of this surrounding luminosity I saw you, Radha, floating towards me with the remembered grace. At first, I could not recognize in you the Radha I knew because earth-time had left its imprint on you. There is wisdom in your eyes, and serenity in your being. And then you transcended terrestrial Time to enter this realm where I have been waiting. Some call it the valley of death, others name it oblivion. I believe it is Elysium. Here all mortal pain is effaced and peace surrounds that phenomenon called the human spirit. From there we watched our son become a splendid young man, who would be torn between the two worlds he had inherited and whose gifts he nobly embodied.

A century passed. Momentous events changed the world. Devastating wars crumbled empires, colonies revolted, armies of liberation carved out new states which gave proud identities to their people. Like Prometheus, these people stole the fire of freedom from heaven. Pandora unleashed impossible hopes upon credulous mankind.

Our sojourn in Elysium was ending. We had been allotted time to gather our thoughts, look back on our decisions and understand why events had taken such malevolent twists and turns. But acceptance is not possible when rebellion brews in one's hearts. Was it Fate that determined the course of our lives, the events and encounters which swept us into the vortex of Time?

The First Day of Spring
London, March, 1961

Alexander Ruthven Courtney, usually walked down Marchmont Street in Bloomsbury enroute to the London School of Economics, where I was reading Economics, Political Science, and International Law. On one side of Marchmont Street were small shops with quaint titles—Home & Colonial Store, Devonshire Dairy. On the other side were Indian restaurants whose names—New Karachi and New Taj—and grimy doors belied newness. But tired of roast beef and Yorkshire pudding at our university Halls, we impecunious students didn't mind spicy curries and *pilafs* at throwaway prices served at these places. The picturesque florist *Buds & Blooms* stood apart from the encircling shabbiness. Young male students from nearby Bentham Hall and Passfield Hall thronged the shop on weekends to buy floral tributes for girlfriends at Canterbury Hall.

The street was quiet in mid-mornings until bobbies mounted on stallions trotted down the road to fight which battles one never knew. Probably they liked being taunted by lusty Leftist women students with cries of 'Oppressors of the capitalist system!'

Sometimes I joined the farce by shouting in a Cockney accent, 'Oi maitey, get off your 'igh 'orse!' Rewarded by their stony faces, these exchanges never failed to amuse me.

On that never-to-be-forgotten first day of spring when I walked down the street, I saw you standing in front of the florist, gazing at, and inhaling the fragrance of spice-scented carnations. The delicate cameo of your face contrasted with the boisterous flowers. How could you know that I had admired you from a distance for many months at lectures given by the celebrated political scientist Professor Oakeshot and historian Professor Manning. I often saw you at the LSE refectory surrounded by classmates and heard your melodious voice or a burst of your merry laughter. Sometimes I passed you in LSE corridors as you walked briskly by on high heels, the end of your sari flowing behind you; a single thick plait followed the line of your spine. I, reading for a postgraduate degree, had been content to watch you, a second-year undergrad, from a distance.

What was the inexplicable force that drew me to you—though we had never been introduced? I could not explain this attraction. I felt I had heard your merry laugh and known you—even before I saw you at LSE. Now on 21st March 1961, I summoned courage and crossed the Rubicon—Marchmont

Street—and went to *Buds & Blooms* to greet you. With fluid grace you turned and offered me a radiant smile. Remembering the words of the Renaissance poet Francesco Petrarca, I thought that the radiance of your smile and the luminous orbs of your eyes swept me towards heaven. But I, earth-bound, plucked a bouquet of carnations and handed it to you.

'Happy Equinox,' I said, trying to be original.

Your luminous eyes rested briefly on my face and tousled auburn hair, as if summoning vague memories. Then you accepted the flowers with a smile, and asked. 'Are you a Druid?'

Puzzled, I asked, 'Why should I be a Druid?'

'The ancient Druids celebrated spring equinox to welcome the warm sun. Modern Brits don't, because they have central heating.'

Intent on prolonging the conversation, I asked, 'Do I look ancient?'

You scrutinized me before saying, 'Timeless would be a better word.'

'And you? Are you also timeless?' I asked.

You shook your head. 'No, I am transient.'

This remark saddened me. 'Then I would also like to be transient.'

You pondered over my words, then murmured, 'Transience and timelessness…these are Western concepts governed by clocks and calendars.'

I listened intently, wondering *where have I heard this idea before?*

Smiling, you continued. 'One should not be morbid on the first day of spring. There are promises ahead...of apple blossoms, Promenade Concerts, Easter vac and of course, exams.' You raised a fragile hand and indicated the road ahead. 'Shall we board a bus for LSE?'

Surprised, I asked, 'How do you know I am at LSE?'

You inclined your head. 'But I see you every day at lectures!' The sparkle returned to your eyes. 'Or do you believe yourself to be invisible—perhaps a socialist phantom haunting LSE?'

I threw back my head and laughed. Then I said, 'Perhaps the phantom should introduce itself. I am Alexander Ruthven Courtney, of Scottish-English descent. One ancestor, whose name I unfortunately bear, distinguished himself in battles, treason and grand larceny in British India.' I paused, wondering if I should divulge a family secret. 'Another ancestor—Julian Ruthven—married an enchanting Indian woman. They were separated during the Mutiny. Julian died during the Mutiny and Radha disappeared soon after giving birth to his son.'

A swift shadow flitted across your face. 'Yes, I have heard this sad tale in our family.'

'It is not entirely sad. Their son, Sir Marcus Ruthven, became a distinguished civil servant in India and won the hearts of Bengalis by opposing Lord Curzon's partition of Bengal.'

You nodded pensively. 'Yes, he was quite a person.' Then your pensive expression changed to amusement. 'And I know about you too, Alexander Courtney.'

'What do you know?' I asked anxiously.

'That you tease the professors with outrageous comments, you visit Lord Bertrand Russell to denounce nuclear disarmament, drink like a fish, smoke like a chimney and…'

'Go on,' I prompted you.

You hesitated before saying, 'And change girlfriends often.'

Astonished, I remarked, 'I say, you would be a gold mine to the KGB for gathering information. Have you enlisted with them?'

'Not yet,' you replied. 'But I may do so if I fail the Part I exams.'

'Excellent! Then I shall join the MI5. We can pass on classified documents to each other at lectures.' Your laughter had the quality of muted bells. To regain the ground beneath my feet I said, 'Enough of banter. Now, tell me your name.'

'Madhusri Chowdhury.'

'How strange,' I said, 'You have the same surname as my ancestress, Radha Chowdhury.'

You seemed disturbed. 'I am of the same family.'

I tried to shake off an eerie sensation. 'But may I call you Laura? She inspired the Italian humanist-poet Petrarca.'

'Why waste your time on economics if you are going to be a poet?' you asked me.

I replied, 'I hope to be a bank clerk by day, like T.S. Eliot, and write dramatic verse at night.'

As we reached the bus stop a double-decker bus came along; my plans to play truant went awry as we headed for LSE. I talked with a friend at the lobby so that I could see you emerge from the cloakroom where you left your cherry-coloured coat. My carnations still rested in the crook of one arm. You bestowed a kindly glance on me before disappearing into a lecture hall…and left sunbeams dancing around me. How I wish that the exquisite spring morning had stayed with us forever!

For several days I avoided running into you, afraid that the spell would break, aware that you had received similar homage from young men like me and found them wearisome. But with the gentle irony and compassion that drew people to you, you did not have the steel to spurn either the fool or the knave. One day as I saw you running to catch the bus to LSE, one of your high heels got trapped in a pavement crevice. I ran towards you as you tried to pull out the shoe. Before I could reach you, a *galantuomo* student knelt, plucked out the shoe and offered it to you.

'Cinderella, I believe?' he asked with a smile and slipped the shoe on your foot. You thanked him.

Watching this, I replied brusquely. 'No. She is Shakuntala, who loses things.'

Rising from the pavement, our comrade shrugged and said, 'Whoever that might be.'

I replied loftily, 'She is the heroine of the great Indian poet Kalidasa's classic.'

Laughing, you boarded the bus, and asked me, 'Have you read Kalidasa's play?'

I leapt into the bus and replied, 'He is greater than Petrarca.'

The *galantuomo* followed and murmured warningly, 'You have got it bad, mate. Beware of fairy tales. Their magic ends at midnight.'

I replied. 'Look around you. It is the hour of dawn.' The prophet of gloom now laughed. As the bus sped past towards LSE, I pondered on the words. Was it really our dawn—or had there been a night before?

LSE had been the nursery of British rebels, innovative economics and politics, where Harold Laski had defined a new egalitarian order before guns fired on imperialist ambitions. LSE continued to be a lively market of ideas, where the economic and political principles of Hayek, Keynes, and Oakeshott warred with each other, where boisterous debates between white teachers and their white, brown, and black students were encouraged.

Once I was addicted to these debates; I was argumentative and enjoyed admiring glances from women students. Now I spent hours in the LSE library, cramming for the much-coveted MSc (Econ) degree that would open the gates to El Dorado. Suddenly, time and purpose had urgent significance. You were the cause of this transformation, which friends and detractors alike declared would not last. I rarely went to pubs with the lads after lectures; instead I returned hurriedly to Passfield Hall to study. I stopped smoking and chewed gum. And I had wearied of both coy and lusty damsels.

I composed a letter and sent it to you:

Dear Madhusri,

Unlike you, I did not have a conventional background. My heroic English father became a pilot in the Royal Air Force. He and my Scottish Ruthven mother married when the Second World War was a mirage away. Our parents' passion brought me and my younger sister, Anna, into the world in quick succession. When we were toddlers, our gallant father was shot down by German gunners when he and his comrades were on a 'dam busting' mission over the River Rhine in 1944. Our mother swiftly recovered to marry a more earth-bound army officer. This alliance did not survive the tensions of the war, so there was a quiet divorce. After the war Mother, still a sensuous beauty, married Henry Bryant, a stolid City banker, who, in the process of acquiring a fortune, had forgotten to marry. Uncle Harry gave us security and commercial values, which I speedily discarded. It was to escape from this atmosphere that I decided to join the National Service even before I was called up.

My mother threw tantrums. 'You have done brilliantly in Advanced level exams! You have a seat at Cambridge! Uncle Harry will happily support you! Why are you throwing away your future?'

'I have a yen to see the world, Mum,' I replied. 'I can go to Cambridge later.'

'After my retirement I shan't be able to support you, Alex,' my step-father informed me apologetically.

'Of course not, you are planning to settle in the Bahamas and blow your savings at the casinos there,' I replied. His face tightened in annoyance.

And so, Madhusri, I joined the National Service, where I was taught how to fight and kill other young men. My group was posted to Berlin where the scars of defeat and despair were still visible. My soldier-friends and I saw the Reichstag and the ravaged Brandenburg Gate, where Hitler's ruinous thunder reverberated and the Gotterdamarung that followed. A song popular in the hit parade that year began with 'My sweetheart is in the army, as handsome as can be,' and ended with the words 'Lay down your arms and surrender to mine.' The War Office raised a furore over such subversive songs and banned its singing, but we cadets sang it loudly at the biergartens until threatened with court martial.

The real excitement came when Egyptian President Gamal Abdel Nasser nationalized the Suez Canal. Hallucinating that gunboat diplomacy was still in vogue, Britain, France, and Israel invaded Egypt, until the United Nations, USA and Russia condemned them. Some of us planned a secret visit to Cairo but the Franco-British troops were ordered to leave. Though it was my first visit to the East, the sights, sounds and scents of the Orient seemed familiar, as if fascination for the Orient was already lodged in my consciousness. India had haunted me even earlier, when my maternal grandfather told me about Julian Ruthven, our rebellious ancestor, in India.

And you seem the embodiment of that India, with its compassion, quiet courage, and gentle resilience.

But how did I guess these attributes when I hardly knew you? Later when I read Rabindranath Tagore's poem 'Endless Love,' it was a kind of epiphany.

'It is thou whom I have loved through many lives and many ages.'

Yours,

Julian

Vernal Days

Spring always dallies with winter in England. The wizardry of spring made us students forget examinations lurking in May. When winds brought rain and sleet we students fled to the warmth of the LSE library and tried to make up for lost time. But I was not studying my subjects nor taking notes from heavy reference books. I sat in a remote corner of the library where books on literature stood in dusty neglect. There I drew out a volume of Petrarca's verses or *Canzonieri* that had taken the Mediterranean world by storm in the 14th century. His *dolce stil novo* (sweet, new style) challenged the sombre majesty of Dante's *Divina Comedia*. The stern piety of medieval Christianity faded and poets returned to the humanism of the classical world. Petrarca was not interested in violence, politics, Inferno or Purgatorio. Life enchanted him; its magic deepened when he fell in love with Laura de Noves, the sad and reluctant wife of Comte de Sade. Even after aeons of time, Petrarca's memories resonate in my mind. He wrote of how on Good Friday in April 1327, sitting in the church of Santa Chiara in Avignon, he had seen a celestial vision in Laura. As she sat ahead in the pew he could only see a lace veil cover her auburn tresses. It was when she rose that Petrarca observed her form and grace. As Laura passed by, the luminous orbs of her eyes rested gently on him. He felt he had gained entry to Elysium.

Good Friday was a week away, Madhusri-Laura, so I decided to introduce you to Petrarca's Good Friday revelations. I rushed out into the clammy cold to W.H. Smith's bookshop on Kingsway to present you with a copy of Petrarca's *Canzonieri*. When I returned to LSE in the early afternoon I saw you emerge from a lecture hall. Detaching yourself from your companions, you came towards me and asked reproachfully, 'I assume you, Alexander, are planning to fail your exams?'

Laughing, I replied, 'Now, why on earth should I wish to fail my exams?'

Trying to conceal your concern you said, 'You have not been seen studying in the library for a few days.'

'I promise to resume studies tomorrow but today I have something to give you.' I held out the beige envelope containing the leather-bound *Canzonieri*. Your tapering fingers turned one page after another; you paused to read a verse, and then gazed at Simone Martini's portraits of Francesco Petrarca and Laura de Noves. Watching you in the neon-lit corridor with the hum of perennial conversation around us, it seemed an inappropriate place to read Petrarca. You read on; your eyelashes shone with tears. Then glancing at me with tear-bright eyes you walked away with the book in your hand.

London University, like other institutions of learning, closed for Easter. I was relieved to learn that you were not going to the country with friends. I told you that I was joining Lord Bertrand Russell's Aldermaston March to protest against the nuclear arms race and support disarmament. You were delighted.

'I think Bertrand Russell is wonderful! To defy his class and creed, and head a protest like this requires moral stamina!'

'And humour. When his Tory comrades asked him angrily if he would like to live under Soviet tyranny he retorted, "Better be Red than dead."'

Your merry laughter rang in my ears.

'Would you like to join the March?' I asked timorously.

You looked wistfully at me. 'I would like to very much, Alexander, but my father will disapprove.'

'He needn't know…in faraway Delhi.'

'The KGB or MI5 will inform him,' you replied.

I had to laugh. 'Perhaps next year then?'

'Perhaps,' you murmured. 'If you are here next year.'

'Oh, I shall be here, make no mistake!' I paused. 'I hope

you will be here—if you pass the Part I exams. But if you don't, will your father make you return to India?'

You sighed deeply and shook your head. 'How much simpler it would have been if my parents had remained a little longer in London. But his assignment ended just as I entered LSE.' You paused. 'Those three years with them was wonderful. I got a glimpse of diplomatic life, discussions and news conferences. The summer garden parties at Buckingham Palace were a treat.'

Eager to know of my beloved's life before she entered my existence, I encouraged her to speak, 'Tell me about it.'

'My mother and I selected appropriate silk saris and jewellery, had rehearsals with hair styles and looked very presentable as we set off for the garden party with Father complaining about the national dress of *achkan-churidar*.' You paused to laugh. 'But the fashions of the guests did not really matter. Everyone awaited the appearance of Queen Elizabeth II and Princess Margaret. There were exclamations of admiration when they appeared. Even the Soviet diplomats and their wives did not conceal their appreciation.' There was a glow on your face as you recalled the royal garden party.

'Do you miss the life with your parents?' I asked anxiously.

Looking wistful, you said, 'I miss my parents, and the life they gave me. But the life I have now…is also wonderful.'

'I hope you will always find life beautiful, dear Madhusri.'

There was a long moment of silence before you said. 'That decision is destiny's…'

Heedless of our destinies, we laughed and strolled down to Burlington Arcade for tea. I showed you the pamphlets supporting nuclear disarmament that we students had printed for distribution to fellow-marchers, spectators, informants and vagrant spies. You scrutinized them, a slight frown on your forehead. I could see you formulating a question which you asked with some hesitation, 'Won't these dissenting activities be an impediment when you enter a profession?'

Amused by your anxiety, I asked, 'What profession did you have in mind, dear Madhusri?'

'Something respectable like a bank clerk or school teacher,' you replied with twinkling eyes.

'Aha! You have not peered into my soul! I do not intend to pursue a respectable career! I intend to be an espionage agent for whichever side will have me—with plenty of money for dangerous activities, dubious lifestyle and …'

Regarding me with a strange sadness, you halted my rhetoric by murmuring, '… and brief romances with ladies of your tribe.'

Clasping your hand for the first time, I said, "My Indian Laura, if you accompany me on my dangerous missions, I shall conduct myself with all propriety. You will inspire me to noble deeds…and lay my laurels at your feet.'

Gravely you murmured, 'Ponder deeply over your words. Then ask me again.'

In that instant our lives seem to have acquired a different dimension. We were no longer students breezing through a carefree existence. Aware of the portentous words exchanged, we walked back in silence through sunlit streets.

The final examinations stared menacingly at us students. As customary during the holidays, I did not go to my stepfather's flat. I stayed on at Passfield Hall which was a three-half-penny bus ride away from LSE, where I crammed for exams in the library.

As Easter bells tolled and sermons on peace were preached, Christian devotees were gathering a formidable arsenal for destruction of Communist infidels. We students joined the Aldermaston March that demanded peace. It was a political success and grabbed headlines across angry NATO nations and the gloating Soviet *Pravda*. But it created problems for me. Along with several fellow students, I was arrested for 'impropriety', which translated, meant we had shouted slogans against Harold Macmillan's Tory government's decision to station Polaris missiles in Scotland, whose trajectory was aimed at Russian cities.

'Will Britannia, once the mistress of the world, become a stooge of Uncle Sam? Should we get incinerated by nuclear missiles?' I shouted.

'Let USA fight its own battles!' my friend cried out.

Another shouted: 'We can deal with the Russkies! They have no quarrel with us. We are all Europeans!'

The placid bobbies accompanying us protesters now closed in and apologised for arresting us for sedition.

'Free speech, mates!' my friend screamed. 'Is this the great democratic Britain where we are clinked for being pacifists?'

Our fellow protesters cheered wildly as we were driven away in Black Marias to a London suburb where we were kept in police custody to 'cool off' on that balmy night. Emulating Lord Russell, my classmates and I refused to pay bail. That also made critical news items. While the Tory papers called us ruffians, the *Daily Mirror* extolled our idealism. Finally, compelled by the sensation students were creating for the London School of Economics, its director, Sir Sydney Cain, came to the police station and read us the riot act. He told the police inspector that the bail money would be sent shortly. We responded with ingratitude and reminded him of the democratic traditions that were being flouted by restricting free speech.

'I am not going to let you pay for bail, Sir Sydney. I am prepared to face trial at Old Bailey,' I replied loftily.

'That will disqualify you from taking your final examinations from London University! And I shall certainly not defend your unruly conduct!' Sir Sydney retorted and stormed out of the police station.

That possibility suddenly sobered me. I could not risk a criminal record or fail to get my postgraduate degree. I had plans to make with you, Madhusri.

As my comrades and I were asked to sign forms stating that we had not been harassed in police custody, there was a flurry at the entrance hall of the police station. Wrapped unnecessarily in a mink coat (considering it was a warm day) my mother sailed in and denounced 'the tyrannical British police'.

The Inspector at the police station focussed beetle brows and glowering eyes on Mother. My sister Anna advised her not to throw tantrums. While this acrimonious exchange continued, you unexpectedly appeared, stern and un-amused. Your coat wet, the hem of your sari creased by rain water, and your hair, glittering with rain drops, was coiled at your neck.

'Laura!' I cried, 'Why are you here?'

'Why else, but to see what sort of trouble you are in?' you replied disdainfully.

Startled, Mother and Anna turned to look at you. I watched them, trying to fathom their facial expressions. Your gravitas silenced the clamour. The Inspector transferred his glowering eyes from Mum and focussed them on you with an anxious frown. Your assumed hauteur convinced him you were a Maharaja's daughter.

'Please Inspector, sir, could you release Mr Courtney? He did not really want to join the Aldermaston March. I challenged him to do so for a silly wager—for a hundred guineas.' You paused, and avoided my astonished stare. 'You see, he is very poor and that sum would have seen him through next year's postgraduation fees.' You glanced at my stylish mother and muttered, 'His…step-parents …are very displeased.'

Mother's green eyes blazed in outrage. 'Well, I never!' she exclaimed.

Playing out the drama, I said mournfully, 'Well, Laura, I have won the bet. I hope you are happy at my humiliation.'

You lowered your eyes in affected misery.

The Inspector, uncomfortable as all Brits are with heavy emotions, rose and sighed. 'All right,' he told his bewildered subordinates, 'release Mr Courtney without delay.' Turning to you he asked, 'Would you mind giving us your name, Miss…?'

'Madhusri Chowdhury,' you replied primly.

Confused, the Inspector exclaimed, 'But Mr Courtney called you "*Laura!*"'

Bending forward to write your name you murmured, 'Mr Courtney hallucinates that he lives in Renaissance Italy and thinks I am Laura de Noves. Not to worry, he will return to sanity soon.'

The Inspector glanced at us in bewilderment. 'You may all go,' he muttered, glad to see our backs, particularly my mother's mink-coated one.

We filed out in silence. There was a problem—Mother's gleaming Vauxhall Cresta parked nearby. I was clearly not the poor student that you, Madhusri, had depicted me.

I whispered to Mother: 'Madhusri, Anna and I will walk to the nearest Lyon's Tea Shop as my tumtum is growling in hunger after a night in the cell.'

Pursing her scarlet lips, my mother got into her car and sputtered, 'Disgraceful! I don't want to be seen with you urchins!'

Seated at a table in Lyons Tea Shop, you, Anna and I laughed uproariously.

'There is no question about your future career, Madhusri,' I said. 'The stage is waiting for you.'

Anna agreed and said, 'I thought you were adorable, Madhusri! The chief cop was entranced.' She turned to me. 'Incidentally, Madhusri and I are lodged in the same corridor at York Hall.'

'Thanks for the belated information,' I replied.

Mother entered like a galleon in full sail. She sat, lit a cigarette, and scrutinized you. The fiery eyes that had enchanted many men were now cold. Did she see in you an innocence that had never been hers? Or was your unworldliness inexplicable to a woman who believed in the here and now? She questioned you about your family, your career plans and was curious about our relationship.

'Are you vagabonds returning to town with me or are you going to march back?' Mother asked sharply.

'I'll drive. You can doze next to me and the girls can sit behind and debate politics,' I replied gruffly, knowing that Mother was afraid of my 'moods'.

'Why should I doze?' She snapped.

'Because, Mother dear, your eyes are bleary from sleeplessness—worrying about me.'

'No need for sarcasm. I was indeed worried! With Uncle Harry out of town, I wasn't sure how we could bail you out.'

'You could have sold your Van Cleef & Arpels earrings,' I suggested.

She turned to bestow a withering look at me. I glanced at the rear-view mirror to see your amused smile, Madhusri.

We three discussed the urgency of nuclear disarmament to halt the arms race between NATO and Warsaw Pact members.

Closing her eyes in boredom, Mother opened them once to mutter, 'Don't worry about the Russian bear. They are no match for British power.'

I was surprised when you, Madhusri, leaned forward to say, 'Don't underestimate the Russian bear, Mrs Bryant.

They crushed the formidable German Wehrmacht during the Second World War.'

Mother stared ahead and said, 'My husband was a courageous RAF pilot and sacrificed his life for Britain.'

Moments of heavy silence followed. One could trust Mother to mention Father to her advantage at crucial moments. Neither Anna nor I reminded her that she took only six months to remarry because Father had left her without a fortune.

Sensing her hidden pain, you leaned forward again and said gently, 'One day when you are not too busy, can we have tea together? You can tell me about Group Captain Courtney. Alexander and Anna worship him.'

To our surprise, Mother nodded. 'Yes dear, I would like to tell you about my husband. He was a wonderful man. I truly mourn him.' In our presence, she never said, *first husband.*

Do you remember, Madhusri, how we three exchanged glances? Mother had slipped into her fantasy world where she was a tragic war widow, struggling against odds. But the battle was won. Mother had agreed to have tea with you and talk about my father.

The tea party at her home was a success. Mother took pains to impress you; she laid out her Irish linen tablecloth, Staffordshire tea set and freshly polished silver. Anna escorted you to the parental flat in Kensington; I ambled in after an hour to see how the dialogue was progressing. It turned out to be a monologue as Mother told you about her wayward youth, her whirlwind romance with Father, his death, the ensuing hardships and the advent of Henry Bryant, who gave us security. I watched you intently, trying to fathom the expression of your face as you listened to my mother's unwritten memoir. Did you feel compassion for a woman who had lived through tempests without an attending poetry?

It was easier to meet after that. Mother had taken to you and was touched by your sensitivity. She frequently drove to Bloomsbury to take us after lectures for high tea at the nearby Savoy.

Do you remember that afternoon when you described life with your parents? My mother listened intently as you spoke and then asked, 'You have led a fairy-tale life, haven't you, dear?' Then, giving me a meaningful look, she said, 'I hope the enchantment continues.'

We looked at each other and smiled, determined that the magic would continue.

Now, as clouds and winds buffet me, I conjure the scene when I was driving you and Anna to a concert. As we passed Buckingham Palace you imitated the Queen of England by slowly waving to delighted passers-by who waved back. A confused policeman sped to us and gestured to me to halt. Peering at both of you, he asked who had waved like the Queen. You confessed to the crime.

'Cain't imitaite 'Er Majesty, Miss,' he growled. 'Against the law, it is.'

'Oh no, officer,' you said sweetly. 'I waved to my ex-boyfriend standing there.'

The bobby retorted, 'E's lucky to be your ex!' and sped away on his motorbike. Our laughter followed him.

Lost in our world, we often strolled through the springtime streets, Sometimes Anna and her current boyfriend joined us. I never knew whether you asked her to tag along or did it just happen that way? Did you feel safer with a *duenna* present? Could her presence subdue the tempest that now swirled around us? Usually, I bought only two tickets for operas at Covent Garden or concerts at Royal Festival Hall so that I could be alone with you, and hold your hand on our way back to our hostels. I longed to bare my heart but dared not.

Do you remember how we students voiced condemnation of colonialism and West's defence of the White Man's Burden when we heard of the carnage in Congo? We all sat on the rim of the Fountain of Eros along with other students, savouring the boisterous excitement.

In September 1961 the assassination of Dag Hammarskjöld, the dedicated Secretary General of the United Nations, left us stunned. Furiously, we speculated which group had perpetrated this crime. As our violent century progressed we were to see many horrible spectacles of the murder of men of peace. International law made no sense against this scenario. I wanted to distance myself from these events and concentrate on economic theories where passions and ideals had no place.

For the first time I was concerned about my future. Though the remonstrations by Mother and Uncle Harry had failed to do so for years, I was now possessed with growing urgency. If I were to offer you marriage, give you a comfortable home, travel the world with you, I had to obtain a first-class degree to enter a good profession. I debated whether I should ask you to wait. You had one more year to obtain the bachelor's degree.

Joining me in the refectory one afternoon for lunch you said, 'Alex, you look very tired. Are you all right?'

Touched by your concern I replied, 'I shall be all right if I don't flunk the exams.'

You looked concerned but replied, 'Of course, you won't flunk the exams!'

'Do you know what I have started reading?' I asked. You shook your head.

'I am reading the renowned Sanskrit scholar Moriz Winternitz's translation of *Kadambari*, the splendid classic by your great seventh century poet Banabhatta. It is an extraordinary love story—of Princess Kadambari and the Moon-god Chandrapida—a romance forbidden between mortals and immortals. They traversed enchanted forests and gardens, dwelt in palaces, watched monsoon storms and full moons. The lovers were separated in this pain-filled world and were then reunited in celestial splendour. There is nothing in Western literature to compare with this classic!'

You listened intently as I continued.

'Even great literature needs powerful empires to propagate it before the world. Had India been an imperial power, millions would have read *Kadambari*! What a loss to the world that few people are aware of this fantastic work. Europe had no vernacular literature in the seventh century. I paused. 'Though I read it for the first time, *Kadambari* seems hauntingly familiar… as if I had read those passages where the lovers traverse magical forests and rivers—sitting by a slow flowing river.'

Your gaze seemed to travel to those distant scenes. I continued. 'Indian philosophy and literature are so vast! The chapter in the *Gita* about the battleground of souls is fascinating.'

Surprised, you asked, 'I did not know you were reading Sanskrit literature. Why are you interested in Hinduism?'

I held your gaze. 'I have always wanted to know about Indian civilization…as if I have to complete some unfinished explorations.'

You frowned. 'What unfinished explorations?'

'Intellectual explorations regarding the final destiny of the spirit. They seem strangely familiar…and keep jostling in my mind, demanding explanations.'

Frowning, you asked, 'Where could you have read them?'

I sighed. 'I cannot remember. Anyway, Hinduism is complex and is not easy to interpret.'

'The Greeks tried,' you replied.

'They could not understand Hinduism, so they turned to Buddhism and created a new school of Greco-Buddhist art in Gandhara. I found fascinating material on this at the British Museum from Central Asian ballads.' I continued. 'After the finals, let me delve deeper into Indian culture.'

Your smile travelled to your lustrous eyes. 'You can start with our greatest Sanskrit poets, Kalidasa, Banabhatta and the modern Rabindranath Tagore.'

'Are they as great as my Petrarca?' I asked, to deliberately provoke you.

'They are both sensuous and sublime. They go from here to eternity...beyond romance and beauty...to themes more profound.'

'What could be more profound than love?'

You murmured, 'Pain and joy, despair and acceptance, life and death.'

The words echoed within me forever.

Rough Winds do Shake the Darling Buds of May*

The final exams for my Master's degree ended in mid-May. I had done better than I expected. I knew it was not due to the cramming but the inspiration that sprang from your presence, indeed, your existence. I wanted to be worthy of your esteem, Madhusri.

Before going to your hostel, I rushed to the parental apartment to tell them that I had done well and hoped to obtain a first or upper-second class degree.

'What about joining me as partner in our investment consultancy firm, son? We—Bryant and Brown—could add *Courtney* to the title,' Uncle Harry suggested. I disliked him calling me son because *my father* was Richard Courtney. Nor did I want to brood over stocks and shares all my life.

'I shall think about it, Uncle Harry,' I replied, reluctant to discuss future plans.

---

* Sonnet 18, Shakespeare.

Undeterred, he said, 'Come over for supper one evening when you are free and we can talk it over.'

Looking at Mother and her third husband I said firmly, 'I want to obtain a Ph.D in Public Finance at LSE and prepare a career in that field. I do not want to be an investment banker in your firm, Uncle Harry. Life would be too cushy there. I want to be in the eye of the storm.'

For the first time Mother eyed me with respect. I was not the wayward wastrel they took me for. She nodded with pride in her eyes. Did I remind her of my father, the man she had loved and forgotten?

'Do what you think is best, Alex dear,' she murmured. I rose from the sofa, hugged her and left the heavily furnished apartment that stifled me.

You, Madhusri, were waiting for me in Cartwright Garden fronting your hostel. I walked slowly towards you, when I wanted to sprint, and took your hand when I wanted to gather you in a tight embrace. Bowing with a flourish I said, 'You see before you a free man.'

'When were you in servitude, Alexander?' you asked ironically.

'The last two months, cramming like a robot.'

'Robots don't cram. They know everything.' After a pause you added, 'I see that you are satisfied with your exams.'

'Far better than I had expected. And now if you will don a gorgeous sari, we shall go for a celebratory dinner at Soho's Chez Auguste.'

'What are we to celebrate, Alexander?'

A life of dreams, happiness and fulfilment. Perhaps a dash of fame.'

'Your new life will give you new interests,' you said quietly.

'We shall discuss it while imbibing ambrosia at Chez Auguste. Dress up and come down while I reflect on the sparkling future.'

I sat on a park bench, gazing at the apple blossoms swaying in the breeze. Were William Shakespeare's words, *'Rough winds do shake the darling buds of May'* a warning? Young women students walked around Cartwright Gardens for their constitutional after studying all afternoon. Tired, tousled-haired young blades came out to smoke and exchange jokes about their Faculty members. I did not have to turn to sense your presence as you walked to where I was sitting on the wooden bench. The spring breeze and my breath merged together as I saw your silhouette in the amber twilight. The wind gently blew your turquoise silk sari around you and caressed your dark wavy hair. An inexplicable vision flashed before my eyes—of you sitting by a distant river, while I, barefooted, in shirt sleeves and breeches, strode towards you. The vision vanished as abruptly as it came. I rose to greet you.

As we walked to Soho, I rehearsed inwardly what I wanted to say. You walked, light-footed, in silence beside me. I might not have known you were there but for the warmth of your hand in mine. As it was midweek, Chez Auguste was quiet, because potential revellers were busy making money in the City. We sat by a window until the *maître d'* accustomed to people like us, took charge and ordered for us.

I broke the silence by asking, 'Will you marry me, Madhusri?'

A rush of colour tinted your cheeks. Regaining composure, you murmured, 'You are very young. You cannot yet be certain of what you want from life.'

'I am twenty-five. After brilliant results in Advanced level exams, I became a patriot and joined National Service for three years, learnt to tote guns and throw grenades. After studying at LSE for five years I feel like an anarchist. I cannot make sense of what is happening around us.'

Smiling, you asked, 'And in this state of mind you want to take care of another confused being?'

My hand tightened over yours. 'No, Madhusri, you are the anchor I have found in my storm-tossed sea.'

Your merry laughter warmed my heart. 'I, an anchor? Oh, Alex, I am so bewildered by life…by events…'

'That makes two of us. But I shall take care of you with my limited wisdom. In return you will inspire me. Is that a fair barter?' You nodded, eyes sparkling with unshed tears.

'I hope to study for a Ph.D in Public Finance at LSE, which holds numerous job possibilities around the world.'

'So, will you remain …in London?' you asked in an unsteady voice.

I shook my head. 'No, not in London but in Elysium.'

You murmured, 'Elysium is heaven. One goes there after one is done here…'

'London then—as you will. Yes, I shall see you every day at lunch or tea and be condescending to a humble undergrad. And I might double up as a tutor on behalf of a weary professor. Your public finance knowledge better be sound—otherwise I shall recommend a pass class for your degree.'

You laughed and I joined in. Hearing our laughter, the *maître d'* sauntered over to us. 'The wine is *très bien*?'

I indicated the bottle and said, 'As you see, Monsieur, it is untouched. We are drunk on our own spirits.'

'It is a happy occasion, *oui*?' he asked.

I nodded. 'This lovely young lady has *agreed to marry* me.'

The Frenchman left and returned hurriedly with champagne. 'For your affiancement,' he said, flourishing the bottle and opening it to the accompaniment of applause from the surrounding waiters. He handed two glasses to us with predictions of eternal happiness.

'My fiancée is only 20. Is she permitted to drink champagne?' I asked the *maître d'*.

He rolled his eyes upwards. 'I will not report you to the police… just for today.'

Beyond that I do not remember the details of that evening, which I believed was ordained in heaven. We had only a few sips of champagne. The ambrosia flowed from our veins into our hearts. I wish I had taken you to a quiet place and that we had taken our relationship further. How different would have been our destinies had I done that, Madhusri!

In Search of Laura
and Petrarca

The year 1961 hovered over a world growing in violence caused by the dismantling of colonial empires. A furious arms race commenced. Western arms manufacturers and Arab purchasers made massive profits. In retaliation, the Soviet Union built a formidable arsenal. The arms industry soaked up their economic resources but it also provided employment to people in townships where armaments were produced. While the Soviet Union maintained military parity, this concentration on arms would come at a heavy economic cost.

Realizing that they were racing towards Armageddon, President Kennedy and Premier Khrushchev sought to halt this by arranging a summit in Vienna in June 1961. Newspaper photographs flashed across the world; people saw a meeting of two adversarial worlds symbolized by their supremos. President Kennedy looked elegant and self assured; his glamorous wife displayed sartorial élan. A proud Premiere Khrushchev made no attempt to compete with the debonair American president.

The homely Nina Khrushcheva, in her plain black dress, neatly combed hair in a chignon, and the maternal smile she offered to Jacqueline Kennedy, made people appreciate her.

Anna observed, 'Jackie needs haute couture to attract attention. Nina stands without adornments.'

Looking at the photographs in *Time* magazine, you, Madhusri, said, 'They represent two different worlds.'

I asked you, 'To which world would you like to belong?'

'Neither,' you said quietly. 'I should like to belong to the world of Rabindranath Tagore...of compassion, courage, and...' You probably wanted to add 'love' but did not. Moved by your words, I replied. 'I think you already belong there, Madhusri.'

In 1961 the world celebrated the birth centenary of the millennial figure of Rabindranath Tagore. Russia and Britain competed with India to honour him and his massive creative corpus of poems, novels, short stories, paintings and dance dramas. London School of Economics organized lectures on him, British students recited his poems, and Indian students sang his songs. I sat in the third row of the LSE auditorium, watching you sit on the stage floor along with your Bengali compatriots, and sing Tagore's soul storming songs from the dance drama *Shapmochan*.

It tells of how a capricious god punished two celestial lovers, Madhusri and Sourasen, for a musical infraction and sent them to earth to atone. Madhusri pleaded not to be separated; so Indra added a rider that they would be united after enduring pain. The two were born in far kingdoms until Fate brought them together. The curse was removed by Madhusri's love for Sourasen. Tagore did not tell us if the lovers returned to heaven. Perhaps not; perhaps they found life in this pain-filled world sweeter than heaven.

The auditorium throbbed with applause and shouts of 'Encore!' Your group sang again. Admirers clustered around your group in homage.

'Does this bring out the Othello in you?' asked a fellow student.

'The young lady is no Desdemona,' I replied curtly. 'She has a mind of her own.'

My classmate responded, 'Make sure she has. Oriental women have a thirst for martyrdom.'

Years later those words haunted me.

The once somnolent Africa became the focus of suppressed rage. The Democratic Republic of Congo exploded into internecine strife as Mobutu Sese Seko and Moïse Tshombe tried to depose the country's first elected Prime Minister Patrice Lumumba, a leftist revolutionary, with the help of diabolic Belgian mercenaries. The civil war stained their land with blood. Former Belgian overlords watched with glee—and hope—that they might resume plundering the rich minerals of the tragic land. Seeing Lumamba's success, the Belgian government arranged his assassination in January 1961, thus eliminating a leader who could have brought stability to the Congo.

In Algeria another battle raged between the Arabs and their French overlords. We read of the Algerian revolutionaries Ahmed Ben Bella and Ben Youssef Ben Khedda pitted against the French armed forces. We heard how the philosopher-writer Jean-Paul Sartre condemned brutalities against a people who wanted their freedom. Derisively he declared: 'The French soldiers who quailed before the mighty Nazis are now showing their might against defenceless Algerians!' News of atrocities and massacres were described in banner headlines. *The Organisation Armée Secrète* or OAS (Secret Army Organization) began killing Frenchmen who wanted an amicable settlement with Algerians, especially General Charles de Gaulle, now President of the Fourth Republic. On 8th January 1961 General de Gaulle had organized a referendum on freedom for Algeria. This resulted in more terrorist attacks by the notorious OAS. General de Gaulle and Jean Paul Sartre were targets of these attacks but both survived thanks to the French security service.

At a tutorial, Dr Manning, Head of the Department of International Relations, praised your paper on African Nationalism. He read out parts which were critical of imperialism and then parts about the fragile roots of democracy in resurgent African nations. Though not a part of the undergrad class, I sat unobtrusively in the hall, watching the proceedings with pride.

Then Dr Manning looked at you with an ironic smile. 'And now, Madhusri, tell us what you think of Mr Nehru's invasion of Goa—in violation of international law. Is this also part of non-violent nationalism?'

There was a ripple of laughter around the lecture hall. I held my breath, fearing the taunt might provoke you. Instead you gave him a smile and replied, 'Professor, I think it is avenging ancient wrongs.'

Puzzled, the illustrious academic asked, 'How so?'

'Portugal conquered Goa through the collusion of Timoji, a local privateer. Goa is inhabited by Indians—Hindus, Christians and Muslims, et al. They want to be part of India. Mr Nehru's move is irredentism rather than nationalism.' You paused. 'Britain applauded when the Indian government asked France to vacate their colony Pondicherry. But then, France is not an old ally of Britain like poor Portugal.'

There was a burst of laughter from the students. Beaming and nodding, Professor Manning said, 'Young lady, I shall recommend you for a UN job. You seem to know the dialectics of international diplomacy.'

My unworldly Madhusri, why did you not pursue this with him after you graduated? What made you believe the goddess of good fortune would come to you, unbidden?

As a long summer beckoned to us before a new academic year began, Anna suggested that we should visit Paris.

Uncle Harry was astonished. 'Paris? There is trouble there.'

'Where isn't there trouble, Uncle Harry?' Anna asked impatiently.

'Madhusri plans to go to Delhi via Cairo and see the pyramids.' The thought of you going so far away disturbed me. In retrospect I should have accompanied you to Delhi and charted our plans for the future. To forestall your visit home, I asked you to accompany us to Paris.

Paris was in silent turmoil. Tourists were few. The older residents said that the atmosphere was similar to that during the Nazi occupation of the city during the Second World War—except that those who instilled fear were not alien soldiers but home-grown fascists who refused to acknowledge that the age of empires was over. The OAS was a right-wing para-military organization established in the Spain of the murderous General Franco. They fought Algerian liberationists for eight years. They organized terrorist attacks, bombings of offices and assassinations of liberals to prevent Algeria's independence from French rule. Its motto was *L' Algérie est française et le restera* (Algeria is French and will remain so.) The FLN or Algerian National Liberation Front fiercely fought against this claim.

You, Madhusri, and Anna visited the Louvre and Hôtel de Invalides while Mother went to look at the latest fashions. Since the votaries of fashion were absent, Mother enjoyed the attention bestowed on her in the haute couture shops. Accompanying her, Uncle Harry wrote cheques with glum resignation. At dusk we strolled along the Left Bank. One warm evening I took you to the Eiffel Tower from where we gazed down at the glistening city below.

'Shall we come here for our honeymoon?' I asked, drawing you close.

You shook your head. 'I would like to take you to Rajasthan, which is redolent with tales of heroism and romance.'

I nodded. 'Yes, I have been reading about those numbskull warriors who, defeated by invading armies, returned home to torch their womenfolk in the name of honour.'

I expected you to explode in indignation and uphold valour and sacrifice. So I was surprised when you said, 'I think the ladies would have preferred to stay alive rather than face death by fire sacrifices.' Then gazing at the Parisian skyline, you said, 'I admire women of the French Resistance who endangered their lives to sabotage the Nazi army.'

'There were also women who collaborated with the Nazis,' I replied.

'If they did, it was for survival. Who can judge?'

I looked at you. 'Would you collaborate with the enemy for survival?'

After pondering over the query, you said gravely, 'If I had given hostages to fortune—then I would collaborate.'

'No moral imperatives?' I asked.

'Loyalty is a moral imperative,' you replied.

'Love? Does that have no claim over ethics?'

When you did not reply I wondered why. If only I had known your response to such a predicament!

After dinner we five strolled back to the hotel. Before adjourning to our separate rooms, we used to sit in the terrace fronting the hotel and drink curacao. Some nights we heard bursts of gunfire, exploding bombs and screams of innocent bystanders. The sounds disturbed me; they seemed echoes of explosions I had heard long ago in another alien soil. I tried to banish these sounds and images but they reverberated around me.

One morning at breakfast, Mother said to you, 'Madhusri, I feel uneasy when you go out in your Turkish dress.' Mother called the salwar-kameez 'Turkish', which was probably its true origin.

You replied, 'My salwar-kameez is north-Indian dress, Mrs Bryant.'

'Dear girl, it looks Turkish. The OAS is stupid. They may mistake you for an Algerian.'

'Mother's geography is unique,' I said. 'She thinks Muslims are one race.'

'Convent schools don't teach geography,' Anna chirped. 'They teach catechism and terrorism.'

Mother pursed her lips and sighed. 'I advise you to wear a sari here and a dot on your forehead.'

I added lightly, 'Wear the *Hare Krishna* dress and chant their *mantras*.' But before the words were out I regretted it. A vague remembrance of such chants rang in my ears.

With quiet anger you replied, 'Imperialism was cosmopolitan. It had to be—to understand the natives. Now it seems we natives have to conceal our identities to satisfy thwarted imperialists.' You paused. 'Perhaps it is safer for us Asians and Arabs to remain in our own countries."

'Come now, Madhusri,' I protested, 'don't make it a racial issue. We are in a besieged city—thanks to Mademoiselle Anna—and naturally have apprehensions about your safety.'

You shook your head. 'No, you former colonials want darker varieties of yourselves—which I refuse to be! I shall dress as I please and if that means the savage OAS will shoot me, well, let them! So much for French culture!'

Uncle Harry put down the French newspaper he was trying to read. 'Hear, hear! Never cared much for the Frenchies. All hot air and flummery. You dress as you like, dear girl! And if Alex can't protect you from the OAS, let us return to safe old London.'

Caught between anger and amusement, you turned to me and said, 'And you, Alexander Ruthven Courtney, don't make fun of *Krishna Consciousness* without understanding it! It was the devotional movement that saved India from Islamic conversion!' You rose and went outside.

As I rose to follow you, Uncle Harry restrained me. 'You and your Mum have offended her. Leave her to calm down.'

I felt a tremor of unease—as if I had experienced these fears before; misunderstandings and resentments between two races that could suddenly surface. Would these turbulent stubborn memories remain with me and cast shadows on our bright days? Did such misunderstandings intrude between my ancestor Julian Ruthven and his beloved Radha? Was it the antagonism of the two races, rather than death, that caused their separation?

In anxious dismay we watched you flag a taxi and drive away. The parents fretted, and Anna made dire predictions to deepen my anxiety. The morning passed in misery. I skipped lunch and wandered along the leafy boulevards designed by Baron Haussmann a century ago. After that I went to the opera house and purchased tickets for Bizet's *Carmen*. Then, driven by instinct, I went to Bibliothèque Nationale de France and entered the high-vaulted main library. And there you were, reading a book on Algerian history by the Palestinian-American writer, Edward Said. I sat some distance away and watched you read, a little frown between your straight eyebrows, wondering what you were thinking, what you were feeling. After a while, you rose and glanced around the reading room until your eyes found mine. I also rose, and waited for you to make a gesture of forgiveness. Shrugging, you walked out of the building. I followed, walking silently by your side until you paused before a traffic light.

'Madhusri,' I murmured, 'I have tickets for the opera tonight. I hope you will come with me, dressed in whatever costume you choose.'

'I shall wear a Chanel evening dress and a Van Cleef & Arpels tiara,' you replied sarcastically.

Puzzled, I looked into your laughing eyes. 'You don't need those things to dazzle other eyes,' I replied quietly. 'But one day when I make good, I shall gift you a diamond as big as the Ritz.'

'I'll remember that,' you replied.

We sat through the sultry songs of *Carmen*, depicting Don Juan's futile passion for the flamboyant gypsy *Carmen*. Their story seemed inappropriate in the sophisticated Parisian setting. You informed me that it was authored by a Frenchman, Prosper Merimee, who also ghost-wrote love letters for Napoleon III to his future wife Eugenie. You mused, 'Powerful emperors do not write love letters while humbler men are better at romancing.'

I replied, 'Because humble men have no power, only passion.'

Paris now throbbed with violence as the OAS and other groups perpetrated terrorist acts. Jean-Marie Bastien-Thiry, a lieutenant-colonel in the French Air Force tried to assassinate President de Gaulle; he was swiftly executed. People scurried to their homes, tourists dwindled away. Armed Gendarmerie patrolled the deserted streets.

'I hope you ladies have had enough of gay *Paree*,' Uncle Harry said angrily.

'I, for one, intend to go home, put up my feet and watch tennis matches at Wimbledon on TV...like any civilized Englishman.'

'Civilized Englishmen play cricket, Uncle Hal,' Anna twitted. 'Tennis is a French game—it came with the Norman Conquest.'

'With your prodigious knowledge, why don't you become a quiz master in ITV programmes?' Uncle Harry asked Anna.

Before leaving France, I had a great yen to see Avignon and Vaucluse, whose majestic scenery had inspired Petrarca. Here, in voluntary exile, he married a local woman who bore him a son. In between domestic felicity he initiated the theme of courtly love in European literature through his *Canzonieri* to Laura de Noves. His fame travelled from this secluded valley to the world. Anna, you Madhusri, and I set off on the journey.

Fontaine-de-Vaucluse is built around a spring near a limestone cliff where ancient cults were observed. We went to see the Musée-Bibliothèque François Pétrarque, which has been erected at the site of Petrarca's home. After seeing old manuscripts and artefacts of a bygone age, we sat by the river bank and watched the swirling water flow downstream. I told you how Petrarca's love for the unattainable Laura kindled his genius. I quoted the famous lines: '*For a woman he would never know, for a woman he could never have, he changed the world forever.*'

Your gaze resting on the river bank ablaze with flowers, you asked, 'How did he change the world?'

'By showing how the unattainable can be inspiring,' I replied.

You murmured sadly, 'Perhaps Laura knew the transience of love.'

In that place of poetic passion where all is forgiven, I kissed you. The memory of that embrace lingers on. I could have held on to you for eternity…which I probably have.

Torrents of Spring

After returning to London we prepared for our new studies. My Ph.D studies began that autumn, while you went on to your second year of the Bachelor's degree. It gave me pleasure to guide you through the formidable subjects on which you would be examined. I gave you my undergrad notes. While discussing the subjects I encountered your intuitive ability to predict events.

LSE holds its annual Commemoration Ball for students and academic staff in early October. Do you remember how I came to fetch you from Canterbury Hall? You were the image of innocence; a shimmering sari draped your slender body, your hair was in a chignon encircled by white roses, and pearls adorned your slender throat. But at the ball you were transformed into a siren. Who would have thought a sari-clad girl could waltz with such ineffable grace, whose dancing eyes could send shivers down one's spine? It was the first time I held you in my arms and felt the warm allure of your body. Or had I held you in my arms before—in another age?

Strauss's waltz 'Tales from the Vienna Woods' began to play. As we whirled around the room, my mind left my body. Images of a marble-veined floor and mirrored hall in a tropical city flashed before me. I saw fireworks illumine the night sky and ancient banyan trees. I, an English magistrate, led you, a demure Indian maiden, to the ballroom of a Mayurganj mansion. Men in British army uniforms or black coat tails, women in crinolines, stopped dancing. Others—Indians and Europeans—watched us in astonished and disapproving silence. For all their enlightenment, the British did not like one of their tribe 'fraternizing with the natives,' even if they were superior in mind and manners. Ignoring them, we drew closer and danced more gracefully than any of them. I remember leading you to the balcony to see the Diwali lamps on your lawn. The balcony whirled around me. Feeling that I was spinning through time, I fainted.

A lifetime later I awoke.

'Alex!' you, Madhusri cried. 'What happened? Are you all right? Open your eyes, Alex, and tell me you are all right!'

I opened my eyes and murmured, 'Radha.'

You shook your head with tearful eyes.

A college friend sprinkled cold water on me. You wiped my face with your handkerchief.

'Had a drop too much, Alex?' The friend laughed.

Since I could not share the extraordinary vision that had caused me to faint, I nodded assent. 'Yes, that and the stuffy room.'

I rose. You stood looking at me with anguish. 'No more dancing,' you said gently. 'Let us return to our hostels.'

We rode through the pre-dawn streets on a milk cart. We sang from the stage musical *My Fair Lady*—'On the street where you live'—until someone from a high window asked us to 'Shut your bloody traps! It's Sunday morning and we are trying to sleep late!' In return for the ride, the milk-cart driver asked us to deliver milk bottles. We laughed in the haze of an autumn dawn.

The New Year—1962—came upon us adorned with hopes and dreams. I enjoyed the grounded reality of public finance and spent long hours at the LSE library reading journals to acquaint myself with the world of finance. I had earlier neglected these for the headier wine of philosophy and poetry. The murkier aspect of domestic and global finance became apparent. Intricacies of international monetary aid provided by the Marshal Plan and World Bank debt traps began to unravel before me.

Since you were also busy preparing for the difficult examinations of the BSc Economics course, we met only over the weekends. Because we stored up all that we had to discuss there was considerable intensity in our meetings. Sometimes this led to chaotic conversations. We went over the notes and essays I had given you.

'Your notes are better than the lectures,' you once said, while we sipped tea at a café near Tavistock Square.

'Really, Radha?' I asked, surprised.

'Please!' you cried out. 'Don't call me by that name!'

Other tea-drinkers turned around to stare at you so distraught.

'Why not?' I asked, feeling the tremors I had experienced at the LSE ballroom.

'I…get nightmares…when I hear that name!'

'Radha is Lord Krishna's beloved. Why should the name distress you?'

'Do you wish to distress me?' you demanded angrily.

'Dear girl, that is the last thing I want,' I replied, bewildered. I waited for you to calm down to resume discussions on international relations.

'The lecturers sometime narrate events without analysis. Your notes are an analysis of events, their causes, their effects.'

Your praise warmed my heart but also set me thinking. 'Have I embarked on a wrong course? Would I have been better suited to an academic career or journalism?'

You pondered over my question. 'Public finance does not bar you from those careers. Imagine, you could become editor of *The Economist*.'

I burst into laughter. 'Young lady, don't encourage me to be too ambitious!'

'What do you want from life? Wealth, achievement, fame?' You asked solemnly.

'Of course, I do but not in that order. First—fulfilment in work and happiness with you. Fame is welcome and wealth is quite unnecessary.'

You laid your hand on mine and said softly, 'May your wishes be fulfilled.'

'Oh, they will be! I have no doubts about that.' I paused, seeing strange glimmers in your eyes. "Have you doubts about our future?'

With sad resignation you murmured, 'We have plans, Alex, and we pursue them. What happens is not in our hands.'

'*Our future is in our hands*—except in times of war or disasters,' I replied.

'Wars and disasters,' you murmured, shivering. 'It was a war that changed our lives.' The faraway look returned to your eyes.

Once more I felt as if the ground trembled under me.

One mellow October morning in 1962 the world woke up to learn that the American President Kennedy had delivered an ultimatum to Soviet Premier Khrushchev to dismantle Russian missiles in Cuba or face nuclear warfare. Though our imperial wars had acclimatized us to violence, we Brits now stared at the spectre of annihilation. Even the exuberant mood of LSE was muted on that autumn afternoon. Excitement visible on their fresh young faces, students clustered together or sat in the refectory to cheerfully discuss the possibility of imminent extinction. They could be seen in varied sartorial styles and all sporting the famed purple and blue striped muffler of LSE as a badge of honour.

Some English classmates defended 'liberty and the pursuit of happiness'. One English student declared: 'Now is the moment of truth. People will have to decide whether they are willing to die for liberty and our way of life!'

'Oh, dry up! Our way of life may not seem great to other people,' I replied.

Trevor, my classmate, son of a Labour Party member, said, 'Better be Red than dead.'

Another Leftist classmate declared fiercely, 'Without life on earth can we trip up to Parliament for debates or scream inanities in Hyde Park on Sundays?'

'Your concept of democracy is elemental,' a stubborn classmate retorted.

Glancing at my friends I murmured, 'The atom bomb will extinguish all elements. A line in an Indian metaphysical text asks: "When the sun, moon, stars, wind and water are gone, what will remain, oh Sage?" We can reply: "When the sun, moon, wind and water are gone only ashes will remain." Is that what you want?'

'Has your Indian girlfriend made you a pacifist—*Ahimsa* and all that tripe?' my Tory friend taunted.

'She is my fiancée, if you please, and she is not a pacifist,' I retorted and walked towards the iron grilled door of the elevator. Reaching the ground floor lobby, I heard words flying; of fear, bravado, and condemnation. Agitated students debated whether they preferred surrendering rather than adherence to principles. I heard students of different nationalities argue heatedly on Kennedy's threat of Armageddon. Most students felt that Kennedy was endangering humanity with brinkmanship.

An African student asked, 'Why does President Kennedy think he has the right to encircle the Soviet Union with ICBMs but that they cannot keep a few missiles in Cuba?'

'Rightly said! Khrushchev should call the bluff!' Trevor exclaimed.

My Tory friend spoke angrily: 'Kennedy will then retaliate. If Khrushchev does not dismantle the missiles soon Moscow will be A-bombed.'

An Arab student retorted: 'And then it will be the turn of New York to turn to cinders. But the fate of millions is hardly a matter for concern—so long as you can practice antiquated gunboat diplomacy!'

I saw you, Madhusri, hurry to the lobby, where students usually met around the big clock. Deeply distressed, you informed me that the Peoples' Liberation Army of China had invaded India's northeast frontier. 'My parents are very anxious. Curfew has been declared in Delhi and Calcutta. Troops are being moved towards the northeast region.' You paused. 'Will Indians be slaughtered again …as they were during the Revolt of 1857?'

As our eyes met, the clamorous lobby seemed to reverberate with sounds of the booming of British cannons and the artillery fire of rebel troops. I clasped your hands to reassure ourselves.

'The East India Company was superior in weaponry. The Chinese Peoples' Liberation Army cannot compare with them. Now, the Indian Army is well trained.' I paused. 'Your Indian generals were trained at Sandhurst.'

'India is in danger!' You exclaimed. 'Russia does not want to offend China and is staying neutral…and that has emboldened the PLA!'

I shook my head. 'If the Chinese advance further, I can bet my last farthing that the USA will intervene. The West cannot afford to have the Chinese in India.' I paused. 'Perhaps now India should have a military alliance with America.' I added ironically, 'Or even a pact with her old enemy, Britain!'

I shall never forget the expression on your face when you said softly, 'We are no longer enemies. The days of the East India Company and Mutiny are over.'

Brushing aside unease that the mention of the Mutiny caused, I said, 'Come, let us see if we LSE gallants can raise a Brigade to halt the Chinese hordes.'

Acrimonious discussions continued at the lobby. Glancing around at fellow students I clapped my hands to demand silence. 'Knights of LSE!' I cried, and used the words (though modified) of Pope Innocent III, who had incited the First Crusade. 'Word has been bruited abroad that the Chinese Peril has invaded India. Who will go to evict the Chinese?'

There was a cheer of assent from the young men. One of them cried, 'Charge of the Light Brigade to India!'

I addressed my friends. 'Please join us at *Three Tons* for a drink and we can draw up plans for an army of intervention against the Chinese.'

With arms linked we stepped out into the October twilight and headed for Three Tons Pub. Between beer and serious discussion, we decided to collect money for the families of soldiers killed by the Chinese troops in northeast India. We senior students tried to reassure you about your native land.

As you and I walked towards your hostel, you said, 'I have never felt like this before…as if I am safe and… belong here.'

'Remember to feel like this always,' I said, drawing you close.

End of an Era

Time flew on wings of joy; you passed the Part I exams with honours. The distinguished academics regarded you as a student with prodigious promise and were happy with your performance. You carried the magic of spring; those approaching autumn frosts were warmed by your vernal charm.

While you entered the final year of the BSc (Econ) degree, I was midway through my postgraduate course. In the interludes of studying, we enjoyed theatres at Haymarket, concerts at Royal Festival Hall, operas at Covent Garden, *avant garde* films at the National Film Theatre. Sometimes on long weekends we went to Stratford-on-Avon to see Shakespeare's plays and stayed in old taverns. Anna accompanied us as a *duenna*. With some annoyance, I wondered if you had doubts about my sense of honour and propriety. Would it not have been wonderful if we had flung aside conventional codes? Does happiness come through discretion or is happiness seized by brushing aside wisdom?

Our seasons in paradise passed in anticipation of bliss. One late morning in November 1963 when we were having tea at the LSE refectory, I tentatively suggested that we make plans for our future together.

'Let us first get through our respective exams,' you said, with a sensible air.

'And then what do we do? Run around like gypsies, looking for shelter? And steal chickens for dinner?' I asked impatiently. Your response was merry laughter. 'You are not a practical person, are you, Madhusri?'

'Why should I be practical when you are here, Alexander the Great?' you replied lightly.

'Then listen to me,' I said sternly. 'First, you must write to your parents about our decision to marry. After that I shall inform Mum and Uncle Harry. Then we shall start searching for jobs and after that, with some idea of our incomes, we can look for a home.'

Sparkles lit your eyes. Normally undemonstrative, you laid a hand on mine, and said wistfully, 'You make it sound so simple—marriage, career, home—as if we have to wave a magic wand and everything falls into place.'

'We are not asking for the moon and stars are we, my love? Just ordinary mortal happiness will suffice.'

'It is easier to pluck the stars than attain mortal happiness,' you said quietly.

'That is not the message of Tagore's *Shapmochan*. Your namesake Madhusri and Sourasen found happiness as mortals,' I reminded you.

You raised your tea cup. 'Here is to mortal happiness.' I clinked my cup to yours. Then I fell silent, turning a thought over in my mind. I said, 'Could you come out with me at lunch break. We have some urgent work to do.'

'Really? What is this matter of such solemnity?' you asked.

'You will soon know,' I replied.

An autumn wind blew around us as we sauntered down majestic Kingsway. I led you to a jewellery shop. As I pushed open the gleaming door, you stopped and asked, 'Why are we here?'

'Don't make a scene, Madhusri. I intend to buy an engagement ring for you. Come inside. I am not taking you to a lion's den!'

Standing there, you looked at me as various expressions passed over your face.

As we entered the shop the modish manager came forward to greet us. I told him what we wanted. He handed us over to a stylish, heavily made-up woman who brought out black velvet trays which displayed eternity rings and diamond circlets. Shaking my head, I said gruffly, 'No, these won't do. My fiancée is from a princely family. The Maharaja, her father, will be furious if I give her a tinselly ring.' I paused. 'He may even withdraw his consent for our marriage.' You, Madhusri, looked at me as if I had taken leave of my senses.

The now anxious manager glided over and brought out another tray on which glittered several solitaires. He moved away for me to make the selection. An inexplicable tension gripped me as a coruscating emerald ring arrested my eyes. Had I searched for this ring through Time? My trembling fingers picked up the exquisite piece. The emerald solitaire was held up by two golden letters, J and R—for Julian and Radha—on either side.

Staring at it, you, Madhusri, whispered hoarsely, 'I wore it…long ago…someone removed it from me when I…drifted into another world…where a beloved awaited me.'

Sliding the ring onto your finger, I murmured, 'Wear it again, my love, until the end of Time.' Turning to the manager, I asked, 'Would a cheque on Barclays Bank do? The bank is next door—if you wish to verify my account.'

Convinced now that I was an adventurer who had seduced an innocent 'native princess', he murmured, 'It will do, sir'.

As I drew out the cheque book from my jacket pocket, I saw one of his lady assistants skip across the road and enter the bank. To gain time, the heavily made-up lady brought us tea. After sipping the dismal liquid, I wrote out the cheque, allowing time for the assistant to return with affirmation about my cash-worthiness. Thus reassured, we implemented the formality of purchase. You, Madhusri, watched the proceedings in distracted silence.

'Where was this ring made?' I asked the manager.

He replied. 'I can't rightly say, sir. The ring is of Indian origin as one may see from the chased-gold band. An Indian gentleman sold it to the owner of this store many years ago. He said it belonged to a young lady in his family who became a widow during the Mutiny. He thought it to be…'

'Inauspicious?' I asked sharply, angry that anything connected to Radha could be inauspicious. My thought took me by surprise. Did I know Radha? Who was this unseen being continually intruding on my thoughts?

The manager nodded. 'It stayed in the velvet box for a long time. Quite by chance I brought it out today…if you wish to exchange it, sir…'

I glanced at you. It seemed as if you were trying to assemble fragments of a puzzle.

Images of Julian Ruthven ordering the ring for Radha at Cavendish Jewellers in Calcutta's Chowringhee Road, now flitted across London's Kingsway—where I saw carriages trundle along the *Sahebi Para* or European area, where memsahibs under parasols walked to swaying crinolines. Indians were forbidden there. Then came the image of Julian sliding the ring on Radha's finger on their wedding night in the storm-tossed barge. I felt as if that barge was swaying beneath my feet. I clutched the table and rebuked myself for the crazy thoughts which had taken possession of me.

'No, no, I replied hoarsely, 'we have searched for this ring through endless Time.'

The store manager gave me a long appraising glance. He seemed to muse, 'This is not an adventurer. He is an educated bloke who has lost his marbles and the young lady is under the spell of this loon.'

I, Alexander, and you Madhusri, stared at your slender hand that bore the emerald solitaire with the initials J and R— as we had gazed at it a century ago.

Mirage

In the summer of 1964 you, Madhusri, graduated with an honours degree in Economics and Political Science. Following my advice, you applied for—and were admitted to—a postgraduate course in International Relations. Now I felt compelled to complete my Ph.D thesis. It seemed as if the sky was our limit. Before settling down to our studies we decided to travel in Italy. Two LSE classmates and Anna joined us. Do you remember those unforgettable days under the amber sunshine that lingers briefly in Europe before the onslaught of cold grey winds?

The English Channel crossing was uncomfortable but once we were on *terra firma*, it was a joy to drive across France, where we stayed at quaint inns of picturesque villages, and gorged on various types of cheese, bread and renowned French wines. Do you remember the drive to the French Riviera, where we breathed the mimosa and myrtle-scented air? We swam in sapphire seas and stayed nights at a small *pensione* with other impecunious students. We laughed when you remarked, 'The French Riviera crowded with people prancing around in near nudity is obscene.'

You became our guide when we entered Milan. You told us of the Viscontis and Sforzas who patronized artists, scholars, engineers and *condottieri*, who made Milan powerful. We halted in Florence to see splendid remnants of the Medici-sponsored Renaissance. While our companions moved through the Uffizzi gallery, I stood before Sandro Botticelli's painting, *The Birth of Venus*, and remarked that you resembled Simonetta Vespucci, the supposed model for Botticelli's immortal painting.

Blushing, you admonished me. 'How can I look like the gorgeous Simonetta who is portrayed without clothes and with only clouds of hair swirling around her?'

I wanted to say, 'I long to see you with only clouds of hair around you,' but dared not. Instead I said, 'Your face is like Simonetta's.'

You murmured, 'Thank you, Alex, but you sound fond and foolish.'

After visiting famous edifices, we five went to the hilltop Piazzale Michelangelo; the breathtaking spectacle of a luminous Florence and bridges over the river Arno enchanted us.

Our grand tour ended in Rome. We had found a small *pensione* near the Palatine palaces and the Circo Massimo.

After a breakfast of *panettone* and *caffe machiato* we roamed around the city of timeless splendour. Twice we went to the spectacular operas in Terme de Caracalla. In later years I would remember that halcyon week in Rome, of walking back through oleander-scented streets at night and the Palatine palaces encased in amber aureoles.

One of the pleasant summer pastimes of Romans is to sit at the outdoor cafés of Via Veneto for after-dinner coffee or liqueur, where people go to see and be seen. The Italian literati and media people sat here. Famous film directors strode down the street with aspiring young starlets. Impoverished Italian noblemen escorted bejewelled American dowagers of uncertain years, before settling into a discreet corner inside. At the brightly lit Café Doney, trans-Atlantic visitors congregated to exchange details of their Roman adventures. We watched the passing parade, then strolled to the Campidoglio, and halted at a café near the Colosseum to drink *granita dei caffe*. Perhaps the umbrella pines and summer breeze heard our words of joy and hope. At Viale Aventino, the last trams glided over the rails and café owners folded up tables and chairs. Silence fell over the eternal city and hushed rumours of the day.

'Can we come here for our honeymoon?' you asked me.

'Why only our honeymoon? I could spend months, even years, here.'

'Isn't that unpractical? How could we earn our living here?'

'I could serve at a Via Veneto bar, where you could sing Tagore songs. Italians might want a break from the doleful arias.'

Our companions who were walking ahead laughed heartily.

We returned as autumn wafted over old imperial London. Hues of North American autumns are flamboyant, while ours are muted, aware that tribulations of sleet and rain lie ahead. But our lives were bright in anticipation of the future.

You entered the postgraduate course with immense enthusiasm. The international relations that you were studying had been transformed. In the past year the international scenario had changed. The hope of the future, J.F. Kennedy, had been assassinated; the Janus-eyed Nikita Khrushchev had been deposed; the pragmatic Harold Macmillan, who wanted to end the Cold War, resigned; and Jawaharlal Nehru, who presided over the non-Western world, had passed away. Only the charismatic Nasser and Tito remained.

The new world leaders had no visions to offer as they trundled from one crisis to another. Paradoxically, we young people preferred the vanished leaders because they had held out hope rather than those who planned cynical games in uncharted terrain. The Cold War was renewed with ferocity through proxy wars in Vietnam, West Asia, Latin America and Africa.

Though these events troubled us, we sailed over dream-laden seas. I spent long arduous hours at the LSE library consulting books for my Ph.D thesis. I also began applying to various organizations for employment. Like my heroic father, I had never been ambitious. Like him, I wanted to win the friendship of the skies, explore the world of men and mind rather than seek status or wealth. After meeting you, I took life more seriously. I wanted to offer you a life of security and intellectual excitement and wished you to find fulfilment in your work. Your parents had sacrificed luxuries to give you the best possible education. You owed it to them to make their sacrifices worthwhile.

Above all, we wanted happiness, which is an elusive and impatient wind or like a restless river that changes courses while heading towards the sea. I wanted to gather happiness and gift it to you. I asked where you would like to live, the children we would cherish amidst our dreams. Your answers were hesitant, as if afraid of asking too much from the Fates. I realized you were not a woman who would confront destiny and demand your dues. Did I sense a philosophic Hindu under the patina of westernization? This made you more attractive.

I was grateful that Mother and Uncle Harry accepted our marriage plans with cheerful equanimity. Not that I would have brooked any opposition to my cherished plans but it was reassuring to know that they not only accepted you, but respected you and wished us happiness. Marriage between people of different cultures is thorny enough without the antagonism of family members.

Sometimes, we would go cycling along leafy lanes of old London. I was amazed at your agility despite the sari billowing around you. One Sunday morning we walked in Hyde Park and paused to sit and watch children sail toy boats on the Serpentine.

A little boy with auburn locks and sapphire eyes caught your attention. Returning your gaze with a strange smile, he walked over and held out his plump little arms to you.

'Hello,' you whispered, taking his hand.

The child laughed and clambered on to your lap. 'Come see my boat,' he chirped. You accompanied him to the Serpentine pond. He indicated his toy boat with a little hand. 'Do you want to sail on my boat?' He asked. You nodded.

Just then his nanny called out, 'Marcus! Come, we must go home.'

Snuggling closer to you he cried out, 'I am home!'

The nanny strode towards us. We surrendered a sobbing Marcus to the virago. Still crying, he turned to wave to you.

As your tears brimmed over, you murmured, 'My ancestress Radha and her husband Julian had a son named Marcus.'

I drew you close, trying to comprehend the incomprehensible.

Sometimes we spent Sundays at my parents' home. 'I hope you are not bored by Sundays at my parents?' I once asked you.

You replied, 'I like them. They represent the best of English traditions.'

'When will I meet your parents?' I asked.

'You can meet my parents when they come to London next June, where Father will represent his ministry at the Commonwealth Prime Ministers Conference.'

'I am looking forward to that. How have they reacted to our plans?'

I remember you hesitate before speaking. 'They asked me to be very certain that we know what challenges our marriage can pose. Of course, they are very impressed by your CV.' You paused again; a smile lit your eyes. 'Mother says you look like an English film star.'

I burst out laughing. 'Which one?'

'She cannot remember their names.'

Autumn turned to winter; Oxford and Regent Streets glittered with decorations. We saved money from our scholarships to buy gifts at Harrods for our families and friends. I watched you ponder over cashmere sweaters for your parents and jackets for your younger brothers. Later you went to the Indian Handicrafts Emporium at Tottenham Court Road to buy Benares silk scarves for Mum and Anna. I bought gifts for your parents, which we sent by registered air mail. Then we bought books for each other at Foyles.

On a December afternoon, sitting by a crackling fire in my parents' home, we read the great Sanskrit poet Banabhatta's *Kadambari*, the world's first work of magical realism. As I read out the hauntingly beautiful passages, you gazed out of the frosted window into the wintry scene outside.

Quietly, you asked, 'Can people really journey from this world to another without losing the identity of their souls?'

There were strange vibrations around us. I felt we had been transported from *terra firma* into another world. Had we lived before? Or were we mere mortals who only asked for some happiness and fulfilment in this existence?

Ah my Beloved, Fill the Cup that Clears, Today of Past Regrets and Future Fears[*]

We welcomed 1965—with hopes and without fears. My final year in the postgraduate course was drawing to an end. I had several good offers from institutions in England and Europe. You were half way through lectures and papers on international relations. There was plenty to study and discuss that tumultuous year. I advised you to apply to international organizations. You preferred to wait until the end of the academic year.

You told me, 'My father will be able to guide me on this. So, let us wait until June.' You had a touching faith in your father's wisdom.

---

[*] Quatrain 20 of *Rubaiyat of Omar Khayyam*. This is the first version of Edward Fitzgerald's translation. Finding no publishers, Edward Fitzgerald printed 250 copies of the poem at his own expense in 1859. Then he translated them again in various versions. Published by The Folio Society, London, in 1970, and bound by W.J. Mackay & Co. Ltd.

That June came—but not in the manner we had anticipated. You received a letter from your father informing you that he was ill and was advised to rest. Your gentle mother tried to cope but she had never dealt with finances or taxes. Your younger brothers felt rudderless. Under the circumstances, he could not attend the Conference of Commonwealth Prime Ministers. I remember that June evening when you stood in abject misery near the LSE clock, where we always met after lectures.

'What is it, Madhusri?' I asked, an old familiar fear clutching my chest, a fear I seemed to have felt across a century, when our parents tried to separate us.

You handed me your father's letter. I read it in growing distress, and paused to look at your sombre face. Though you disliked any 'public display of affection,' I gently led you outside, where you sobbed in my arms.

'Your father's illness is curable,' I said firmly. 'A course of iron injections will do.'

Pleading for assurance, you asked, 'Do you really think so?'

'Yes. Let us go to my parents' place. They will advise us what to do.'

When we went to my parents' place, you announced that you must go home to Calcutta to be with your parents. Mother embraced you and murmured gently, "Of course, dear child.'

I was utterly astonished when Uncle Harry drew me aside and said, 'Go to India with Madhusri immediately after the term ends. She will need strength now. I will pay your airfares.'

In profound gratitude I hugged my stepfather, the stolid, unromantic, hard-nosed banker. My parents asked you to make trunk calls from their place. You came twice a week to speak to your parents, to ask about their health, and reassure them that you would return home in July.

We were surprised when your mother sent a reassuring message. 'Complete your studies. A few months will not make any difference.' She was obviously not in agreement with her husband.

But you, Madhusri, shook your head. 'Mother is anxious. I can sense her sadness. I must go…if only for a few weeks… after writing the exams next month.'

'Would you like me to accompany you?' I asked anxiously, yet hesitant to intrude.

You blinked back threatening tears. 'I would like nothing better but perhaps my family would…'

I nodded. 'I understand. Sometimes, a family wants to be left to themselves in the midst of a crisis. I will be a stranger at the gates. But if I can help…let me go with you.'

Looking at me gravely, you said, 'I shall phone you after seeing how things are at home.'

Apple blossom time arrived in England. I marvelled at the manner in which you composed yourself and wrote the postgraduate exams. The time came for you to leave for India. We sat together in your hostel room on the evening before your departure. I told you to be brave for both your and your parents' sake.

'I lost my father when I was five. Life goes on relentlessly and opens other doors,' I said, embracing you, as if that would nullify the imminent separation.

As I drove you to Heathrow Airport the next morning, sunlight flirted with the clouds and danced on verdant trees. We waited in the lounge until your Air India flight was announced. I held you in my arms—for a minute and an eternity. Then I watched you walk across the tarmac, wisps of wavy hair flying around the sad cameo of your face, the end of your sari blowing towards me in reluctant farewell. Halting, you turned to wave. As you stood motionless looking at me, I had a wild impulse to run to the tarmac, board the plane and fly together to our destiny.

You telephoned me from Calcutta a few days later. To hear you was to hear music! But the music faded as you told me briefly about your father's condition. 'The doctors think it may be something more serious.'

'Doctors are prophets of doom,' I replied tersely. 'That is how they make their living.'

'But one has to take their advice.' You paused and said, 'I wish you could be here—with your optimism.'

'I am ready, waiting, and willing,' I replied, imitating Eliza Doolittle's father.

You laughed. The sound warmed my heart and dispelled my inner fear. You hesitated before describing the chaotic atmosphere at home; one wayward brother and the other who had plunged into melancholy, your mother's weariness and the disorderly servants.

I waited eagerly for your letters, sometimes brief, sometimes long, imbued with dignity, never asking for sympathy. You described the *kalbaisakhi* storms that were prelude to monsoon. Those descriptions stirred memories of distant forgotten *kalbaisakhi*s. One letter described your visit to a Nabadwip temple by the Ganges on Lord Krishna's birthday, of *bhajan*s chanted by the devotees. Remembering our argument in Paris, you added mischievously, 'The place was swarming with Krishna Consciousness votaries.' I smiled, visualizing my sophisticated, high-heeled fiancée in that setting. Your last line moved me. 'I prayed for our dear families––and for you, dearest Alexander. The ashram gave me peace. I felt I had come here once before to seek peace.' This also brought unease; I recalled family accounts of how Radha Ruthven had sought sanctuary in Nabadwip after Julian's death and after their son Marcus was taken away to England.

Your letters were delayed when war broke out between India and Pakistan in August 1965. There was fighting in Kashmir, West and East Pakistan. Major cities were under curfew. It was difficult to get telephone connections, letters went haywire. How I feared for your safety through that terrible month! Confused memories of war disturbed me. Was it of World War II or something older? Frantically, I read news of the Indo-Pakistan war. I wrote asking if I should come to India. I received no answer.

Things Fall Apart

When does Fate take a devious turn and decide a future neither of us wanted? Is there something perverse in human existence that our dreams and hopes, our strivings and efforts, are cast aside for the amusement of the jesting Almighty? When did I sense that something was going wrong? Was it when your letters became infrequent or when they no longer brought me joy? The day I read the last letter it seemed as if the ground trembled beneath me and that the sky caved in.

You informed me that your father had arranged your marriage to a young engineer from a good family. Your father's deteriorating health made this necessary. Should he die…the young man would take care of not only you, but your mother and younger brothers. Something apparently which I, a foreigner, could not do.

I have never forgiven Anna for not revealing what you wrote to her in torment. 'I have agreed to this marriage with a heavy heart. How will I live with memories? How will I surrender my dreams? Don't tell Alex anything. He cannot help me. Thank heaven life does not go on forever.'

Why did Anna keep her vow of secrecy and not inform me of Madhusri's desolation? Women truly are women's worst enemies.

Your father used his illness to persuade you to marry this man. He cited cases of mixed marriages which had ended in disaster for Indian women. 'If the glamorous Shanta Rama Rao could not keep the brilliant Faubion Bowers' fidelity, how will you, an innocent unworldly girl?'

There were other arguments as well. "The cosmopolitan university world is not the real world. You will live in an alien atmosphere where racism lies beneath the surface. You will have to face and fight discrimination if you want to progress, and encounter resentment if you succeed.'

Then your father said that if you married me, Alexander, and lived far away, your mother and younger brothers would face an uncertain future in case he died. You were gently reminded that it was your duty to look after them…even if was at the cost of your own happiness.

Marriage and martyrdom—what a lethal recipe for disaster!

Far away across two continents, your marriage was arranged by your father. The man selected for you was from a 'good family', which I presume in your society meant respectable and stable. How the respectability of family ensures happiness for people was beyond my comprehension. The young man did not share your intellectual interests. Nor did he possess your memories. He liked the good life and led a surface existence.

So, my foolish Madhusri, you renounced happiness not only for yourself but for me as well.

Everything that happened afterwards still remains vague and chaotic. I could not understand the reason for your decision, nor accept why after three years of weaving dreams together, you prepared to tear apart the tapestry of those dreams. Why did you not write to me before you took this decision? Why did you not ask me if I would share your family responsibilities? I oscillated between rage and pain, between love for you and a growing hatred against you.

There came a time when I drank myself senseless every evening and flung myself into joyless iniquity to obliterate your memory. I neglected my work at my organization and failed to keep deadlines, which prompted my seniors to question my suitability and stability. Then I composed myself because work was all that remained in my barren life. In fact, I worked hard for success—no longer to lay my laurels at your feet but in the hope that you would hear about me, regret your sacrifice, and that you would realize what you had thrown away and renounced for a spurious sense of filial duty.

Once, walking on Hampstead Heath, you had told me of the great poet Kalidasa's verse drama—*Messenger of the*

Clouds—where separated lovers sent messages through the clouds. I would spend hours on the terrace of whichever city I was staying, staring at the clouds, like some crazy mystic, desperately waiting for some message. I heard only the sound of howling winds and imagined taunting laughter.

Hesitantly, I made enquiries from university friends if they had heard from you. They shook their heads in astonishment that you and I who were so close had severed our ties.

'Write to her,' one friend advised. 'Madhusri might be waiting for you. Perhaps she feels hesitant to write after...'

'After jilting me,' I retorted.

Frowning, the friend said, 'These Orientals are astonishing. Heaven knows what made Madhusri run away. Was she afraid?'

Banishing pride and summoning courage, I wrote to you—a bland letter of friendship, enquiring after your health, about your parents, whether you were working or studying. I sent the letter to your parents' address because no one knew your present address. The envelope was returned marked 'Addressee not found'.

All communication with you ceased; you could not write to me because my letters never reached you. There were class friends who wrote to you and whose letters were returned in the same manner. This tore to shreds the remnants of my bruised heart. You became my beloved phantom.

I remembered the poem 'To Marya' composed by the great Russian poet Pushkin before his death. He also lost his beloved to another man.

> *Whatever changing fate I knew,*
> *The memory of words last spoken*
> *By you, and your sad wilderness,*
> *Have been my only sacred token,*
> *Sole refuge and ultimate redress.*

And in thy Joyous Errand Reach the Spot, Where I Made one Turn Down an Empty Glass[*]

Five years went by. I passed through Time like a sleep-deprived somnambulist waiting for dawn. I hoped that in some distant city you would hear about me, and remember me with love and regret in forsaking me. But I also hoped that by the very magic I found you standing at *Buds & Blooms* on spring equinox, I would miraculously find you in a city far away, where Fate would bring us together.

In between, weary of hoping against hope, bored by my affluent vagabond life, I decided to marry, though I knew that it was unfair to expect a wife to live under the shadow of an unfulfilled love. After a year of married misery, the lady and I parted amicably and went our different ways. There were no children from this barren union. The dream children you, Madhusri, and I planned, who would have 'blue eyes put in by a smudgy hand' and dark auburn locks—remained the other beloved phantoms of my barren existence.

---

[*] Quatrain 75 of the *Rubaiyat of Omar Khayyam*

Tryst by a
Sacred River—Once More

In the summer of 1971, I was assigned by a British development agency to explore possibilities of establishing small industries in East Pakistan. It seemed an odd time to contemplate such a project when a full-blown revolt had begun in East Pakistan against its West Pakistani overlord.

West and East Pakistan were separated by 2,000 km of Indian territory. Though both professed Islam, East and West Pakistan had cultural, linguistic and ethnic differences that impeded nationhood. It made a mockery of Jinnah's two-nation theory. Though West Pakistan was proportionally in a minority, it attempted to dominate East Pakistan and impose its will on the majority Bengalis.

The people of West Pakistan both feared and hated the majority East Bengalis who despised the 'uneducated and unrefined' West Pakistanis. The Bengalis cherished their world-famous writers: Rabindranath Tagore (whose ancestral home was on the banks of the River Meghna in East Bengal),

Kazi Nazrul Islam, scientists, economists, artists, musicians, weavers of exquisite textiles and their revolutionary traditions.

As language was a contentious issue, Bengali intellectuals and litterateurs were kept under surveillance. Allocation of funds and resources was the other. East Bengal's jute, cotton and rice were sequestered and exported; foreign exchange earnings went to West Pakistan. The Bengali producers did not receive their dues. Economic exploitation, political injustice and cultural tensions incited revolt.

In December 1970 Sheikh Mujibur Rahman's Awami League got an absolute majority in the General Election and justly expected to form a popular government. To avoid rule by Bengalis, West Pakistan overruled the election results. On the orders of Premier Z.A. Bhutto, the army prevented convening the assembly session that would have proved Mujibur Rahman's claim to form a new government. Islamabad made another mistake by making the hybrid Urdu the official language in East Bengal. That the language of Nobel laureate Rabindranath Tagore should be so insulted was the last straw for the culturally proud Bengalis.

As opposition mounted, Islamabad imposed martial law, reinforced by oppression and violence. Sheikh Mujibur Rahman was arrested; from prison he declared secession from Pakistan. East Bengal's War of Independence began in right earnest.

Members of the army in East Bengal who sought freedom from West Pakistan's domination, paramilitary forces, and civilians joined the mutiny. They began subversive activities, blew up power plants and railways to cripple the West Pakistan-backed government that responded with a brutal Operation Blitz. The West Pakistani air force strafed rebel-held areas. Bengali rebels sustained heavy losses; homes were set ablaze, women were mutilated and raped, children massacred. A relentless genocide began. Survivors of the East Bengali army fled to India and lost contact with clandestine organizations that guided the resistance.

By mid-1970 the Bengali forces set up a government-in-exile in Calcutta at an encampment called Mujib Nagar. Bengali dissenters from the Pakistani army set up a command structure in key areas: Faridpur–Potuakhali–Mymensingh, Chittagong–Noakhali. To escape the savagery of West Pakistan's army, more vicious than the Nazi's, millions of mainly Muslim Bengalis fled to neighbouring Hindu West Bengal, where after Partition, East Bengali Hindu refugees after Partition had settled. The burgeoning population had led to severe shortage of food, resources, shelter, unemployment—and unrest.

The Indian government assessed the situation. At first, Prime Minister Indira Gandhi's government maintained neutrality and treated the revolt as an internal matter of Pakistan. There was unrest in West Bengal with the activities of Naxal-Marxist 'revolutionaries'. The army was tasked to deal with their violent acts. The Indian government feared that the Naxals might join forces with kindred-soul-rebels in East Bengal. But India could not treat the insurrection in East Bengal as an internal matter when the growing revolt in East Pakistan brought millions of stunned, hungry, homeless refugees across a 2,000 km border. War between India and West Pakistan became inevitable.

Mujibur Rahman, leader of the opposition movement, went underground on 26th March 1971. A full-blown revolt began. *The Mukti Bahini* (army of liberation) fought the West Pakistani forces.

Richard Nixon visited China in July 1971—the first US President to do so since the Chinese communists took power in 1949. There, Premier Zhou Enlai informed US Secretary of State, Henry Kissinger that in the event of an Indo-Pakistan war over East Bengal, Beijing would launch military attacks against India. So now Nixon's government gave full support to Pakistan for atrocities in East Bengal. Pakistan warned India to refrain from interference in East Bengal.

It was at this stage that I, Alexander Ruthven Courtney, arrived in Dhaka, capital of East Bengal. Members of the international media reported news of the genocide; many nations offered sympathy to East Bengalis but no assistance. NATO's slogans of the 'free world', 'democracy', and 'human rights' stridently chanted in Hungary and Czechoslovakia were forgotten when thousands of ragged, hungry, homeless, Bengali men, women and children were slaughtered by Pakistanis.

The government of India encountered an acute predicament. Should it watch the slaughter of unarmed Bengalis and the exodus into West Bengal of survivors of the carnage? Prime Minister Indira Gandhi and her cabinet colleagues consulted General Manekshaw, head of the Indian Army, on the feasibility of assisting East Bengali freedom fighters and the consequences of war against Pakistan. General Manekshaw asked for additional resources, ammunition, spare equipments and for time.

Then Indira Gandhi undertook a campaign to influence world opinion and garner international support to restrain West Pakistan. In the summer of 1971, the Indian Army joined the Mukti Bahini in guerrilla warfare against Pakistan. On 4th December 1971 Pakistan attacked India.

I witnessed the onslaught of the Indian army on Pakistani forces. Alarmed, the US Seventh Fleet sailed to the coast of East Bengal to assist Pakistan. The Soviet Union responded by sending several cruisers, destroyers and a submarine armed with nuclear warheads to the Bay of Bengal. The Seventh Fleet withdrew. In a few days the Pakistan army surrendered. The people of East Bengal, now Bangladesh, began returning home. A new nation was born through carnage and courage.

This war made me wonder if in the bloody end justice is delivered to the oppressed?

My evaluation reports had been well received by the development agency, though some on the Board felt that I had displayed a partisan spirit.

I left Dhaka for Calcutta. Though I had never been to Calcutta, I felt I had once seen these British Raj edifices, British officers and stylish Memsahebs drive past in smart carriages. Vague memories stirred within me—of Cavendish Jewellers on Chowringhee, where I had ordered an emerald ring; a mansion on Alipur Road where I had lived; a massive neo-classical style Government House where my parents attended receptions.

How did I come here? This was the land of my beloved Madhusri, whom I had not seen or heard of for five years. She had vanished. Was she still in this world? I wondered if the spirit of Radha Ruthven had merged with that of Madhusri. She had told me about the Ruthvens and Chowdhurys. These people had long haunted me.

I decided to confront these phantoms of the past. Then, perhaps I would be liberated from misery and begin a new life. Leaving Calcutta, I set off in search of the Chowdhury estate at Mayurganj, where on the two banks of the River Ganges, the Ruthvens and Chowdhurys had their estates and mansions, where they had fought as antagonists in the 1780s, been friends and collaborators in the 1830s, until their sons Julian Ruthven and Dilip Chowdhury, once devoted friends, declared war on each other during the Indian Mutiny. Here, Radha Ruthven had heard of Julian's death during the siege of Delhi. Broken by grief, she had lived on to give birth to Julian's son, who became Sir Marcus Ruthven, and secretly sponsored Bengali 'terrorists' (the Indians called them 'freedom fighters') in 1905! With Marcus' passing, the Ruthvens' connection with the Chowdhurys had ended. But had it? Why was I here, carrying memories of another age?

Twilight was settling over the river bank and ancient spreading trees. The old mansion seemed familiar; I seemed to hear echoes of laughter, music, and animated debates. Did I see Julian and Radha strolling by the eternal river?

'Stop!' I screamed inwardly. 'You are becoming insane!' But a persistent voice whispered I had been here before. I recognized a banyan tree under which Dilip and Julian had played cards, while Radha and Isabel looked on.

With excitement and trepidation, I walked towards the mansion. Perhaps a new generation of Chowdhurys lived there. Or perhaps it now had new owners. Inside, numerous people were engaged in animated discussions. During my six months in Dhaka I had learned to speak Bengali fluently. This astonished people. They were amused when I used Sanskritised words that had fallen into disuse. From where did I receive this knowledge? From the conversation in the house I learnt that it was the office of an organization that was engaged in relief operations for Bangladeshi refugees.

I stood there, unable to move or assemble my thoughts. Should I leave before I made a fool of myself before those busy people? Or should I go inside and tell them of the horrors I had seen in Bangladesh? Should I inform them of the districts most affected by Pakistani violence and brutality? Would they resent my intrusion? After all, the British government had never said a word in support of the Bangladeshi freedom fighters.

'A stranger is standing at a corner of the garden,' one of the men said loudly. 'Looks European.'

Another man sneered. 'They will come now…to establish business houses, banks, and other means of garnering what riches remain in poor Bangladesh.'

A woman added, 'This fertile sub-division was where a marauding Ruthven came to seize the Chowdhury lands for starting an indigo plantation. But the Sanyasi Rebellion of the 1770s made short work of his plans.'

There was some laughter on this. Then a man looked up from his papers and mused, 'There was also a Julian Ruthven who was posted here at the time of the Mutiny. He made improvements in the revenue system. Defying everyone, he married Radha Chowdhury. Sadly both died during the Mutiny.'

As if seized by pain, a young woman suddenly stood up, sending her chair crashing to the floor. Her agitated voice broke into my bewildered mind. 'I am going out…for fresh air. Please continue sorting out the clothes and food packets.' She came to the colonial-style pillared veranda and looked upwards at the December sky where the first stars glimmered. Then she walked to the flower-filled garden and sat under a blossoming *shefali* tree. Resting her head on her raised knees, she began to cry softly, and then in heart-wrenching sobs.

Had I once seen Radha sitting like this, head resting on her knees, weeping by a river, under a *shefali tree*? I walked slowly to where you sat, head bowed. 'Radha? Or is it Madhusri?' I whispered. 'Can you not recognize me, Alexander-Julian?'

Startled, you looked up at me, unable to believe what you saw. Then you cried out, 'No! You are a phantom of the past! You have been entering through the doors of a dream world, and then returning to an abyss. Please, I entreat you, do not torment me like this!'

I sat and drew you close. 'I have been searching for a beloved I had lost aeons ago. I thought I had found Radha in London but you fled to Calcutta…and disappeared. Now that I have found you, nothing and no one will come between us again. No husband, no children, no rules, no codes. Do you understand?'

I was astounded when you replied—between laughter and tears. 'I have neither husband nor children. When I realized that I had no affinities of mind or dreams with the young man chosen for me, I ran away from home and sought refuge at the ISKCON ashram in Mayapur. There no one asked questions. I organized discussions and musical events and sang Shri Chaitanya's songs.' She paused. 'Do you remember how you once made fun of the Krishna Consciousness group?'

'I ask your forgiveness,' I replied contritely. Smothering my anguish, I continued, 'Why did you not inform me that you had not married?'

Your profile was framed against the sky. 'Because I heard you had married.'

I sighed. 'Yes, I thought it best to forget you. But I couldn't. The marriage lasted only a year.'

'I endured the days with pain and courage—not the courage extolled in battlefields but a more difficult one…when my tears could have drenched a fisherman's net.' The sadness in your melodious voice brought me shafts of pain. I replied, 'Life is not acceptance and sacrifice! Life is the quest for fulfilment and happiness!'

You, Radha-Madhusri, now turned to look at me. Had time stood still? Your eyes have remained luminous, your slender form seems untouched. You still wore the emerald solitaire mounted by the gold letters J and R. It required great restraint not to gather you in my arms and kiss you fiercely, as I had done when I left you at the district magistrate's bungalow while the violence of the Mutiny raged around us.

We sat there, hands clasped, gazing at each other, at a loss for words, heedless of the curious stares of spectators who had come out of the house. Then we rose and walked towards the river bank, remembering the barge where we had spent our wedding night in another existence.

Now, after many ordeals, we had found each other...and perhaps this time we would find happiness. I recited from Omar Khayyam's *Rubaiyat*.

> *Ah Love! Could thou and I with Fate conspire,*
> *To grasp this sorry Scheme of Things entire,*
> *Would not we shatter it to bits—and then*
> *Re-mould it nearer to the Heart's Desire.*[*]

This time we would do just that!

---

[*] Quatrain 73 of the *Rubaiyat of Omar Khayyam*.

 II
WAIT! 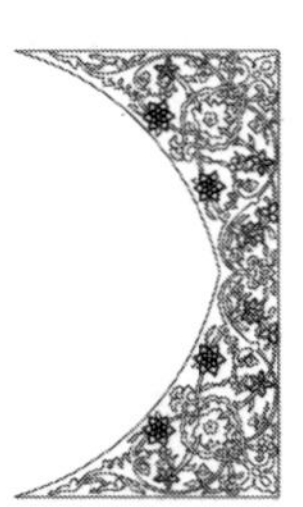

This story is dedicated to
the proud, suffering and courageous people of Afghanistan
who have waited endless years for peace.
May peace be finally upon them!

Wait!

The Merry Month of March — 155

Italy, the Paradise of Exiles — 167

The Eternal City — 176

Roman Fountains of Hope — 188

Dispatches from Kabul — 197

The Promised Bride — 217

Tangled Destinies — 226

Turbulent Journeys — 237

A Game of Errors — 254

The Darkest Dawn — 266

The Prisoner of Kandahar — 278

Messenger of the Clouds — 288

Winter of Despair — 297

The Jailer's Daughter — 302

Storm over Kabul — 309

In Search of Rustom — 319

Russia Comes to Afghanistan — 329

Chains Unbound 343

Sweet Thames, Flow on Till I End My Song 356

Rome, the City Eternal 364

The Tempest of Time 372

Wait For Me

Wait for me, and I'll come back!
Wait, when dreary yellow rains
Wait when friends tell you,
you should not.
Wait when snow is falling fast.
Wait when summer is hot.
Wait when yesterdays are past.
And others are forgot.
Wait, when from that far-off place
Letters don't arrive.
Wait, when those with whom you wait
Doubt if I'm alive.

Kontstantin Simonov[*]

---

[*]'Wait for me' by Konstantin Simonov (1915–1979), translated by Sergei A. Karmalito.

The Merry Month of March

Spring came early in March that year. It caught the skeletal trees and frosted ground unprepared but knowing the fickle English sunshine, unfurled leaves and blades of frozen grass soared sunward to thaw themselves. Outside the International Law Faculty of University College, London, students debated whether to attend the lecture or play truant. Beyond the cobbled Foster Court a park was clamorous with a rush of migrant birds.

Rustom Ferghani, lecturer and assistant to Professor Schwarzenberg, stood outside the lecture hall. After incessant rains, the spring sunlight conjured images of his native Kabul where spring bursts suddenly upon its denizens, prompting flowers to peep through craggy stones and causing melted snow to flow down hillsides. Rustom turned to see the illustrious professor coming down the cobbled path, his stout figure swaying slightly as he conversed with a debonair Ivy League student. The professor greeted Rustom and asked, 'Waiting for me, Mr Ferghani?'

Rustom nodded, 'Yes, sir, and also enjoying the spring air.'

'Come in then,' the professor commanded.

Rustom nodded but waited for a slender sari-clad young woman student who was approaching the lecture hall.

Reaching him, Minoti asked with a smile, 'Is spring really here?'

Rustom's deep-timbered voice was tinged with nostalgia. 'We Afghans also wait for our cruel winters to end,' he said, and then entered the crowded lecture hall. Minoti followed.

Sitting behind a large table, Dr Schwarzenberg waited for the cosmopolitan students to take their seats. Rustom sat nearby. The professor's astute eyes, behind rimless glasses, grazed over his assistant and disciples.

Rustom was educated in France and England and had graduated from London University. Aspiring young African politicians and Arab diplomats sat in respectful silence. Across the aisle were affluent Ivy League American students who wanted to study with the doyen of international law. British students sat behind them exchanging departmental news. Three English women students and Minoti sat at the back of the lecture hall. Intimidated by the professor who hurled caustic questions, the students always responded politely because the illustrious maestro of international law could find placements for his favourite students in renowned law firms or international organizations.

'Shall we start?' The professor asked. Framed as a question, it was a command for halting murmured conversations. Without preamble, he delivered acerbic commentaries on the Vietnam War and asked the students to cite landmark judgements of international law to condemn combatants on both sides. The eager beavers trotted out their knowledge to impress the maestro. Rustom thought of Afghanistan, where jurisprudence struggled with tribal warfare.

The professor strode up and down the aisle and stopped near Rustom. 'You are pensive, Mr Ferghani,' he observed in a guttural Wurtemburg accent.

Rustom nodded. 'I was thinking of the invasions of my country in violation of international law—but Afghans always defeated invaders.'

There was a flicker of interest in the German-Jewish eyes. 'An interesting point. One wonders if history makes its own laws.'

Before Rustom could respond, the professor's eyes darted to Minoti's bent head; she was sketching birds in flight. This was not the first time he had caught her displaying indifference to his wisdom. Striding down the hall, he halted by the timorous young women. One of them nudged Minoti, who raised her head and saw 'old Schwarz' glowering at her. Swiftly, her hands covered the sketch.

As if about to unleash the Spanish Inquisition on her, he asked 'Who was India's greatest political adviser?'

Many male heads turned curiously to look at Minoti because she was an elusive figure. Rising, Minoti replied, 'Chanakya, sir.'

'Wrong!' came the sharp riposte. 'Try again!'

Stubbornly she repeated, 'Chanakya is India's greatest political thinker.'

The irate professor came closer. 'Were I my friend Professor Ayer, I would ask you to leave the class but I don't insult pretty women. Only Nazis do that.' This comment was greeted by male laughter. Satisfied, the professor said, 'Last time, Miss India, what is the name of the great Indian adviser?'

Minoti remained silent.

Dr Schwarzenberg shook his head. 'You do not know? It is Kautilya!'

Rustom had been anxiously watching the exchange; now he rose and said quietly, 'Sir, Chanakya was given the sobriquet Kautilya, which means "The Wily".'

Surprised by his junior's effrontery, Dr Schwarzenberg asked, 'Really? This is epiphany! Thank you, Mr Ferghani.'

There was uneasy silence in the hall; some students smiled with vicarious pleasure that 'Old Schwarz', who believed in his infallibility, had been corrected.

Then Dr Schwarzenberg turned to the grim-faced Minoti. 'My apologies, young lady. An Afghan knight in tweeds has come to your rescue.' More male laughter. He gave her a sardonic smile. 'I trust India and Afghanistan are friends?'

A flushed and angry Minoti did not reply.

Rustom replied for her with an ironic smile. 'Yes, sir, our nations are friends. Kautilya advised that one's enemy's enemy is a friend. We have a common foe in Pakistan.'

The students laughed uproariously and then quickly composed their expressions into rapturous interest when the professor returned to his seat.

Vigorous debates began on the raging Watergate scandal. Minoti stared pensively at the bare trees. When the lecture ended, she waited at Foster Court for Rustom. When he finally emerged she murmured, 'Thank you for informing the Infallible One that Kautilya is Chanakya.'

Laughing, he took her book-laden briefcase. 'Do you feel like minestrone? The little Italian café at Tavistock Square serves a tolerable one.'

They walked in silence in the spring sunshine. Rustom's intervention brought to the surface a turmoil that had swirled around them for some time. They reached the café, sat down and ordered minestrone.

Rustom observed: 'When one grows up amidst persecution one tends to be aggressive. That has happened to our good professor who grew up in Nazi Germany.'

'I would have thought persecution makes people submissive,' Minoti replied.

Rustom shook his head. 'A peoples' response is determined by their temperament. Despite many invasions, Afghanistan has never been subdued.'

'I did not know that people outside India knew about Chanakya-Kautilya and his works,' Minoti said.

'The Indo-Iranian people of Afghanistan—the Kurus, Khambojas, Gandharas—were culturally part of *Indica Magna*. The word *Gandhara* was first mentioned in the Sanskrit *Rig Veda*, then in the *Ramayana* and *Mahabharata*. One of the names of Lord Shiva is Gandhar. His devotees settled in today's Kandahar.'

Minoti listened intently. He continued: 'India, Afghanistan, Iran and Central Asia comprised a vast unitary civilization where Hinduism, Buddhism, Zoroastrianism, and Hellenism flourished. The Hindu Kush range is named after the first settlers. A province there—Kaffiristan or place of infidels— still remains Hindu. These are our cultural legacy.'

Minoti said, 'I had no idea of these affinities! How did it all change?'

'Islam drew up frontiers of the mind which divided people,' he replied.

'Do you regret it?' She asked.

Rustom replied. 'Of course. Frontiers create barriers.'

'So, once we were all one people,' Minoti mused, as if resolving an inner conflict.

Rustom nodded. 'Please remember political frontiers are temporary.' Minoti realized he was trying to remove barricades between them.

For sometime now, Rustom and Minoti had greeted each other before lectures and exchanged pleasantries. Since members of the academic staff were discouraged to fraternize with students, they met only at the three weekly lectures on international law. Sometimes, they stole away to the café atop Dillon's Book Store. After taking tutorials for first year students, Rustom studied in the vast Law Library of University College. Sometimes they walked through Bloomsbury to their university hostels.

At University College, Wednesday afternoons were set apart for sports. Thus freed, Rustom and Minoti strolled by Victoria Embankment and discussed international events. After crossing the barrier of formality, Rustom told her about his father, who was adviser to King Zahir Shah, and of his mother and sisters.

His father expected him to return home after he obtained a doctorate in international law to join Afghanistan's civil service. Hearing this, Minoti concealed a furtive pain. Observing her darkened eyes, he asked her gently, 'What are your plans for the future?'

'My parents live in Rome, where my father works for an international organization. My brother lives in America and my sisters are married to successful men in India. After I obtain my bachelor's degree, I am expected to follow suit.'

Fearing she might drift away, Rustom asked, 'Don't you want to pursue a career?

Minoti shrugged. 'Our destinies have been charted out. Our frontiers have been drawn.'

Looking intently at her Rustom replied, 'No destiny is charted out. We can make our own.'

As the sun slanted westwards a wind blew in from the Thames. They returned to their hostels, wondering what lay ahead.

Students tried to resist the wizardry of spring because university examinations came at the end of May. Minoti studied and took notes at the UCL law library; sometimes Rustom took her to 'Sicilian Avenue', a restaurant in Burlington Arcades. Glancing around the elegant ambience he described wooden tea-houses in rural Afghanistan where people sat around trestle tables, drank amber tea, cracked walnuts and inhaled opium from bubbling *hookahs*.He mused that with luminous eyes, delicate features, and black hair coiled in a chignon, she looked different from the sternly beautiful Afghan women.

'It sounds picturesque,' she said.

'One day you might see such tea-houses,' he said wistfully. Then changing the subject, he asked, 'How is the cramming going?'

'When I meet classmates and start discussing the exams, I feel nervous.'

'Don't worry, I shall give you my notes on case laws. Professor Schwarzenberg likes answers laced with the case laws he argued at The Hague —and won.'

'Thank you. Do you have notes on the breakdown of the League of Nations?'

'I have a whole pile. But treat them carefully. One day I intend to write about it.' He paused. 'When Afghanistan became a member of the League of Nations in 1934, my father accompanied young King Zahir Shah to a session of the League.'

'How sad that a small country like Afghanistan was a member of the League while India, a large nation with millions of people, lived under British rule!'

'How did ten-thousand Englishmen subjugate three-hundred-million people?' Rustom's voice was sharper than he intended.

Pained, she replied, 'You are being discourteous to my country.'

He stretched his hand and laid it on hers. 'I am sorry...I did not intend to be rude. I have wondered how your great nation came under foreign rule. We have always helped Indian revolutionaries like Subhash Bose.' He paused. 'Do you know how two *Kabuli-wallas*, as Indians call people of Afghanistan, came to the Bose mansion on Elgin Road to sell their famed dry fruits? To enforce Subhash Bose's house arrest, a large police contingent encircled the house. The police chaps searched the big bags of the *Kabuli-wallas* and found nothing objectionable. They also helped themselves to handfuls of walnuts and apricots. The two *Kabuli-wallahs* entered the house. One *Kabuli-walla* gave Subhash Bose his clothes, turban and a false beard. Swinging their empty bags the genuine *Kabuli-walla* and the Bengali *Kabuli-walla* jauntily walked out of the house. They walked for a while, hailed a taxi for Howrah Station and there boarded the waiting Kalka Mail for Pathankot where 'Frontier Gandhi's' disciples were waiting to receive them. From there the men travelled to Kabul, where King Zahir Shah organised Bose's escape on the old Silk Road to Europe, where Subhash began raising arms for the future Indian National Army.'

'That is why we Bengalis love *Kabuli-wallas*. Rabindranath Tagore has written an enchanting story of a *Kabuli-walla* and a little girl.'

Rustom nodded. 'I saw the film based on the story.'

Minoti smiled. 'Now tell me about your King Zahir Shah.'

Rustom continued. 'Our king attended a school for the

nobility in Kabul and then studied at the Pasteur Institute and University of Montpellier in France. King Zahir Shah and his family tried to bring law and order to Afghanistan. He served as deputy war minister and minister of education. Like many educated Afghans he spoke English and French as well as our Pashto. He had friendly ties with Russia, cordial relations with Britain and France, as well as Germany and Italy. But he maintained Afghanistan's neutrality. So, Kabul became a centre of international espionage during World War II. After the war he sought assistance from both the USA and the Soviet Union for the development of Afghanistan. He promulgated a constitution, established a parliament or *Loya Jirga*, free elections, universal suffrage, and emancipation of women.'

'I wish our rajas and nawabs had been as enlightened as your king,' Minoti said wistfully.

'The king wants me to join our diplomatic service,' Rustom said quietly.

Minoti nodded. 'Your education, knowledge of international relations and numerous languages, makes you most suited to that profession.'

'Your education and upbringing also makes you suited to diplomatic life,' Rustom replied.

Minoti sighed and shook her head. 'In India there are stiff entrance exams for that, entailing slogging for years. I would rather work in a law firm.'

He took her hand. 'Would you like life with an Afghan diplomat?'

She had never thought of a future with Rustom because he had never expressed his sentiments. And here he was offering marriage without preambles! Composing herself, she replied, 'There are numerous barriers between us.'

He spoke gently. 'Barriers can be pushed aside with a little effort. Our affinities are stronger than the differences.' He paused. 'Think about it, Minoti, and give me your answer before you go home for the holidays.'

The entreaty in his voice moved her deeply.

Rustom paused. 'I need an educated wife to guide me in international relations.'

Minoti laughed. 'Is that why you are offering marriage?'

Rustom nodded.

As they walked back to their respective hostels, Rustom drew Minoti close to shield her from the lashing rain. Minoti murmured, 'I feel spring has burst upon us.'

He quoted lines from a Pushkin poem.

'This is magic indeed! How did it come to us, unsought and undeserved!'

Italy, the Paradise of Exiles

Minoti stayed on in London until the results of her examination were announced. She passed with honours. Rustom obtained his postgraduate degree in jurisprudence and international law with *summa cum laude*. After the first transports of joy at the thought of their marriage, they realized the daunting task that lay ahead—of convincing their families.

Rustom decided to go to Kabul in August to announce his plans to his father. He decided that if his father opposed his marriage with Minoti he would nevertheless marry her and pursue an academic career at a European university. He had one trump card—the affection of King Zahir Shah—who would intervene on his behalf. They decided to spend a few weeks in London together before leaving for their homes.

It was a piquant situation; a Afghan academic and an Indian student finding sanctuary in the capital of a country which had waged wars of conquest on both their nations. In Minoti's parents' nomadic existence, London provided the semblance of a home. For Rustom, it was a place for learning and training before he returned to his native land.

'I feel like a passenger on the Silk Road caravans that passed across Central Asia, India, Afghanistan, Iran, and Turkey on their westward journey,' Rustom mused. 'As travellers exchanged culture and commerce with alien people, their diverse identities dissolved and they became eclectic voyagers.'

Listening with interest, Minoti observed, 'If only mankind had stayed that way.'

'Occidental scholars have underplayed the achievements of the Orient to fortify their claim to supremacy. Take the British. Afghanistan was only a part of the Great Game…a buffer state between the Tsarist and the British empires. I doubt if Britons knew anything of Afghan poets, philosophers, mystics, centres of learning, our rich and eclectic civilization.'

Minoti smiled. 'I see you are an ardent Afghan nationalist.'

Rustom nodded. 'We defeated many invading armies. That is why Afghanistan is called the graveyard of foreign empires.'

Minoti said, 'I must learn about your country and customs.'

'Start with the Vedic times, when our affinities and divinities were the same. Buddhism followed. Then came Hellenic culture. Read our great poet Jalaluddin Rumi, who infused Islam with Hindu mysticism, which became Sufism. He fled from Koyna to Turkey at the time of the Mongol invasions, scattering his verses along the way, where they were recited by the inhabitants for many centuries. Reading his verses, you will never guess Rumi was Muslim.' He recited:

'I sought Thee in a temple
Then in a mosque
And in other places of worship
There was no need.
I found Thee in my heart.'

Minoti realized that he was telling her that he was not a bigot nor an atheist and that in between international law and jurisprudence, Rustom had read about Hinduism and Indian history.

'Afghanistan has also been the fulcrum of empires. We keep ourselves informed both about foes and friends,' Rustom said.

Staring at the flowers in the park where they were sitting, Minoti asked sombrely, 'Do my people come under the category of friend or foe?'

Laughing, Rustom replied, 'Oh, friend, definitely! I would not dare take you to Kabul were you a foe!' Beneath the banter there rippled the anxiety of reconciling alien worlds.

But the days passed on wings of joy as Rustom and Minoti strolled over bridges, wandered across heaths, went to hear soul-storming music at Festival Hall, operas at Covent Garden, and explored restaurants in Soho. They walked through streets illumined by northern lights. Both had lived for many years in London but now it seemed as if they were seeing the city through dream-filled eyes. The day of parting drew near. Rustom prepared for the journey home and the dreaded encounter with his father. Minoti told her parents that she was coming home soon and feared the waiting storm when she would announce her betrothal to Rustom.

On 17th July 1973, Rustom was stunned to hear on BBC radio that while King Zahir Shah was in Italy for eye surgery, his cousin Mohammed Daoud Khan had staged a coup d'état, announced deposition of the king, and declared Afghanistan a republic, with himself as President. Previously, as Prime Minister, Daoud Khan had supported militias on the Durand Line and this had prompted Pakistan to close its borders. Receiving scant support from the USA, which was an ally of Pakistan, Daoud Khan had turned to the Soviet Union for economic and military assistance, which was duly given. Daoud Khan intensified tension with Pakistan. Fearing a war, the King had dismissed Daoud Khan as Prime Minister in 1963. He, in turn, had waited for revenge.

King Zahir Shah had introduced a new constitution in 1964 whereby elected representatives would form the *Loya Jirga* or grand assembly. He established a Constitution, excluded members of the royal family from the Council of Ministers, and removed their royal powers. He introduced reforms that took time to implement. Wanting to reform Afghanistan's medieval customs and laws, the King declared that the laws passed by

Parliament would supersede Sharia law. This angered Muslim clerics. King Zahir Shah was revered by his people because he had brought peace and stability. They called him '*Baba*' (Father). Amidst the welter of tribal feuds, he was the symbol of unity.

Fervently Pashtun, he intimidated Pakistan by proposing a Pashtunistan that would fragment Pakistan. The King implemented development projects in irrigation and communication. By taking both Soviet and American assistance he retained Afghanistan's neutrality. However, economic progress slowed down when drought and famine adversely affected the country in 1971–72. This led to food shortage, inflation and discontent. Taking advantage of the unrest, Prince Daoud Khan deposed his absent royal cousin.

After hearing the news Rustom went to Minoti's hostel, which was now almost empty because most students had gone home for the summer vacation. He asked the concierge to inform Minoti that he was waiting.

Hurrying down from her room, Minoti saw him pacing the porter's lodge. 'What is it? You look very anxious,' she asked.

'Anxious! That is an understatement! Afghanistan is in turmoil! Our good King has been deposed and his cousin Prince Daoud has declared a republic, with himself as President!' He paused, distraught. 'I wish I could do something to help King Zahir. He is like a father to me.'

Minoti was concerned; she realized that Rustom had lost a powerful ally and asked, 'What do you intend to do?'

Rustom glanced around him. 'Let us go somewhere we can discuss this.'

'We can sit in my room and talk quietly.'

'A man in your room could tarnish your reputation.'

'I never know whether you are serious or being amusing.'

'I try to amuse you. You are too serious for your age.'

They sat in Minoti's room, where a vase of daffodils stood on the window ledge. Her sketches of birds in flight embellished the grey walls. 'This is a tranquil place. I wish I could come here more often,' he murmured.

'You can come when you are in need of tranquillity.'

Rustom's expression changed. 'I may not be able to visit you in the near future.'

Minoti asked with sudden dread, 'Why?'

'I must go to Rome—to meet the king. He is recovering from eye surgery in a villa at Olgiata, a Roman suburb.'

'Rome!' Minoti exclaimed. 'That is where my parents live!'

'But of course! So now I can meet your parents and ask for their blessings.' Rustom saw her eyes darken. She was afraid of her parents' reaction. He asked, 'Will there be difficulties—my being an Afghan and Muslim?'

'Don't worry about that now. Meet your king and make your future plans.'

That evening Rustom informed his father over the phone that he was planning to meet King Zahir in Rome. General Ferghani had recently pledged allegiance to President Daoud Khan. So he spoke angrily to Rustom. 'Have you taken leave of your senses? Prince Daoud will regard this as treason!'

Rustom retorted, 'Treason, Baba? What the Prince has done to his liege lord is the highest treason!'

General Ferghani warned Rustom. 'Be careful of your words, my son. We live in uncertain times.'

A few days later Rustom Ferghani went to Rome by a BEA flight and drove to the villa in the stylish suburb of Olgiata, where Zahir Shah was recuperating. Armed *carabinieri*s paced the grounds as the Italian government feared assassination attempts on the King. After Rustom's credentials were verified, he entered the villa and was led up the marble stairs by an Afghan attendant who spoke excitedly in Pashtu. He entered the room where King Zahir Shah sat on a brocaded armchair, wearing an elegant suit and striped Pashtun turban. Upon seeing Rustom, the haggard royal face creased into a smile.

Rustom bent his head over the king's extended hand. 'I am here to serve Your Majesty,' he said sombrely.

King Zahir Shah rose and embraced Rustom. 'I see you are a true son of Babur's Ferghana. But I want no sacrifices. You have many achievements to attain. That will not be possible if you join me. Return to Kabul and make peace with Daoud.

The future is with him, now the ruler of Afghanistan—not with an exiled king. Join the civil service or the diplomatic service. Marry one of Daoud's nieces and you will prosper.'

'Prince Daoud is married to your sister. Did that help?' Rustom asked grimly.

The King sighed in resignation and narrated the events that led to declaration of the republic and his deposition. 'My policy for progress did not proceed well. The elements went against me. There was drought and famine, shortage of food and high prices. Maybe I should have checkmated my cousin long ago. I failed to sense the danger.'

But Rustom sensed something else in the resigned attitude—as if the King was happy to be relieved of the weight of the throne. Interestingly, Daoud Khan had not harmed family members or adherents of the king. Rustom's father, General Ferghani, had been retained in the important position in the defence ministry. These were not customary in the aftermath of a coup. Had the two patriotic princes agreed to this bloodless coup to save Afghanistan from civil war?

Affirming Rustom's thoughts, the King said, 'I want no bloodshed in my name.' He paused and asked, 'I sense you are troubled. What is it?'

'I want to marry an Indian girl studying at University College. When my professor is busy, I take her for tutorials now and then. She is 21, well born and well educated.' Rustom paused. 'I would like Your Majesty to meet her and give us your blessings.'

Frowning, King Zahir asked, 'I gather from your hesitation that she is not of our…creed?'

Rustom replied, 'No, Sire. She is…Hindu.'

For some time, the king looked solemnly at the garden below where the purple wistaria tumbling over gates swayed in the summer breeze. Then he turned to Rustom. 'You have my blessings. I am not religious. But your father? He is proud of the Babur-Ferghana lineage.' There was a touch of sarcasm in the king's voice.

'So he says. What happened in Babur's harem is anyone's guess. And Father's concubine, the former actress, what is her lineage?'

'Neither she nor her son are expected to continue family traditions, Rustom. You are his heir. Anyway, I would be happy to meet your fiancée and assist in any way.'

Rustom stayed with the exiled King at the villa filled with royal family members and his entourage who refused to return to Daoud Khan's Republic. Rustom felt happy to be with his compatriots, converse with them in Pashto, to eat the kebabs and tandoori bread he had missed. All this suddenly made him yearn for Kabul and the Hindu Kush range looming over the town.

The Eternal City

Arriving in Rome a few days after Rustom, Minoti disarmed her parents with accounts of her studies and the postgraduate course for which she had been admitted.

When Rustom telephoned her parents' home, he was happy to hear Minoti's voice and narrated what had transpired. 'Would you like to meet the king? Is Olgiata far from your parents' home?'

Minoti said she would meet him the next morning.

After her father, Nihar Ray, left for his office and her mother, Leela, sat down for morning *puja*, Minoti left home, saying she was meeting visiting university friends. The taxi took 40 minutes to negotiate the traffic on Via Cassia to reach Olgiata and the villa, which was known as 'Casa del Reggio de Afghana' or House of the Afghan King. Rustom awaited her at the flower-festooned gate. Only a week had transpired since he had left London but it had felt like a lifetime. Oblivious of spectators, Rustom embraced Minoti. Curious members of the king's entourage watched the tall, rugged Rustom and the sari-clad Minoti walk towards the royal villa.

King Zahir Shah rose as the duo entered the opulent sitting room. His sapient eyes scrutinized the young Indian woman. Listening to and watching her, the king realized why Rustom had embarked on an unwise journey. They discussed everything except future plans of the young people. By the time post-lunch coffee was served, the king was won over. As the summer sunshine mellowed, the king broached the subject. Master of conducting high-level negotiations, he told them of the difficulties they would encounter, the tensions that could disturb their harmony and the conflicts that could erode their affection. 'Such a situation requires the support of both families. Obtain that and then proceed with your dreams,' he said.

Next evening Rustom Ferghani arrived at the Rays' well-appointed apartment, on Aventine Hill. It indicated the sophistication of its *padroni*. Many international civil servants lived there.

Minoti went down to the courtyard to receive him and murmured hurried instructions. 'I have told my parents that you are a good friend. If we announce our engagement now, there will be a furore. Let them meet you several times before we announce our engagement.'

'This is not right!' Rustom protested. 'We must be honest with our parents.'

Minoti disagreed. 'I know my parents, especially my father. Please do as I say.'

Minoti's parents were warm in their welcome. Because of their support to Subhash Bose, Afghans are popular with Bengalis. The housekeeper, Lucia, served aromatic coffee and *millefoglie* pastry. Nihar Ray was agitated by news of Zahir Shah's deposition and drew Rustom into a political discussion, to which Rustom responded eagerly. Both criticized Daoud Khan for the coup.

'I expect you know that your King is residing in Rome?' Mr Ray asked.

While Minoti feigned ignorance, Rustom replied, 'Yes sir, I know. I am staying with His Majesty at Olgiata.' Seeing the astonishment of the Rays, he added, 'I am a sort of godson to His Majesty.' Rustom paused. 'The King took an interest in my education and suggested that I study International Law at London University as this would be useful in a possible diplomatic career.'

'Is your father of the royal Durrani family?' Mr Ray asked.

Rustom shook his head. 'No, our family came from Ferghana with Babur—hence our name. Our family stayed in Afghanistan, while Babur's other followers settled in Hindustan.'

Leela's serene eyes sparkled with interest in historical drama.

'Hmm,' Mr Ray muttered, not quite favouring the drift of the conversation because it reminded him of Muslim rule, which pained him, an ardent Hindu-Brahmin. Vaguely troubled, he went to the mahogany liquor cabinet and brought out a bottle of martini, instructed Lucia to bring wine glasses, ice, lemon peel, and maraschino cherry. Moodily stirring the martini, he asked Rustom. 'Do you drink? I know Islam forbids alcohol.'

'Yes, he does,' Minoti replied. 'Once he drank himself silly at a university party and danced the tango and rumba for hours.'

'Minoti exaggerates,' Rustom replied with a furtive tenderness that made Mr Ray frown and pause in stirring the martini to glance at his daughter and the young Afghan.

They discussed the duel between the West and the Soviet Union. Rustom expressed hope that the neutrality of Afghanistan would continue under Daoud Khan. After another round of martinis, Rustom rose and bent his head over Leela Ray's extended jewelled hand. 'Thank you, Madame, for a wonderful evening.' Turning to Mr Ray he said, 'Sir, would you care to meet our King? He would enjoy a political discussion with you.'

'I would be honoured to meet the man who assisted Subhash Bose's escape to Europe to raise funds for the Azad Hind Fauj,' Nihar Ray replied warmly. He added that he would like to bring his friend, Senator Fuschini, from the Italian Christian Democratic Party because this could help the King, should he wish to form a government in exile. Rustom promised to arrange a meeting.

A few days later, Minoti and her parents, accompanied by Senator Fuschini, met the deposed Afghan king, who cordially welcomed them.

He told them: 'Let me tell you a few things about my country. The first thing you have to know is that we are and always will be a mosaic of many different languages and cultures and ethnicities and approaches to Islam. There are 14 ethnic groups recognized in our national anthem—Pashtuns, Tajiks, Hazaras, Uzbeks, Balochis, Turkmens, Nooristanis, Pamiris, Arabs, Gujars, Brahuis, Qizilbash, Aimaq, and Pashai. We have Sunni, Sufi, and Shiite Muslims. The reason the country was relatively peaceful under my leadership, until my idiot cousin toppled me, was that people saw me as a unifying symbol to whom they could all relate.'[†]

While the three men talked in the large drawing room, a lady-in-waiting took Leela Ray to meet the stately Queen Hamira. This left Rustom free to stroll with Minoti in the flowering gardens. Motionless tall cypress trees cast shadows on the ground. Glancing around, Minoti murmured, 'It all looks like a Tuscan painting.'

----

† This was King Zahir Shah's actual statement.

Rustom asked, 'Why don't we organize a trip to Florence? I have been there before but the trip would give me an excuse to extend my stay here instead of rushing back to Kabul. We could take along a few escorts to avoid gossip.'

'You would find Southern Italy more interesting, especially the Costiera Amalfitana, where Arabs established principalities after conquering Spain.'

Rustom laughed. 'We Afghans don't care much for Arabs but we shall go there if you wish. I believe the scenery is breathtakingly beautiful.'

Minoti nodded. 'Those who settled there never returned to their original home.'

He spoke sombrely: 'I will then be an exception. I want to return home and work there.' He added. 'Your presence will inspire me.'

As they drove back after dining with King Zahir Shah and Queen Hamira, Leela Ray said, 'What a charming young man is Rustom! If only he was Indian I would ask him to marry you, Minoti.'

'Not only Indian but Hindu,' Mr Ray added heavily, glancing at the rear-view mirror to gauge Minoti's expression. Laughing, Senator Fuschini said, '*Mio amico, tu sei un fanatico*' (My friend, you're a fanatic).

'Yes, that would have been nice,' Minoti murmured. She realized that her father had drawn the battle lines.

A few days later Minoti told her parents that she was going to Naples with some university friends who had arrived in Rome. She dared not inform them that dreading the impending separation, she wanted to be alone with Rustom. He took a car from the royal garage and set off with Minoti for Amalfi.

The Costiera Amalfitana or Amalfi Coast is breathtaking. The winding road follows the contours of the hills glowing with olives, lemon and orange. The ubiquitous Tyrrhenian Sea lay below. Standing on jutting promontories *Torre Saraceni* or Saracen Towers were built by Moorish barons whose soldiers kept vigil for invading ships from Sicily and North Africa. Rustom and Minoti stopped for lunch at Amalfi. Standing on the pier by the Moorish style cathedral they got a panoramic view of the town with its yellow and orange-walled, red-tiled houses and the harbour lined with small sailing boats. After *zuppa de frutta dei mare* (soup of the fruits of the sea) and *caffè macchiato* they sat in silence, watching tourists from many lands. Seeing Minoti's pensive face, Rustom asked gently, 'Are you afraid? Would you like to return to Rome? I do not want to…dishonour you…'

'Is there dishonour in love?' Minoti asked.

'Not in the love I have for you.' He rose and held out his hand. 'Let us go. I don't want to drive along the curving road after dusk.'

They drove along the highway until they came to the little port town of Positano where Minoti asked Rustom to stop. 'I want to show you the place where the poet Robert Browning and his bride Elizabeth Barrett strolled after eloping.'

Rustom replied, 'I am ready to elope if you are.'

They strolled to where artists were sketching the scene. 'One day we shall return here when you can make sketches of the promenade,' Rustom said, as they ascended the bougainvillea-lined steps to the road.

The sun was setting in many-hued splendour over the sea when they came to the picturesque hill town of Ravello. They went to Pensione Torre dello Ziro, a villa that had been built by a merchant-baron centuries ago. Perched on a hill, it was built in Moorish style with pointed arches and round windows. The hotel manager gave the *Coppia Indiana* (Indian couple) a room with a curved balcony overlooking the sea. Amused, Rustom looked at Minoti and asked in broken Hindi. 'Should I tell him that I am an Afghan warlord?'

Minoti laughed. 'He will then raise the charges.'

Rustom and Minoti stood on the balcony, deep in thought, looking at the scene before them. Then they went to the picturesque terrace where dinner was being served. Guests sat at tables, drinking local wine, while musicians in *jongleur* costumes strummed on guitars. A baritone sang Tosca's farewell song, *'E lucevan le stelle'* (And the stars were shining). After dinner they gazed down at illumined houses, streets and ships on the small harbour. Neither touched the complimentary wine placed before them.

'This is the most beautiful place I have seen,' Rustom murmured.

Minoti nodded. 'I have been here before but wanted to share it with you. It seems more beautiful with you.'

As night deepened the lights below twinkled off, leaving the sea in darkness. When the terrace became empty, Rustom rose and said, 'It is late and the restaurant staff are waiting for us to leave. Tomorrow you can show me around Ravello and see paradise blooming.'

They discovered another paradise that night. Months of physical yearning culminated in the encounter. As words had been exchanged, now caresses were offered and taken. Unspoken thoughts were finally expressed. Yearning ignited flames until a deeper fulfilment of the spirit quenched the flames. Rustom and Minoti fell asleep in each other's arms. A fragrant mimosa-scented breeze wafted over them like a benediction.

They woke to the sound of travellers on the breakfast balcony and others walking down the slope below, laughing and planning the day's schedule. Rustom ran his hands through her wavy dark hair, and traced over her features.

Opening her eyes, she asked, 'Was it all a dream?'

'I think so. That is why I am touching you to ascertain whether you are Minoti or a phantom of my imagination.' He paused. 'I have fears that you might vanish…that something like this cannot last.'

Minoti smiled. 'We must be careful. Spirits of Christians and Moors who fought on these hillsides still hover here. The Moors came here and to Sicily after they were defeated by your Indian-Afghan ancestors. Shall we go to Sicily?'

Rustom's eyes darkened. 'We don't have much time to spend here, my love. I have to return home soon.'

Minoti sighed. 'I know. Well, let us start the day. After breakfast I shall take you to Villa Ruffolo, redolent with romance and violence.'

Perched on a high hill, Villa Ruffolo was the residence of the lords of Ravello during medieval times. The low ceilings and arched doors were decorated with Moorish geometrical designs. Standing by tall casements, they looked down on the sapphire sea which met the azure horizon. In between, terraced gardens cascaded from one level to another. They strolled around, breathing the mimosa and myrtle-scented air.

'The manager of our hotel told me that there will be a moonlit concert in the garden tonight. Would you like to attend it?' Rustom asked.

Minoti nodded. 'It will be unforgettable.'

Seated on a raised platform, musicians were tuning their instruments when Rustom and Minoti arrived. Moonlight encased the audience seated in a semi-circle flanked by ancient Roman fountains. Cicadas hummed from shrubs. The young lovers sat listening to Grieg and Paganini. When the concert ended, Rustom and Minoti walked back to the Pensione through undulant streets where brooding medieval villas emerged from shadowy gardens. Reaching their hotel room, Rustom threw open the balcony door to let the scented air and moonlight enter and be witnesses to their joyous turmoil.

Two days later they left Ravello and returned to Rome. They spoke little on the journey. It was as if they were afraid of saying or doing something that might dispel the magic of their brief idyll when the past and future were discarded in the ecstasy of the present. They wanted to preserve images of their idyll as a talisman into the future. Nearing Rome, they realized that the future was full of uncertainty. This intensified their attachment.

In the week that they had been away dramatic developments had taken place. Zahir Shah was informed by his cousin Prince Daoud, now President of Afghanistan, that he would not be allowed to return. Had the King opposed Prince Daoud, many would have been ready to fight for him but Zahir Shah did not wish to plunge his beloved country into a civil war. King Zahir Shah formally abdicated his throne in August 1973.

President Daoud did not possess the tact of King Zahir Shah, who gave the impression of humility by cultivating pears and apples in his orchard, nor the patience which he practised when stalking deer and wild goat on arid Afghan hillsides. King Zahir Shah did not believe in confrontation; he had obtained his goal by exercising power with wisdom. In later years Rustom mused that Zahir Shah's abdication changed the fate of Afghanistan and hurtled her towards a tragic and interminable chaos.

Roman Fountains of Hope

Returning from Costiera Amalfitana, they decided to announce their engagement but King Zahir handed several telegrams that General Ferghani had sent Rustom, urging him to return to Kabul.

Also, in a letter to the deposed King, the General entreated him: 'Sire, please dissuade Rustom from joining you and your followers in dangerous politics of establishing a government-in-exile in Italy. What will my son do as an exile? I have given Rustom an excellent education so that he can serve Afghanistan, make his contribution in governance, and carry on family traditions. His mother and I have selected several possible brides for him. I would like to see grandsons continue our bloodline. Is all this to be nullified because the reckless boy wants to walk a lonely road? Please, Sire, send him home! There is much he can do here.'

One day Rustom said he had to discuss plans and asked Minoti to drive with him to Ostia, an ancient Roman port, now a resort. *Sporting Beach*, the popular café (so named to please Anglo-Saxon tourists) was full that night. The juke box played the current winning song of the San Marino contest—*Vagabondo*. The lilting music contrasted with the sound of waves crashing on the beach. Seeing Rustom's sombre face, Minoti realized that he was unhappy at what he had to tell her. After ordering the café's summer speciality—*granite di caffe con panna*—she stared at the white crested-waves rushing towards the shore. It seemed as if something sinister was approaching them.

Rustom broke the silence. 'My father has been sending telegrams asking me to return home.' Staring at the waves, Minoti nodded. He continued. 'I sent back a telegram saying that I was settling down to an academic career in the International Law faculty. After sometime with Dr Schwarzenberg's sponsorship, I could join the International Court of Justice at The Hague.' Rustom waited for Minoti's response; having none he said, 'For heaven's sake, say something, Minoti!'

Blinking back tears, she turned to look at him. 'What would you like me to say? "Return home as your father commands" or "Ignore his pleas! Design your future as you wish!"'

Shaking his head, Rustom raised his hand and beckoned a waiter. '*Signor*, could you get me a glass of Strega?' The waiter nodded, pleased to be called *Signor* instead of *garcon*.

Minoti smiled through tears. 'I didn't think Afghans needed Dutch courage to break bad news.'

Rustom shook his head.' 'It is not entirely bad news, Minoti.' Bringing out a little box from his jacket pocket, he opened it. Minoti saw an exquisite sapphire ring. 'Family heirloom,' he said. 'My grandmother gifted it to me and asked me to give it to a woman who would illumine our house.' He slid the ring on her finger and clasped her hand in his. 'I shall go to Kabul for a while, then return to London to take you to our home in Kabul with its gardens of tulips and pomegranate trees, encircled by the snow-crested Hindu Kush ranges. We will get married there.'

'Will you really return? Or will you be the forgetful Rustom of Firdausi's *Shah Nama?*'

Minoti's sad query pained Rustom; he almost changed his mind about returning home. 'I am going for a short time. I shall return soon.' He paused. 'If my name bothers you, give me a new name—a Hindu name.'

Minoti shook her head. 'A Hindu name would not suit a rough Afghan like you.' Silently, they gazed at the sea that would soon separate them.

The young lovers no longer made up stories for their meetings. Rustom's determination to marry and take her to Afghanistan emboldened Minoti. They met at the Ray home and then went out for dinner to *trattoria*s, or she would go to the deposed King's villa at Olgiata and spend the day with Rustom where no one disturbed them in the large sunlit room on the second floor. In between passionate interludes were hours of interesting conversation.

Once, Rustom said, 'Why didn't I grow up as an ignorant, violent warlord? Why has knowledge brought me the predicament of warring dreams?'

'When you talk like this, you remind me of Crown Prince Dara Shikoh, son of Emperor Shah Jahan, who liked exploring philosophical ideas and theology. Had he lived to rule India, our history would have been different. He was no sinner turned saint like Ashoka or the megalomaniac Alexander.'

Rustom laughed. 'Sitting in this imperial city of violence and massacres are you questioning the greatness of warriors?'

Minoti replied, 'None of them were great. Military campaigns that cause massacres have nothing to do with greatness.'

Rustom nodded thoughtfully. 'Yes, the humility of the soul brings us closer to knowledge of the universe, of divinity and our real identity. We should discard puerile theories of past preachers.'

'The Upanishads attempt to offer answers,' Minoti said.

Rustom replied, 'The composers of those treatises had no names. They revelled in the anonymity of their souls which were in quest of truth.'

These discourses would be broken by royal attendants summoning them to dine with the former king and queen, where there were animated discussions on current politics.

Autumn comes slowly to Mediterranean lands. The effulgent sun is reluctant to leave the hills and valleys, towering cypress trees, medieval castles, renaissance palaces, and cobbled streets. One by one sea-side villas close down as their *padroni* move into their town houses, and pavement café owners move the chairs and tables inside. The *tramontana* blows from the Alps and scatters gold-brown leaves from trees. Mediterranean autumns lack the drama of northern autumns where nature pours forth its most glorious colours in anticipation of winter gales.

Foreign visitors who cross the frontiers in summer, gather to drop coins at the Fontana de Trevi in the hope of returning to Rome. 'Drop a coin to make sure the nymph of the fountain brings you back,' Minoti suggested to her fiancé. Laughing, Rustom gathered a fistful of coins from a pocket and scattered them in the fountain. He told her: 'I have seen urchins come after dark and scoop them from the nymph's lap. This custom must have been initiated by those boys.' They sat for a while with the merry-making tourists and then rose reluctantly to return to their car.

As they drove back, Rustom asked, 'Won't it be wonderful when I no longer have to say good night? When I can take you to my windswept room where we can see the Milky Way spread over the Hindu Kush?'

Minoti replied quietly, 'Yes, that is something to dream about.'

He glanced at her. 'Don't dream about it! Help me to make it happen!'

Minoti went to see off Rustom at Fiumicino Airport, where a cluster of Afghan officials from the king's entourage had gathered to bid him farewell with advice, suggestions and warnings. Rustom listened to them politely and thanked them for their dire predictions. Then he took Minoti to a quiet corner and held her close. Resting her head on his shoulder, she murmured, words from Verdi's opera *Aida*—'Ritorna vincitor'.

After seeing him board the coach that took him to the waiting Boeing 707 aircraft, she was reluctant to converse with his Afghan friends. So, bidding them polite good-byes she hailed a taxi and told the driver to take her to the Roman Forum. There she sat on a broken column surrounded by ancient edifices. Here, Time had stilled the tempest of empires. Sounds of power and glory echoed in the ruins, while images of heroes were gathered in the indiscriminate dust.

When Minoti was with Rustom she felt certitude about the future. Now she felt at a loss. Afghanistan was a distant, unknown land in the midst of turmoil. Would Rustom get drawn into the vortex of events that would distance him from her?

Soon after, Minoti prepared to leave for London. University College had admitted her for a postgraduate degree in international law. A few days before her, departure her father, Nihar Ray, broached the subject of her relationship with

Rustom Ferghani. Leela Ray sat embroidering on the sofa as this precluded participating in the conversation.

'Now that the young man has returned home, as I knew he would, I trust you will put this… unsuitable romance…behind you and think seriously of your future?'

Anticipating this conversation for some time, Minoti was prepared. 'I am very serious about my future. That is why I obtained a scholarship for my postgraduate course. After I get the degree I shall apply for a suitable job.'

'Your brother wants to introduce you to a very eligible young man who works in New York. He has expressed interest in marrying you.'

Minoti wanted to laugh. Was father so obtuse that he had not seen the attachment between her and Rustom? What would father do if she informed him that she and Rustom were lovers and she now wore his betrothal ring? Suppressing her impulse, she said lightly. 'Oh, that's nice.'

Mr Ray paused. 'Not that he is doing you a favour. Indeed, a young lady with your education, accomplishments and family background would be an asset for him in the corporate world.'

Minoti could not resist teasing her father. 'Why, Baba? Is he a rough diamond?' Leela raised her eyes from the embroidery and smiled.

Mr Ray continued. 'Don't be silly. An ambitious man wants a smart, pretty wife.'

'Ambitious men should be careful. Rustom told me a Russian proverb: *Beware of fair wife / Fair wife is too often / Asked to the feast.*'

Leela stopped embroidering and glanced at her husband, whose face tightened in anger.

Heavily, he said, 'I am sure you will not give Naveen cause for disquiet by frivolity.'

'Who is Naveen?'

'Your brother's friend… the prospective suitor.'

At this point Leela paused in her embroidery to glance at her daughter.

Minoti wanted to disarm her father before escaping to London. 'No, I shan't give the young man cause for disquiet… because I am not fair and I don't like feasts.'

'Glad to hear that. So, when Naveen goes to London you will meet him and then we can arrange an engagement ceremony.'

Minoti's eyes clouded. She realized her father was in earnest about her marriage to this eligible suitor. Gripped by fear, she played for time. 'Well, let me meet him and see if I like him. I cannot marry a man I do not love.'

'Marriage,' Nihar Ray said curtly, 'is a social contract. Men and women marry to have a home, raise a family, and have stability in their lives.'

Anger gained momentum in Minoti. 'And love? Don't men and women marry for love?'

'Love,' he said derisively, 'is a malady experienced in adolescence. Some call it spring fever. No sane person builds a life on maladies.'

Leela glanced at her daughter with a silent plea not to argue for a lost cause. She had sensed Minoti's attachment for the Afghan lecturer.

Minoti was not to be cowed. 'It is curious that men and women who marry to fulfil a social contract are usually unhappy. Men go philandering and their women compensate themselves with baubles.'

'And those who marry for what they delude themselves as love, are usually ruined. Don't be ruined by Jane Austen's specious stories.'

Minoti was going to make a harsh retort but her mother's tear-filled eyes pre-empted the words. Going to her mother, she dropped a kiss on the head of silky hair and murmured, 'Whatever happens, Ma, give me your blessings.'

Leela nodded, filled with apprehension about her daughter.

Dispatches from Kabul

Though Rustom Ferghani was sent to study in France and England, he never lost touch with Afghanistan. Sitting on the lap of his grandfather, Iskandar Khan of Kandahar, little Rustom had listened to stories of conquests and invasions, of romance and chivalry. Iskandar relished telling Rustom: 'Your great-great grandfather helped to vanquish the British Army of the Indus.' This gave Rustom deep pride in his family and people.

He learnt how for many millennia his country had been the fulcrum of empires. Its name was derived from the Sanskrit word 'Avagana' or the Sumerian 'ab-bar-gan', which means high mountain. Since 'Avagana' was believed be to the homeland of Indo-Aryans, the country also acquired the name Ariana. Some six millennia ago the vast Indus Valley civilization encompassed India, Afghanistan and Iran, whose people shared common beliefs and customs. The Maurya emperors of *Indica Magna* brought Buddhism to this land. The Indian-Afghans carved giant statues of Lord Buddha at Bamiyan. Invasions by

Parthians, Scythians, Macedonians, and Mongols despoiled the land but none could subdue this land of wild grandeur or its formidable people. When Islam came in the 10th century, Afghans were reluctant to accept a creed so different from the Vedic and Buddhist faiths.

Rustom's father's family came from Ferghana with Zahiruddin Babur, who, after losing Ferghana and Kabul, went south and founded the Mughal Empire in India. Rustom's ancestors took a new name—Ferghani—and stayed on to make their fortune in Afghanistan.

Iskandar Khan told Rustom of how Britain and Russia competed for eminence in Afghanistan. This was the Great Game—at the expense of the Afghans. The British waged and lost two disastrous Afghan Wars. Later, mutual fear of German militarism in Central Asia compelled Britain and Russia to sign the Pamir Convention; Russia came into large possession of the Pamir territory and extended control to the River Oxus.

The Russian incursion into Central Asia had beneficial effects. Travellers recorded how Russian influence had 'brought a breath of fresh air to a land despoiled and impoverished by centuries of despotic rule'. Several years after the Russian Revolution the Central Asian Khanates became part of the Soviet Union. Russia believed that a strong and friendly Afghanistan would make her a reliable ally of the Soviet Union and fostered good relations with its government. Despite being poor and feudal, the Afghans remained fiercely independent. The different races became as unruly as they were antagonistic to each other.

The disastrous Partition of India in 1947 also adversely affected Afghanistan. The Afghans declared null and void the treaty that established a border line, a partition agreed upon by King Abdur Rahman Khan and Sir Mortimer Durand, after whom the border between Afghanistan and Pakistan was called the Durand Line. The arbitrary territorial division disregarding ethnic and tribal divisions weakened Afghanistan; it created perpetual conflict between Afghanistan and Pakistan.

Rustom remembered how Daoud Khan, then Prime Minister, requested the USA for aid, which was refused—to please its ally, Pakistan. When the Helmand Valley Project ran into difficulties. Afghanistan turned to the Soviet Union, who readily offered economic and military aid, with a $25 million arms deal and an economic aid package worth $550 million. Roads were built between Kabul, Herat, and Kandahar that outflanked the Hindu Kush, tunnels were constructed through gaunt hills, grain silos for stocking food grains were built, and investments were made in small-scale industries. Afghanistan's modernized Ariana Airlines regularly flew between Kabul and Moscow. Defence personnel were trained in Russia, and 40 percent of Afghan exports went to Russia, including the famed Karakul lamb wool. Young Afghan men and women received medical and technical education in Soviet universities, and the Russian language was in wide use. Russia invested in a friendly, neutral Afghanistan on the frontier of Soviet Central Asia.

It was to this scenario that Rustom arrived in Kabul in the autumn of 1973. From Rome he had flown to Islamabad, drove to Peshawar and then through the Khyber Pass and Jalalabad. Mathew Arnold's poem *Sohrab and Rustom*, had inspired Rustom to journey through this region. He drove on the high roads of Asia and the Silk Road, where adventurers and invaders had traversed on horseback and camels. He stopped at villages to drink tea at picturesque *chaikhonas* and at dusk halted at *musafir-khanas* in Pashtun villages, and set off in the mornings through the mist-blurred landscape. The magnificent Hindu Kush dominated the scene; its snow-frosted pyramidal peaks soared skywards while the arid plains stretched to Iran, Elburz, and the Caucasus.

Meanwhile, tossed by doubts and uncertainty about the future, Minoti returned to London. She now stayed at Goodenough House, the well-appointed hostel for postgraduate students. It fronted Mecklenburg Square in Bloomsbury. The Germanic name had provoked a patriot to hurl a bomb there during World War II. This had damaged some buildings. Minoti walked through several parks to University College's Foster Court, where International Law lectures were held and brought images of meetings with Rustom. Sometimes, her mind wandered at lectures as she visualized her fiancé in Kabul.

In between busy hours, Rustom wrote to Minoti and informed her of events in Afghanistan.

Dear Minoti,

The political atmosphere in my country is different from yours. While India, after nearly two centuries of colonial rule initiated parliamentary democracy, Afghanistan, which has never been under colonial rule, has a troubled story. Afghanistan had no opposition parties to check and balance the exercise of power until a party with purported socialist agenda, the People's Democratic Party of Afghanistan, filled the vacuum and gained popularity. As the journalist John Griffiths writes, 'In the heady days of democratic fervour after World War II, Afghanistan had a brief flirtation with a siren called democracy.' The youth of the country formed the Afghan Mellat to initiate democracy. It was a great idea and a greater leap forward to agitate against government corruption and the insidious encroachment of Islamists into our public life.

I am surprised to find that despite the coup, President Daoud is a popular figure. Earlier he had used military force to bring rebellious tribesmen to heel and forced them to pay taxes. As Prime Minister he abolished the use of purdah for women and encouraged their education. His economic reforms required money, which was readily provided by the Soviet Union in order to retain Afghanistan's friendship. The old warlords resented the socialist tilt. He expedited development projects such as the Helmand Valley Project. This improved conditions in south-western Afghanistan. As an ardent Pashtun, Prince Daoud proposed the reunification of all Pashtun people in Afghan and Pakistani territory, which delighted the Pashtuns but caused anxiety among the Tajik and Uzbek minorities, who feared that a powerful Pashtunistan would marginalize them. That fear still persists. By shedding his royal title and declaring the country a republic, Doud has come closer to the Afghan people.

I look forward to the day when you and I can be together in my beautiful country,

Yours,

Rustom

On a cold rainy afternoon Minoti received another letter.

Dear Minoti,

I understand now why King Zahir Shah abdicated with alacrity. His loyal followers got wind of Prince Daoud's plan to seize power and tried to abort it. Though they planned a counter-coup against Prince Daoud, he shortly seized power and took action against this group. Anticipating danger, my father hastily joined President Daoud. I did not know all this when I was in Rome.

There is much to observe and learn here and I look forward to discussing it all with you. I trust your studies are going well.

Yours,

Rustom

Minoti waited anxiously for his letters. She also feared for his safety in that turbulent land which had been the graveyard of empires. She had read how a former minister was arrested and tortured; what guarantee was there for the safety of an outspoken, westernized young man?

Early in 1974, Rustom wrote enthusiastically:

My Dear Minoti,

President Daoud is anxious to modernize the Afghan Army. He has concluded aid agreements with the USA to provide funds for this. Hearing of my specialization in international relations and law, the President has selected me as member of the delegation that would discuss terms and conditions of the memorandum of agreement. I am thrilled about this and am trying to acquaint myself with the armament requirements of our defence services.

I am intently watching the President's parleys with the General Secretary of the National Awami Party. As an Indian you should wish him well because he hates Pakistan and is encouraging Baluchi tribesmen in Western Pakistan to oppose and secede from Pakistan. Afghan army officers are training Pakhtun Zalmay and young Baluchis to end Pakistani rule. When questioned by the Western media, President Daoud stated that his army is responding to the subversive activities of the Pakistani Inter Intelligence Services (ISI), which has commenced a proxy war in Afghanistan.

I am glad that you are studying in London and far from this turmoil. After you obtain your postgraduate degree, we can consider where to settle.

Yours,

Rustom

Minoti wrote back:

My Dear Rustom,

I find your narrative fascinating. I would so much like to be with you in Kabul. I can get a postgraduate degree in international law from any university. It is not necessary that I remain in London.

Yours,

Minoti

Rustom replied in haste:

You have the privilege of studying International Law with a world-renowned professor. When you obtain a good degree in this subject, many roads will be open to you. Don't trifle with this opportunity. If you work in England, it will be that much easier for me to join you.

Annoyed by this unromantic response she wrote back:

What about the wind-swept room where you will take me to gaze at the Milky Way spread over the Hindu Kush? Or was that just random poetry?

Rustom replied:

My Dear Minoti,

Unlike Persians, Afghans do not indulge in random poetry. We fight for freedom and struggle in this unruly land. After our wedding you will certainly come to your new home. But there is no harm in keeping other roads open in the event of turbulence in Afghanistan.

Yours,

Rustom

From the tenor of Rustom's letters Minoti sensed that he was enjoying the excitement in Kabul. In guarded language he hinted at the predicaments of the new regime. His distrust of Prince, now President, Daoud, was turning into respect. This had brought about reconciliation with his father, General Ferghani, who now belonged to the President's Military Council. He wrote to Minoti:

Dear Minoti,

Prince Daoud envisages an expanded Afghanistan by bringing Pashtuns of Pakistan into a confederation with Afghan Pashtuns. By fomenting unrest in Balochistan province, the Afghan President hoped to bring the oppressed Baloch people closer to Afghanistan. Balochi rebels began guerrilla warfare against Pakistan when it sidelined tribal leaders. Massacres of Balochi separatists followed.

Yours

Rustom,

Afraid that Rustom would get involved in this dangerous game, Minoti wrote:

Dear Rustom,

Your academic experience and knowledge of international law and political philosophy are obviously not being utilized. You seem more interested in playing dangerous games than governance.

Yours,

Minoti

Rustom evaded a reply. Instead, he told her of social events, of meeting Terence Rowland, First Secretary in the British Embassy. Terence shared his views on international politics. They also enjoyed horse riding. General Ferghani maintained a stable of small, swift horses from ancestral Ferghana. Rustom and Terence rode on the mountains, where they paused to admire the dramatic scenery, explore old forts, and return at dusk to dine with guests of consequence at General Ferghani's table.

Terence was keenly interested in Afghanistan; his great-great-grandfather had been one of the few survivors of the ill-fated Army of the Indus sent by Lord Auckland 'to subdue Afghanistan' in 1839. Though it was the first time Britain's imperial pride had been humbled in Asia, Britons had a residual fascination for Afghanistan.

'Your father's friends are aloof with me,' Terence complained to Rustom, who laughed and replied, 'They still harbour fear and distrust of British intentions after the Anglo-Afghan wars of the last century.'

'Good Lord, all that happened a hundred years ago! Things have changed.'

Rustom shook his head. "Afghanistan does not have military power but has strategic importance now—because it stands on Soviet Central Asia's frontier. Britain and the new imperial power, USA, want a foothold here. I earnestly hope these powers will leave us Afghans to shape our own destinies.'

'That will depend on your leadership,' Terence observed.

'I have every expectation that President Daoud will succeed,' Rustom replied.

Rustom's other diplomat friend was Ivan Suvorov at the Soviet Embassy. Affable and courteous, Ivan, like his compatriots spoke warmly but with measured words about Afghanistan. Soviet Union had apprehensions when Prince Daoud deposed their trusted ally, King Zahir Shah. Russians were wary of President Daoud who wavered between cordiality and coldness, coupled with a growing interest in America, which was searching for new footholds in Asia after their defeat in Vietnam. Ivan spoke fluent Pashto and Farsi and held a Ph.D in Afghan history.

Ivan was a frequent guest at General Ferghani's dinner parties, where animated discussions on international politics continued into the early hours of the morning, when amber tea was brought in by sleepy orderlies to douse the fires of wine and cognac. Sometimes, the three bachelors—Rustom, Terence and Ivan—met at picturesque teashops to discuss politics. They also gathered information from each other.

Rustom's subsequent letters to Minoti were light-hearted. He described the places he had visited and the people he had met at his parents' home. Among them was Princess Zubaida, a niece of the President's wife, who wanted Rustom as nephew-in-law. An invitation to the family estate at Herat could not be refused. To abort matrimonial negotiations, Rustom invited Terence and Ivan to accompany him. He described the visit to Minoti.

My Dear Minoti,

Herat was once the capital of Afghanistan. Wheat fields shimmer green and gold in the spring sunshine, and grapes planted by Persian settlers ripen in the vineyards. The city's wide streets are lined by cypress, poplar and elm trees, public parks and gardens are redolent with Turkish tulips and Indian lilies, while bazaars display fruits that are the speciality from Kashmir to Kandahar—cherries, plums, peaches, apricots, grapes, pomegranates. I told Terence about Queen Goharshad, a princess of Samarkand, who married our King Shahrukh in the 15th century. For all her achievements and power, she met a gruesome end. When the queen was of 80 years, she was beheaded by her nephew Abu Said, who hated her vision of an enlightened Islam. I feel ashamed that an Afghan could do this to a frail, old woman.

We were warmly welcomed by the warlord and his family in Herat. Zubaida's father regaled us with sly stories of how the then vagabond Babur visited Herat to meet his sophisticated Timurid cousins, who made the future Emperor of Hindustan feel 'to be laggard in showing me respect was unreasonable.' They served him roast goose, which Babur did not know how to eat! The future poet-emperor wrote 'In Herat a man can't stretch his leg without touching a poet's backside.' (These lines are from the Babur Nama.)

Yours,

Rustom

Minoti brooded over Rustom's visit to Herat and his meeting with Princess Zubaida. 'What could be more natural than for them to be united in matrimony,' she thought sadly. 'There would be no tension, no friction between families, no conflict of creeds—of which King Zahir had warned us in Rome. Rustom would be well allied, and would continue the family traditions with a woman of the same race.' She toyed with the thought of writing to him to forget her and marry the princess to further his career.

While she was in this mood, her elder brother in New York wrote to her that Naveen Sen would be coming to London on work and would like to meet her. She thought angrily: 'Since Rustom is meeting Zubaida, why should I not meet Naveen Sen? I might like him and might agree to marry him!'

A week later Minoti saw a self-assured Naveen Sen standing at the foyer of Goodenough House. Seeing Minoti, he joined his hands in a *namaskar*. She responded likewise, unable to summon appropriate words with which to greet a man who was considering marrying her. After the first awkward moments he asked her where she would like to have dinner. She chose a nearby restaurant to avoid Soho and Burlington Arcade, where she and Rustom used to meet.

Naveen told her about his work at Goldman Sachs investment bankers in New York, of his prospects and travels. Subtly, he indicated that she would have a comfortable existence. He enquired about her interest in international law and wondered of its relevance in a lawless world.

Minoti half listened, staring with unseeing eyes at the pleasant man before her, while she conjured images of her beloved Rustom sitting across a table and regaling her with amusing anecdotes or engaging her in discussions on profound subjects—of human existence, the universe with its cluster galaxies, the Great Game in Central Asia, of mystic poets and murderous warriors.

'Would you like to write to your parents that we have met?' Naveen Sen's question dispelled remembered dialogues.

Panic seizing her, she asked, 'Write to them? Yes…of course…'

Naveen continued. 'Perhaps you could write to my parents. They would like to get acquainted with you.'

Minoti felt that she was sinking into a pool of quicksilver. This confident young man was deciding events that were hurtling her towards a situation for which she was unprepared. An exchange of letters would seal her fate. Once more she had to rely on her elusive ally—Time.

'Perhaps we should reflect on matters…before I write to your parents…and I cannot marry until I obtain my postgraduate degree. That is two years away.'

'Two years is a long time,' he murmured.

She replied stubbornly, 'I have worked hard to get this scholarship. I must get my Masters degree.'

'What will you do with this degree?' Naveen asked.

'Work in an international organization perhaps…or in a firm where they require personnel to deal with international transactions.'

'After marriage?' He asked with a frown.

A gust of anger made her think: 'So he has assumed I will marry him…that I will do his bidding from now on!' She rose abruptly and put on her coat. 'My hostel gate closes at 10:30. I must be going…'

Naveen Sen also rose and strode to the cashier's desk to pay the bill. Minoti stood outside the restaurant, stamping her feet and rubbing her hands to keep off the cold. A tipsy pedestrian passed by, murmuring, ''Ello, black eyes.'

Accustomed to these harmless overtures, she replied, 'Good morning, blue eyes. Go home safely to your Mum.' The man laughed and walked away with an unsteady gait.

Emerging from the restaurant Naveen asked, 'Do you normally talk to strangers?'

She nodded. 'Haven't I been talking all evening to you, a perfect stranger?' At that he laughed and hailed a taxi to drop her at Goodenough House.

A few days later he took her to see Agatha Christie's play *The Mousetrap* at a theatre in Haymarket.

Minoti informed Naveen that the play had been running to full houses for years. 'If one likes something, one does not tire of it.'

The tone of her voice troubled him. Was she missing something or someone? He firmly pushed away the thought because diving into other people's thoughts entailed dealing with their predicaments.

After the play, at Minoti's suggestion, they went to Schmidt's Restaurant, renowned *for Wiener Schnitzel* (Viennese veal steak). Minoti watched with a mischievous smile as Naveen toyed with the half-cooked steak.

'Good Hindu, aren't you?' She asked. 'I apologize for bringing you here.'

'Ancient Hindus ate venison and horse-meat. But to kill a baby calf...' he replied with distaste.

They conversed more easily this time because Minoti did not wish to offend this well-bred stranger. After a few days of seeing her, Naveen informed Minoti that he would be going to Rome to meet her parents and then would be flying back to New York. Tremors of apprehension possessed Minoti. Between her father and Naveen, they might settle her future. While she debated how to discourage him, he said hesitantly, 'I see you are as accomplished as your brother said you were.' He paused and added. 'I am glad to have met you.'

Guilt overwhelmed her. She wished Naveen Sen had been arrogant and ill bred. It would have been easier to refuse his proposal of marriage. Then a vagrant thought nudged her. What if Rustom had begun to forget her? Immersed in exciting work in Afghanistan, the proximity of a princess close to the citadel of power, and their affinities of race and creed, could erase memories of an alien forbidden love. So why not keep this new amity alive?

Looking at Naveen, Minoti said warmly, 'I have enjoyed these few days. I hope you enjoy your visit to Rome. It is the grandest city in the world. Arrivederci.'

Though Naveen displayed no sign of attraction to Minoti, she sensed that he was drawn to her. 'I hope to see you soon,' he said quietly. Minoti stood at the entrance of the hostel watching him go, musing that he seemed a refined and honourable man. She knew it was wrong to deceive him and let him go to Rome to discuss marriage plans with her parents when she was betrothed to Rustom. Impulsively, she ran towards him crying, 'Mr Sen! Naveen! Stop! I must talk to you urgently!'

Naveen turned, astonished by her frantic words and the sight of her running towards him. When she reached him, he asked with bewilderment, 'What is it?'

She said, 'Can we go somewhere and talk …I cannot go on deceiving you!'

'Deceiving me?' He echoed, even more bewildered.

Minoti nodded miserably.

Naveen considered the matter and indicated the garden fronting Goodenough House. There they sat on a bench.

Frowning, he asked, 'Now, what is this deception about?'

Looking at him she pleaded, 'I implore you to treat my confession with utmost secrecy.'

'Minoti,' Naveen asked anxiously, 'are you involved in some crime—murder, theft, forgery?'

Minoti burst into laughter. Then she said sombrely, 'No— it is more complicated.'

Exhaling deeply, he said, 'I shall not divulge your secret— though I shudder to think what it is.'

Hesitantly, Minoti told him about Rustom Ferghani, and their plan to marry, of how she had tried to deflect her father but he insisted that she marry Naveen because marriage to Rustom—a man of a different religion—would be unacceptable to both families. Minoti saw various expressions pass over Naveen's face.

Staring at the sky, he murmured, 'So I have come on a fool's errand.'

'I humbly ask your forgiveness. It was wrong of me not to tell you this earlier.'

Naveen nodded. 'You should have saved me an unnecessary journey. Thankfully, I need not go to Rome to meet your parents.'

'Oh Naveen! Please go to Rome, and meet my parents, I implore you!'

His bewilderment turned to anger. 'You can't be serious!' he exclaimed.

'Please tell them that we have met and that you agree to give me time to complete my studies…by which time Rustom and I…can make our plans. Please! I beg you!'

Naveen spoke sternly. 'I have no wish to marry a woman who loves another man. But I advise you to be certain of Rustom's intentions…'

Tears gathered in her eyes. 'He cares for me…I cannot imagine life without him.'

Naveen nodded. 'In between these emotions there are the imponderables of time and distance, difficulties and predicaments. Make sure Rustom returns soon to marry you. The waiting game is a gamble…and distance brings oblivion.'

Rising, Naveen asked ironically, 'Until then am I expected to pose as your fiancé? And when do I get jilted?'

She tried to laugh but tears stung her eyes. 'A man like you will never be jilted. Pretend for a while and then announce that you have changed your mind about me…that I am frivolous…or vulgar …or whatever you feel like saying.' To his astonishment she hugged him and said, 'You are so noble and generous! I wish I had met you earlier!'

He held her—briefly. Then releasing her, he said grimly, 'Fate has decreed otherwise. I hope you find happiness. I don't know why I am collaborating in your crazy scheme.'

His inner voice told him why.

The Promised Bride

After meeting Minoti's parents in Rome, Naveen Sen told them that he agreed with Minoti that she should complete her postgraduate studies.

'I don't believe in long engagements,' Nihar Ray said unhappily.

With a sardonic smile, Naveen replied, 'Neither do I. But Minoti's education will help her future progress.'

Leela Ray frowned. There was something in Naveen's manner which troubled her. Despite praising Minoti's mind and manners, he seemed in no hurry to marry her. Had something gone wrong? Was he postponing the wedding because he had an American paramour?

The Rays showed him around Rome, took him to the opera and elegant restaurants. During those few days, Naveen experienced a sensation he had not known through many years of security and success. He had wanted a 'trophy wife'. But after meeting Minoti he wanted a wife whom he could respect and love—a woman unworldly and brave, like Minoti, he thought ruefully. Returning to New York, Naveen informed Minoti of all that had transpired in Rome, through a long letter.

In the course of browsing through your father's books, I found an English translation of Manzoni's famous novel, The Promised Bride. *Serendipity! So, my promised bride, study hard, keep well and take my advice—get married before distance and time dissolve both your dreams.*

Underneath the banter, Minoti sensed sadness. She replied by thanking him profusely for agreeing to the charade and asked forgiveness for wasting his time. She ended with a benediction—that the Almighty would reward him with great happiness. Then strange thoughts came unbidden. 'If only I could feel for Naveen what I feel for Rustom, life would be much simpler!'

Rustom's letters were now less frequent but those he wrote were suffused with tenderness, hope, and anxieties about the future of his country. He described Kabul, its stately mansions, offices, shops that sold clothes, carpets, and confectionery. All seemed staid against the drama of the snow-topped Hindu Kush range that ringed the city. He told her of family picnics at the citadel of Bala Hisar, which had been home to Afghanistan's Durrani kings. He visited the imperial garden laid out by Babur, founder of the Mughal dynasty in India, and saw the marble mosque built in the conqueror's honour by his descendant Emperor Shah Jahan. Rustom wrote:

Dear Minoti,

After working in the President's office, I drop in sometimes at Hotel Kabul on Pashtunistan Square. The solid two-storeyed hotel with an austere façade has been recently built by Soviet engineers. It is a rendezvous for the Kabul elite and the cosmopolitan crowd stationed in our capital—diplomats, media people, affluent Afghans and westernized Afghan women. Warlords and merchants wearing circular turbans, bushy beards and fierce countenances may be seen glowering at clean-shaven Afghans wearing western clothes. The bar is crowded with Afghans, Indians, Russians, British, American and Chinese citizens. My diplomat friends Terence Rowland and Ivan Suvorov come here with colleagues. In that Tower of Babel one can hear mingled sounds of many tongues.

The drinking and bonhomie is a charade for information gathering. Those who know I work in President Daoud's office strike up political conversations. I remind myself that this is Kabul, not University College lecture halls, and the audience does not comprise free-speaking students and liberal academics but people with questionable agendas. Many I suspect are espionage agents. The people gathered here remind me of characters from an Eric Ambler thriller. It is as if intrigues and conspiracies are swirling around us. I listen intently to learn what is happening outside the well-guarded Arg or Presidential palace.

To gather information, I go to the bar and chat with the famous barman of Kabul—Abdul Chugtai. Since he is also an accomplished singer, he is called Abdul Bulbul or Nightingale. With slanted eyes and tawny skin, he is the most inventive barman in the world. After he mixes drinks and infuses slivers of walnut bark and poppy seeds into your martini, one feels luminous. Fluency in several dialects enables him to eavesdrop on conversations of important people. While polishing long-stemmed glasses, his narrowed eyes scan the stylish clientele. When I asked him for information about several men in the room, he gave me thumbnail sketches of those prominent people. I requested him to pass on anything of interest he hears. 'The President will be grateful,' I told him.

'I preferred the old King,' Abdul the Bulbul muttered mournfully. 'But I will help you…if you tell your tribesmen not to bother my people.'

My tribesmen?' I asked, surprised. I had never regarded myself as a member of a tribe.

Abdul the Bulbul polished a few glasses and nodded. 'The badmash landlords abduct our women and try to grab our land. They get the Mullahs to intimidate the peasants with threats of perdition if they resist the warlords.'

I never knew this, Minoti. Have I been living with illusions, oblivious to the situation here? What is the relevance of

International Law and the International Court of Justice, when there is scant regard for law or justice in my own land?

To assess the situation, I visited rural areas where development has been slow and sporadic. During these visits I saw disturbing disparity between the rich and the poor. Now that the people are exposed to egalitarian ideas they resent the disparity. There is a palpable alienation between the privileged and the deprived. The country's economy is primarily agricultural, but little has been done to increase food production. Seeing the numerous rivers—Kabul, Amu Darya, Harirud, Oxus—and abundant mountain streams which empty into rivers, water can be harnessed for irrigation and hydro-electric power. I wrote reports for the President that projects to irrigate the peasants' fields should be taken up urgently. The Arghanabad and Kajakai Dams were built in the 1950s during King Zahir's reign but they are inadequate. Scanty irrigation resulting in shortage of food grain can have serious consequences.

On the way back from a mountain-girded village I sat by a swift-flowing mountain stream. Nearby clusters of violets, tangles of wild blueberries, giant purple rhododendrons and pines soared to the pellucid sky. May a day come soon when I can bring you to this enchanting place,

Yours,

Rustom

In 1975 Nihar Ray completed his tenure at the international organization where he had worked for 15 years. Leaving Rome was a wrench for him and Leela. They had struck roots in the alien soil and discovered that the roots could not be easily plucked out and transplanted elsewhere. Moving physically from one city to another, one country to another, is not only dismantling of home and furniture; it is a transformational movement, something akin to transmigration of souls. The traveller acquires a new identity in the new terrain; it demands adjustment of outlook like readjustment of wristwatches in different time zones. Memories of the past dispel of their own accord as the mind aligns itself to new realities.

Minoti went to Rome that summer to assist her parents in moving and packing. She also went there to take leave in silent remembrance of things past—of a carefree youth, of holidays with parents and siblings, of sultry summer afternoons by the seaside and evening strolls along Via Veneto, of discovering the tapestry of Italy embroidered by many civilizations growing out of each other. Amidst of all this welled out the memory of Rustom's passionate tenderness and invitation to unite her fragile existence to his sturdy one. Images of their magic days and nights were attended by nostalgic pain because those images had to be surrendered since they could not be retrieved in their original form and mood.

Without informing her parents, Minoti went to King Zahir's villa at Olgiata to take leave of him. King Zahir and Queen Hamira received her with warmth. Numerous visitors, or 'hangers on' as Rustom called them, were also present.

After tea, the king invited her to take a stroll with him in the gardens. 'Come and see the pomegranates I have grown here,' he said.

She sensed that the king wanted to know about Rustom, who now wrote infrequently to the king.

'How quickly one becomes redundant without the panoply of power,' King Zahir lamented.

Minoti shook her head. 'Your Majesty, please do not misunderstand Rustom! He venerates you. But he has to be careful in the new ambience. Your…successor…is suspicious of conflicting loyalties.' She paused. 'His letters to me have grown less personal. He describes visits to various places, the development projects and his hopes for Afghanistan's progress.'

Glancing at Minoti, King Zahir asked quietly. 'What are your plans?'

Looking at him she replied. 'Rustom and I have decided that we can marry after I complete my postgraduate studies. That is another year.'

The king stared ahead. Something in his granite face alerted Minoti but she was afraid to ask. Zahir Shah drew in a deep breath. 'Rustom's plans will be nullified by the ambitious

General Ferghani. He wants to fortify his position through his son's marriage to President Daoud's niece-in-law.'

Minoti concealed her distress with a sad smile. 'Princess Zubaida. Isn't that what you advised him when you met here in July 1973?'

The king's granite face softened. 'That was before I met you, dear child.'

The royal kindness moved her to sudden tears.

The king muttered. 'Murderous lot, that Herat tribe. They side now with Pashtuns, and then with Persian-Tajiks, even with the Shiah Hazaras. Rustom would be ill-advised to pursue that path.' The king took out a briar pipe from a pocket of his elegant Foa jacket and slowly ignited it, during which time he gathered his thoughts. After inhaling from the pipe, the king asked: 'Why don't you go to Calcutta with your parents and ask Rustom to meet you there?'

Minoti looked at the king. 'Your Majesty, if Rustom wants to marry the princess to further his career, I will not resort to strategies to deflect him.'

'Spoken like a truly foolish and proud woman,' the king murmured.

'You do not have to resort to anything—just inform him that you will be in Calcutta when your parents return in a few months.' The king paused. 'I have no knowledge about romantic marriages. We princes marry where we are told to marry. But as a king I know one thing—act swiftly when fortune shines.' He stubbed out the glowing embers of the pipe with a thumb and spoke pensively, 'Save Rustom from a dismal marriage.' With egalitarian chivalry the king escorted Minoti to the taxi parked by the gate, followed by three armed guards. He kissed her hand and said, '*Khuda hafiz*, dear child.'

Tangled Destinies

Nihar and Leela Ray arrived in Calcutta after Prime Minister Indira Gandhi had declared Internal Emergency in order to 'protect the country from disruption and disunity, fomented by opponents in the pay of foreign hands', she said. West Bengal had fallen into chaos when a group of Marxists staged riots and murders in the name of achieving equality and fraternity. The state government could not control the violence and disruption unleashed by the group known as Naxals. Emergency gave the state government the authority to deal sternly against the self-styled revolutionaries.

The Rays settled in their 19th century mansion on Alipur Road, which had been built by an ancestor who traded with the British East India Company. Their son Tarun and his family returned from New York and also lived in the mansion. Amidst this bonhomie, Leela felt anxious for Minoti living alone in London. She prayed Minoti would soon obtain her postgraduate degree and come to Calcutta, so that preparations for her wedding could begin.

Briefly, Minoti felt insecure after her parents' departure for India. Their beautiful home had been transported thousands of miles away. This displacement deepened her yearning for a home with Rustom. But he too was far away. 'It is only a few more months before I obtain my postgraduate degree,' she consoled herself. 'Then I shall join my fiancé in Kabul.' She had not formulated details of this reunion but the prospect lightened her days.

This blissful mood was disturbed when Nihar Ray wrote to her in early 1976.

My dear daughter,

In a few months' time, you will be completing your postgraduate studies. I am sure you will obtain a good degree in international law. After that you will return to India. We are now settled in Calcutta. Tarun and his family have returned to India. He is assisting us to organize your wedding.

Please book your tickets soon so that we can fix the wedding date. You will be happy with Naveen, who assured us that you will be able to put your education to good use. He has waited two years for you to complete your education. He is 33. Most of his friends are married. You are 24. After a few years you will be, as they say, 'put on the shelf'.

Your concerned father,

Nihar Ray

Profoundly shaken by this letter, Minoti went for a long walk through the spring-time gardens of Bloomsbury. She had been playing for time for three years since that morning when Rustom came to her rescue at the lecture hall. It had not been a sudden epiphany. She had long been impressed by Rustom's refinement and idealism. He had shown her special courtesy, while maintaining the formality required between academic staff and students. That March morning had awakened the sensations that had slumbered within them. And from these encounters there developed a deep attachment.

Minoti decided to inform her parents in her next letter.

Dear Father,

Rustom Ferghani and I are engaged to be married. Our relationship has withstood a separation of two-and-a-half years and a distance of 5000 miles. Rustom has waited for me to complete my studies even though his father had wanted him to marry a woman from a powerful family. I met Naveen Sen only to pacify you both. I am not attracted to life in America. I prefer a challenging life in Afghanistan with a man I love and admire.

Your loving daughter,

Minoti

She knew the letter would change the direction of her young life. But she did not anticipate the furore that it would provoke. Her father wrote of his astonishment that she could even contemplate marriage to a Muslim!

My dear daughter,

The sophistication which has enchanted you is skin deep. He is of a race that invaded our country for many centuries. They scorn us because they conquered us. Islam is intolerant of other creeds and recommends conversion at sword point. Do you wish to cast aside the cultural heritage of 5000 years and the magnificent faith in which you were raised? If you marry Rustom Ferghani you will never be allowed inside a temple. No relation or friend of yours will invite you to their religious ceremonies. You will be an outcaste from your own society!

And what can you expect from Rustom's world? They will tolerate you—no more. Not all your education and accomplishments will bring you the honour or recognition that you would receive in your own world. Then when the powerful husband wearies of you he will declare 'talaq'—the arbitrary decree and freedom that the Sharia law gives to a man to abandon a blameless wife. We have seen this happen numerous times. Will you then return to your baper-bari [father's home] hurt and humbled? Will you bring your children to us, shell-shocked and abandoned? Or will you be forced to leave them behind in the Ferghani mansion to an Afghan stepmother?

Think very clearly, Minoti. There is a clash of civilizations between Rustom's world and yours. Nothing can obliterate the antagonism, overt or covert, that has accumulated over a millennium. You have been away at London University for many years. Loneliness obscures one's vision. Once you are in your own environment you will realize that what I say is valid. Do not embark on this dangerous journey. If you do so, we shall disown you.

Your father,

Nihar Ray

It took Minoti many days to recover from her father's terrifying message. Thoughts which had never occurred to her now rose like intimidating phantoms. Doubts crept in like a dark tide at night; then one awakes to find a sheltered shore inundated with swirling waters. She often sat gazing at Rustom's photo on her desk. His sapient blue-grey eyes seemed to penetrate her mind with many reproaches.

So, my timid Minoti, he seemed to say, *I see that you can be easily swayed from your purpose. Well, so be it. I shall find another love. Perhaps our love was never a sturdy bloom anyway. Perhaps the seduction of the Tyrrhenian Sea, mimosa-scented air, Rome's amber magic played tricks with our fickle hearts.*

No, she would whisper in reply. *I am somewhat disturbed. Hold on, give me time to strengthen my resolve. You are so far away. Perhaps we should discuss these conflicts before we embark on an uncharted sea.*

Two things happened that affected the course of Minoti's and Rustom's lives. Leela and Nihar Ray never divulged Minoti's 'reckless infatuation' for Rustom Ferghani. Knowledge of this fact, they felt, could damage Minoti's matrimonial prospects. And Minoti again made the mistake of relying on an unreliable ally—Time. Hesitant to tell her parents of her resolve to marry Rustom, no matter what the dangers and difficulties, and reluctant to endure another paternal diatribe, Minoti left them to think that she would obey them.

Rustom was also encountering pressure from his father to make a marriage of convenience with a niece of President Daoud's wife. Zubaida had opulent beauty and belonged to a powerful family. Men who wanted an alliance with the ruling elite sought her as a bride. Like many affluent Afghan women, Zubaida was well educated. Since 1950, when the Afghan Constitution guaranteed equal rights, girls attended school, half the university students were women, 40 per cent of doctors were women, 70 per cent of teachers were women, 30 per cent of civil servants were women, and some were even judges and members of parliament.

General Ferghani told Rustom of his wish; Rustom should marry Princess Zubaida. President Prince Daoud would approve of the match and would assist Rustom to rise swiftly in government service.

Rustom listened in silence. Relieved that he could now inform his father of his Indian fiancée he said, 'I am engaged to be married—to a young Indian lady who was my student at University College. I am waiting for her to obtain her Master's degree. Then we will marry in Kabul, if you permit, or in her home town, Calcutta.'

General Ferghani heard his son with incredulity. When Rustom completed his brief announcement, the general exploded. 'I do not believe this! That you, who are a descendant of Zahiruddin Babur, conqueror of India, want to marry an obscure *kaffir!*'

Rustom had expected this and had prepared his reply months ago. 'Baba, are you certain about our ancestry? Or is it a legend to fortify our status in society?'

The general's face was inflamed by rage. 'How dare you speak like this! How dare you denigrate our lineage! Curse the day your mother bore such a son!'

Rustom offered his infuriated father an indulgent smile. 'All right, even if Emperor Babur is your ancestor, why should I not marry a well-born, educated Hindu girl?'

The general shouted, 'People will think you are mad!'

Rustom nodded, unfazed. 'My fiancée's father is equally averse to our relationship. But being a suave international diplomat, he pretended not to know that I love his daughter.'

The general thundered, 'So you have met the young lady's father? You kept all this concealed from me! This is not the honourable Pashtun code!'

'My fiancée's parents live in Rome. I met them when I visited King Zahir. Minoti met our king.' Rustom paused to deliver a Parthian shot. 'His Majesty approved of my fiancée.'

The general loosened his necktie. 'Do you want to commit political harakiri by allying with the deposed King? If so, destroy yourself—but do not drag me down with you! If you pursue this path I will disown you!'

Rustom rose and bowed before his father. 'This is exactly what I feared you would say, Baba. I have no taste for politics and intrigues. I was privileged to be assistant lecturer to a great professor, content to learn and teach, happy to plan a future very different from what you want for me. Please give me your blessings to return to England and pursue the career I want and marry the woman I love.'

The general was accustomed to minor mutinies amongst his unruly soldiers. He knew he had to take a few conciliatory steps backwards to prevent a full-blown revolt. 'Do you want to live as an émigré among the *feringhi* British when you can live proudly with a princess-wife in your own land? We defeated those *feringhis* in three wars ... and ruled the *kaffir*s of Hindustan for a millennium.'

Rustom replied: 'The *feringhis* are still a world power while we live in medieval times. The *kaffir*s as you call them, look down on Muslims. Their women torched themselves rather than fall into hands of Muslim invaders.'

'Have you so lost your pride that you are exalting them!' The general roared. 'All right, go then! I disown you! Never set foot in this country again! Do you hear? I shall shoot you with my own hand if you do!'

Rustom looked at his father in pain that this once proud warrior was trying to fortify his position through matrimonial intrigues. Rustom spoke with suppressed anger. 'Name my half-brother Javed as your successor. He cannot boast of lineage since his mother was a nightclub singer. But I suppose Emperor Babur had his *nautch* girls as well.' Rustom paused. 'I shall leave Kabul in a week's time.' Bowing again, he left the opulent sitting room.

Hearing of this showdown, the general's friends advised him to make peace with his son. 'Rustom has impressed our President with his knowledge of international politics, his fluency in English, French, and Russian, his hard work and dedication. The President wants to utilize his expertise in the Foreign Ministry and in a few years will post him as Ambassador to an important capital. Rustom is your protective talisman. Don't contemplate severing ties with him! And don't speak against Indians! They are our true friends. After his visit to India last year our President wants closer ties with India—to counter Pakistan and to get military support from Prime Minister Indira Gandhi's government.' The adviser smiled mischievously. 'It may even help Rustom to have an Indian girlfriend.'

'If it was a girlfriend I would not object. But to marry her!'

'Play for time,' the advisers said. 'Eventually, Rustom will settle down with a bride of your choosing.'

The general shook his head and exclaimed, 'That we, a race of conquerors, should come to this!'

So, Rustom was persuaded to remain in Afghanistan but he made a condition—that he would marry Minoti. 'I shall serve my country with my life's blood but I will marry the young lady who has claimed my heart.' He related these happenings to his beloved without the bitter details.

Dear Minoti,

So now it is all in the open. I have announced our engagement to my parents. After Father's initial resistance he has accepted my decision. I am puzzled by this sudden change but shall not delve deep into this. My mother, bless her, wants your photograph. So please send me a photo of yourself—in a gorgeous sari, your hair in a long plait, a jewelled dot on your forehead.

The Afghans are vain about their looks. They claim descent from Parthians, Kushans, and Greeks. You can see this legacy in slanted blue eyes coexisting with tawny hair and snub noses. The Ferghanis want a pretty bride—for the sake of progeny. I assured them that you are not only good looking but very talented. I do not anticipate any further problems about our marriage.

What a joy it will be to see you again! When I think of those magic nights in Ravello, those afternoons in Rome, I am tempted to leave my country and take the swiftest aircraft to London. But that is not a practical plan, is it? So, I count the days, like the melancholy lovers in fairy tales who count rose petals to know how soon they will meet. You should inform your parents that we are engaged. Hopefully, the two families can reconcile themselves to the disgrace of their offspring marrying undesirable partners!

Yours,

Rustom

Little did Minoti know of the blandishments of power that had persuaded General Ferghani to accept Rustom's decision. Minoti neither informed Rustom of her father's diatribe against him nor did she inform him that she had written an evasive reply. She was afraid to complicate matters by informing her fiancé that to mollify her father she had met an eligible suitor whom she had no intention of marrying. Instead, she wrote:

Dear Rustom,

Wait until I have obtained my Master's degree. Then I shall inform them and they can attend our wedding, which we shall plan in our own way.

Yours,

Minoti

Turbulent Journeys

President Daoud made a grave political mistake in early 1976. When USA made overtures to Afghanistan, he responded enthusiastically and sent his trusted diplomats to Washington to enquire what benefits the USA would offer Afghanistan. The group comprising senior diplomats, economists, and Rustom Ferghani went to Washington in April 1976 to discuss Afghan–American cooperation. The American government agreed to assist the Afghan government in the development of Helmand Valley and strengthening the Afghan National Army. This involved purchase of arms amounting to millions of dollars. When the Afghan delegation demurred, the American negotiators assured them that weaponizing the Afghan army was for the safety of the nation. 'By the Baghdad Pact we provided military assistance to Iran, Jordan, Saudi Arabia—to protect them against the Soviet Union.'

Rustom saw his Ambassador's face tighten. He retorted, 'The countries you mention are feudal monarchies.

Afghanistan is a socialist republic. We don't need protection against Russia, who has been our friend for centuries. What we need is economic assistance, which a wealthy nation like you can easily give.'

The US team agreed but with a conditionality; the USA wanted bases on the Afghan–Uzbekistan border. The Afghan delegation realized that this would give USA an invaluable foothold on the Soviet Central Asia frontier. Afghanistan was also told to renounce the Pashtunistan project as the price for friendship with the USA. Pakistan would wrest bigger military advantages by her army's cosy relationship with the USA. Five years earlier in 1971, Pakistan had brought about amity between the USA and China against their common enemy, Russia.

Before returning home, the Afghan delegates were shown around the majestic American capital and then they visited fascinating New York. The visit of the Afghan delegation seeking economic assistance from USA made headlines in the *New York Times*. America's plan to have a base on the Soviet Union's frontier was succeeding!

Reading Rustom Ferghani's name in the *New York Times* article, Naveen Sen decided to meet the man who stood between him and Minoti. Employed at Goldman Sachs, he easily secured an invitation for a meeting of investment bankers with the Afghan delegation. Naveen met Rustom amidst the opulence of the Waldorf Astoria Hotel, and engaged him in cordial conversation. Friendship between their two nations encouraged this cordiality. Mischievous Fate deterred Naveen from mentioning Minoti, as this might create complications for all three. Instead, he discussed US investment in Afghanistan, especially the Helmand Valley and Daura projects. Glancing around anxiously, Rustom said, 'There are difficulties, Mr Sen. There are many negative strings to US aid.'

Naveen smiled. 'But think of the benefits, Mr Ferghani. All benefits have a price.'

Rustom frowned. 'I would not have expected an Indian to be cynical. That is a Western quality.'

'How much do you know of India?' Naveen asked gravely, wondering if he was stepping over landmines.

Rustom replied, 'India is a vast and complex country. Afghanistan shares a civilizational past with her. I have read your history and classical literature.' He hesitated before saying, "My fiancée is Indian. I have, therefore, tried to understand her country.'

Naveen looked away, trying to smother an unfamiliar pain. But Rustom claimed his attention by drawing out a photo of Minoti from his wallet. Naveen drew a deep breath to calm himself. Glancing briefly at the image of a radiant Minoti, he murmured, 'Very nice.'

'I am waiting for her to complete her postgraduate studies before we get married,' Rustom said.

Summoning generosity from his bruised heart, Naveen replied, 'Don't wait too long. Distance can bring detachment.' Touched by Naveen's advice, Rustom suggested that they could meet for lunch the next day. Naveen declined, saying that he would be out of town. He did not want to hear about a romance that had clouded his life. In later years he realized how different would have been their destinies had they both discussed their predicaments.

Rustom sought permission from the head of the delegation to halt in London to meet Minoti but his request was refused. As President Daoud wanted their immediate return, the delegation flew home, hoping to forge an economic alliance with the richest nation in the world.

Once more, Fate played a trick by preventing Rustom from meeting Minoti.

The bureaucrats and diplomats who had worked under King Zahir Shah were disturbed by this abrupt departure in Afghan foreign policy. They informed President Daoud that in the 1960s, USA had reneged on its promise to expedite the Helmand Valley Project. Soviet Union had stepped in to offer funds and technical assistance. Afghan military personnel, medical students, and engineers were being trained in the Soviet Union on generous scholarships. Afghanistan was receiving advanced weaponry from the Soviet Union.

'Russia helped us in their interest,' retorted President Daoud.

'In our interest as well,' responded an Afghan general. 'Without their weapons, aircrafts and tanks, we would have been overrun by USA-backed Pakistan.'

'Why are the Soviets supporting Afghan socialists?' the President asked testily.

'The socialists are not harming our national interests, are they?' asked an Afghan diplomat.

'They are Trojan horses,' President Daoud snapped irately.

'They will become Trojan horses if they are persecuted,' a bureaucrat responded. 'Look at India, whose Communist party rules important states like Bengal and Kerala but no one doubts their patriotism.' The civil servant paused. 'The Soviet Union does not want a military alliance with Afghanistan. They are content to have a friendly non-aligned Afghanistan— like India. Why not maintain the status quo?'

Sensing President Daoud's inclination towards the USA, the anxious Soviet Premiere invited the Afghan President to Moscow for discussions on irrigation and road-building projects, which allayed the suspicions of President Daoud. He took a group of seasoned diplomats and defence personnel with him to Moscow. Rustom Ferghani was selected as a member of this delegation because of his knowledge of the Russian language.

Like most members of the Afghan intelligentsia, Rustom was in favour of non-alignment. He was interested in Russia, the Janus-eyed Eurasian neighbour who looked at both the continents it straddled. He had always wanted to see Russia, a vast unknown land; a *terra incognita* that defied comprehension by the Western mind.

Ivan Suvorov, the Russian diplomat stationed in Kabul, was also attending the conference in Moscow. Standing at Red Square with Rustom, he replied, 'Yes, there is grandeur in this square that has withstood the worst times. You will see this grandeur in the Kremlin Museum where I will take you tomorrow.'

Ivan Suvorov and Rustom Ferghani walked through the Kremlin gardens on the way to a Soviet-Afghan conference. Ivan hesitated before asking. 'Why has your President suddenly changed course to flirt with USA? Soviet Union has been a trusted friend of Afghanistan. We have supported her stand on the Durand Line, on Baluchi separatists, on Pashtunistan. Unlike USA we have never sought bases in Afghanistan.'

Rustom sighed. 'Seasoned bureaucrats, diplomats, and army officers have cautioned our president about an alliance with the USA but he appears to think that alliance with the West will bring benefits.'

'Better than what we offer?' Ivan asked sharply.

Rustom sighed. 'Perhaps President Daoud does not like the Kremlin supporting the People's Democratic Party of Afghanistan, which is gaining in strength.'

Ivan continued. 'The Indian government does not object to Russian support to India's Communist Party.'

Rustom nodded. 'That is the general feeling in Kabul. Let us see if President Daoud's meeting with President Brezhnev has a positive effect.'

Russian officials did not express their disappointment with the Afghan President's attitude. They hoped that greater economic cooperation and increased trade with Russia would dampen President Daoud's infatuation with USA.

Later that day Ivan took Rustom sightseeing. At dusk they went to a picturesque old part of Moscow, where, at a quaint tavern, they had a meal of cabbage soup and black rye bread. Until the early hours of the morning they discussed the strategy for fortifying the Russian–Afghan alliance. Both Ivan and Rustom hoped that the old friendship between their nations would remain. But both were aware that they were minor actors among the dramatis personae which would change the history of their nations.

Before returning to Kabul, Rustom went to see his ancestral home at Andijon, a small town in the Ferghana Valley, famous for its fruits, especially the mouth-melting melons for which Emperor Babur yearned in Delhi. Roadside shops displayed fruits—grapes, peaches, plums, persimmons, walnuts, and almonds. He visited a *chaikhona* (tea shop) and spoke to the Uzbek owner. There was a sprinkling of Russians there, who struck up conversation with Rustom. Later he visited the Babur Foundation. Looking at the artefacts and manuscripts that narrated Ferghana Valley's links with ancient Persia, the Mongol and Turkic invasions, Rustom tried to resolve his identity.

Returning to Kabul he told his father about their Ferghana Valley homeland.

General Ferghani was pleased to find Rustom returning to his roots. 'Our family will go there next year,' he said.

In mid-1976 President Daoud resumed his Pashtunistan project. Both the socialist People's Democratic Party of Afghanistan (PDPA), as well as the conservative Pashtuns put pressure on the President to achieve this. This ignited a proxy war with Pakistan, which in turn affected trade and commerce between them. The Pakistani army and Inter-Services Intelligence (ISI) retaliated by inciting *jihad* against Afghanistan's secular government. President Daoud evicted Islamists from Afghanistan. With remarkable foresight he knew that such a movement would create disruption in the country.

Rustom wrote to Minoti.

Dear Minoti,

For all my regard for King Zahir, I wonder if he would have dealt so effectively against this pernicious Islamist movement. President Daoud has asked the state police and army to round up the mullahs and provocateurs that Pakistan sends to our land. If Indians are bewildered by Pakistan's antagonism for Hindu India, how will they explain Pakistan's morbid hatred for a fellow Muslim nation? How can a nation live on a diet of hatred that corrodes their minds?

But there is a bright side to this development. President Daoud has invited Prime Minister Gandhi to Afghanistan on a state visit. Pakistan's depredation on Afghan soil has been a catalyst for the visit. Both leaders want to unite against their common hostile neighbour. My colleagues and I have been tasked with preparing documents on the areas in which Afghanistan seeks cooperation and assistance from India.

Yours,

Rustom

To prepare for the Indian Prime Minister's state visit to Afghanistan, representatives from the two nations prepared documents for discussions and meetings between the two leaders. President Daoud selected Rustom as a member of the Afghan team that went to New Delhi to discuss the agenda with their Indian counterparts.

Rustom had read widely on the rich ancient civilizations that spanned Central Asia, Iran, Afghanistan, and the Indus-Ganges plain. But as his youth was spent in France and England, the trajectory of his travels had bypassed India. While his Foreign Ministry colleagues were enthusiastic about fortifying amity with India, Rustom regarded India with a different sensation. India was Minoti's native land. Eagerly, he informed her of his assignment in New Delhi.

Dear Minoti,

It might be difficult for you while preparing for your final examination but please try coming to Delhi or Calcutta so that we may meet and finalize plans for our wedding. As my father has accepted my decision, you could persuade your parents to do the same. Since you will be completing your studies in a few months, the two families can agree to a date anytime after that. I can hardly believe that events are unfolding in a manner to unite our destinies! In the three years that we have been parted, I sometimes thought our romance was a phantom of my imagination, of our letters flying over seas and mountains like migrant birds lost in the vast horizon. Sometimes I feared not seeing you again, that you would be claimed by forces beyond our volition. But now going to your country I feel that happiness is within our reach.

Yours,

Rustom

A fortnight before the final examinations Minoti went to Devon with a college friend to study in the peace of the countryside. The two women sat on the rolling downs to prepare for their final examinations. Rustom's letter arrived in London after she had left for Devon; it was misplaced by a careless concierge. So fragile is Fate that the careless act of a stranger can alter peoples' destiny.

A blazing summer greeted Rustom and his senior colleagues when they arrived in Delhi in May 1976. He was thrilled to be in India's majestic capital, where Mughal mausoleums jostled against hybrid-classical British edifices. Discussions at the Foreign Ministry in South Block, adjacent to Rashtrapati Bhavan, the Presidential Palace, were absorbing. He composed proceedings of the discussions and circulated the notes he and his colleagues had prepared on Indo-Afghan economic and military cooperation. When the discussions were over, Rustom explored Delhi, undeterred by the heat and the blistering desert air that covered everything with a patina of dust.

However he was troubled by Minoti's silence. If she was busy preparing for her examinations and could not come to India, why did she not respond to his letter? One night he booked a trunk call to Minoti from his room at the grand Ashoka Hotel where visiting foreign delegations were usually lodged. There was no reply from the phone in her room. Disappointment turned to hope. 'She must have gone to Calcutta as I told her I could meet her there.' Next morning, he asked permission of the leader of the team if he could take two days off to visit Calcutta before returning to Kabul because he wanted to meet a close friend there. The senior colleague was surprised by this request but agreed on the condition that he should return to Kabul quickly as they had to prepare for the forthcoming visit of the Indian Prime Minister. 'President Daoud will be displeased if you are absent now.'

After the Afghan delegation left for Kabul, Rustom took an Indian Airlines flight to Calcutta with every hope of finding Minoti waiting for him. He checked in at the Great Eastern Hotel on Chowringhee Road. He was amused by the hotel's attempt to maintain the old British Raj atmosphere; a band played music of the pre-World War II era, while turbaned bearers waited on guests. In the late afternoon, Rustom went in a taxi to the address of Minoti's parents' home on Alipur Road. He glanced around at the edifices of Calcutta that bore witness to British rule and felt proud that the poor and territorially small Afghanistan had remained free by defeating Britain's Great Game in three ruinous wars.

The Ray house was a three-storied mansion built by 19th century ancestors, who had commercial connections with the British East India Company. The fortunes of the family had diminished since then. Descendants of the rich merchants were now employed in government service or in commercial firms. Alighting from the car, Rustom gazed at his fiancée's home. Minoti had once described the evening rituals that were performed in the ancestral house. He stood at the gate, heard the blowing of a conch-shell emanating from the house and saw a retainer waving a brass holder containing sandalwood embers. Scented smoke wafted towards him. When the ceremony ended, Rustom opened the high iron gates, walked to the front door and rang the doorbell.

A dhoti-clad, tousled-haired retainer opened the door and in Bengali asked Rustom's name. As the name 'Rustom' was unfamiliar, he asked, 'Whom do you wish to see? *Boro-babu* (master) is not here but the *Chhoto-babu* (junior master) is here.'

Rustom understood and asked in English: 'I came to meet Miss Minoti.'

'Minoti-*didi*? But, she is in England.'

Rustom was puzzled. If she was in England why had she not replied to his letter in three weeks?

Hearing this exchange, Tarun Ray, Minoti's elder brother, came to the high-ceilinged foyer lined with porcelain vases. He looked at the tall, grey-eyed stranger. 'Can I help you?' Tarun asked politely.

Rustom shook hands with Tarun. Hesitantly, he said: 'I am Dr Rustom Ferghani…Minoti's…friend…from London University days. I now live in Kabul. My senior colleagues in the Afghan Foreign Ministry and I came to Delhi to prepare for the state visit of the Indian Prime Minister to Afghanistan.' He paused. 'Since my work is completed, I thought I'd see Minoti. I assumed that Minoti had returned to India…she was not in London when I telephoned.'

Later, and many times, Rustom regretted that he did not introduce himself as Minoti's fiancé. How different would have been those locust-eaten years! But he was reluctant to declare their relationship to a stranger in an unfamiliar house. 'Ah yes, I remember, Minoti mentioned you in her letters. No, Dr Ferghani, Minoti is still in London but she is expected home soon. But would you like to join us for a drink and dinner?'

Rustom walked with the junior master to a drawing room embellished in heavy *fin de siècle* style. Upon entering the drawing room, he saw several men sitting there. Tarun introduced Rustom to his friends. 'Dr Ferghani and Minoti studied together in London,' he said by way of explanation.

Rustom told them, 'Actually, she was my student. When her professor was busy, I took the classes.'

After pleasantries were exchanged, Tarun told Rustom that the family was waiting for Minoti to complete her exams and return home for her wedding. 'Naveen Sen, her future husband, is expected here soon.'

Rustom was stunned; he felt as if his life's blood was spilling out of his body.

Traditions of courtly conduct came to Rustom's rescue as he sat there, his mind unable to absorb Tarun's words. Was Minoti to marry Naveen Sen, the investment banker he had met in New York? How did Sen discuss Afghanistan's politics and economy, Indian-Afghan affinities, watch Rustom bring out the photo of Minoti and say nothing except, 'Don't wait too long.' Could any man be so devious? Did Naveen Sen enjoy seeing Rustom make a fool of himself and rejoiced in his triumph over the alien intruder?

Tarun was confused by the stunned expression on Rustom's face. But as a good host he asked, 'Now, Dr Ferghani, would you like whiskey or wine?'

Rustom Ferghani struggled with a wild impulse to announce that Minoti and he were betrothed three years ago, that they loved each other and wrote to each other regularly. Then a terrible thought held him back; what if Minoti had indeed *agreed to marry* her compatriot? What if she had renounced Rustom after giving him her body and soul? The Afghan pride—which fought without fear, which killed without mercy, that preferred death to defeat, now came to his rescue.

Stoically, he replied, 'Thank you, Mr Ray, but I have to get back to the hotel. My diplomat colleagues are waiting for me. Tomorrow we return to Kabul.'

'Did you come to Calcutta to meet Minoti?' Tarun asked, as if the thought had suddenly struck him.

Rustom replied with effort, 'No, I had some other work.'

As Rustom stood up, Tarun also rose and said, 'It was very nice meeting you, Dr Ferghani. I wish you could have stayed for dinner and told us about your country.'

Suppressing his fury, Rustom replied coldly, 'That would take more time than a dinner party to narrate.' Then, afraid of losing his composure, he hurriedly said goodbye and strode down the gravel path which he had crossed with such hope half-an-hour earlier. Entering the taxi, he bent forward and held his head in both hands, wondering if what he had learnt was indeed true or was it a passing phantom of fear that came to him now and then?

'Where to, Saheb?' the chauffeur asked, looking with concern at Rustom's bent head in the rear-view mirror.

'Anywhere,' Rustom muttered hoarsely.

The old chauffeur had experienced many such incidents; he also knew the remedy. Steering the car around, he drove towards a quiet place on Outram Ghat, where despondent lovers sat and where vendors sold jasmine garlands to perfume lovers' wounds. Rustom sat back, trying to breathe evenly. A deep fury gathered momentum and took possession of him. How could Minoti, the embodiment of honesty, have played such a devious game? How could she be so cynical to relinquish a man she loved and who loved her, for what was obviously a good match with one of her own race? And how could a seemingly decent man like Naveen Sen meet him without revealing that he was Minoti's future husband? Nothing made sense.

Alighting from the taxi he paced the river bank. The lights on the ships glittered in the hot starless night. When the ships sailed away they left behind dark empty spaces. Rustom sat on a bench and thought: 'This is what the black holes of the universe must be—offering oblivion and emptiness, the end of existence and cognition—and peace!'

Lovers and flower vendors walked away, ships anchored on the river dimmed their lights; a weed-scented wind rose from the sacred river. Spent by pain and anger, Rustom walked slowly to the waiting taxi. Wearied by the summer heat and lulled by the river breeze, the old chauffeur had fallen asleep. Gently, Rustom roused the old man and drove to the Great Eastern Hotel. Asking the chauffeur to have dinner and wait, Rustom went to his room, packed hurriedly, settled the hotel bill with the astonished manager, and then took the same taxi to Dum Dum Airport. Rustom thanked the chauffeur and gave him a handsome tip. Dawn was breaking when the first Indian Airlines flight took off for Delhi. There he waited for the afternoon Ariana Airlines flight to Kabul.

Dusk was falling over the Hindu Kush range when Rustom arrived at the Ferghani mansion. Standing in the flower-filled garden, he mused, 'This is where I dreamt of bringing Minoti as my bride. And now that dream must be dispelled,' he thought bitterly. 'Was it a phantom dream?'

A Game of Errors

President Daoud awaited the return of his officers from Delhi. Something of a recluse, he depended on civil servants and military men for news and took advice only from close counsellors. Of royal birth, he had abolished the monarchy and claimed to rule as a democratic representative of the people.

That June afternoon, President Daoud waited for the officers to discuss agenda papers and also to gather information of the Indian government's attitude to his government. President Daoud scrutinized Rustom and his senior colleagues when they entered the impressive room. When the officers bowed, he gave a cursory nod. They knew that if he was pleased with their work he would display more warmth.

President Daoud was pleased by the documents prepared by his officers for the forthcoming visit of Indira Gandhi. The President conveyed his appreciation of Rustom's analysis of Indian politics; he also wondered why there was such intensity in recommending friendship with India. Thus encouraged,

Rustom flung himself into work. The lights in his room at the President's office burned long after others had gone. At home he sat through the guest-filled elaborate dinners, listening but rarely participating in the conversation. Tiring of these parties, he devised a means of avoiding them. Returning home late, he went directly to his room and asked one of the retainers to bring food on a tray. After dinner, he read and wrote notes late into the night and then slept from sheer exhaustion.

With a mother's concerned eye, Madame Ferghani had observed his altered mood and wondered about its cause. A month after his return, Madame Ferghani came to his room one night, sat on an armchair and asked. 'What aches you, darling?'

Surprised, Rustom replied, 'Why should anything ache me, Maman?'

'I see it in your eyes which no longer sparkle. You no longer laugh, and seem to be far from us all. It is not I alone who has noticed this. Others have commented how you have changed after your visit to India…how sombre and taciturn you have become. It is as if we have lost the cheerful Rustom. Tell me what has happened. I will try to heal your pain as I did when you were a little boy.' She paused. 'Has it anything to do with the young Indian lady?'

Turning away from her sapient gaze, Rustom stared at the outline of the far mountains. 'I have no wish to talk about her. I am fighting memories and want to forget the ill-starred episode.'

Madame Ferghani shook her head. 'Don't fight memories. Turn to new hopes and dreams. The sad memories will soon vanish.'

Rustom nodded. 'That is what I am trying to do—working for my country…to see Afghanistan become a modern society. That will bring me fulfilment.'

Looking intently at him she said, 'Work alone is not enough, Rustom. You need to fill the empty space in your heart with another…'

'I have done with all that nonsense!' he snapped angrily. 'Long ago I read a poem where love is described as the great vandal!' Sadly, he turned to her. 'You are a wonderful mother. As long as you are near, I am happy. Now, go to sleep, Maman. I have work to do. Indira Gandhi is coming soon on a state visit. You and Baba have been invited for the state banquet where you will meet the formidable Indian empress.'

There was great excitement in Kabul when Indira Gandhi arrived there in July 1976. Lining the streets, Afghans of all classes gave a tumultuous welcome as the cavalcade with President Daoud and Prime Minister Indira Gandhi drove past. Deeply moved, she waved and won them with her heart-stealing smile. Old bonds between the two nations were being revived by new needs.

Afghan diplomats and bureaucrats had spent months preparing for this visit. In the evening President Daoud hosted a state banquet at his palace where he paid warm homage to the 'ancient bonds between India and Afghanistan that have nothing to do with politics'. Those who knew the need of the hour smiled. President Daoud said,

Friendship between Afghanistan and India is neither a new phenomenon, nor is it born out of the compulsions of time. This friendship existed between our two countries and peoples, centuries before the advent of colonialism. In this region great intellectual movements have spread shining civilizations from one country to another and thus helped the process for scientific, cultural and commercial exchanges, which in turn have contributed to efforts for progress and prosperity of our societies. Although colonialism and its sinister impacts halted progress and development in our countries and our two nations were forced to employ all their efforts and resources to combat this great evil, but colonialism did not succeed to divide the Afghan and Indian nations. On the contrary, our two peoples joined their efforts and supported each other in their struggles against colonialism until they achieved full independence. So, it was natural that with the elimination of colonial rule, friendship and cooperation between independent Afghanistan and free India be resumed.

Madame Gandhi nodded and applauded. President Daoud smiled and continued:

Similarity of our economic and social problems and our determination to solve them as well as our adherence to non-alignment, have led to the further consolidation of friendship and to the expansion of cooperation between us. We note with satisfaction that friendly relations and wide cooperation between Afghanistan and India have grown to the benefit of our two peoples in the interest of peace and security of the region and in the world and are bearing fruitful results. This friendship and cooperation, which has risen to a new level with the establishment of the Republican regime in Afghanistan, has afforded our peoples the opportunity to benefit from each other's experiences and assistance in different fields of economic and social development, as well as to endeavour to build a new and prosperous life for present and future generations.

The President looked at the stately Prime Minister before saying:

During my friendly visit to your beautiful country last year I witnessed that the hard-working and energetic people of India, under an able and enlightened leadership headed by Your Excellency, are engaged in an enormous struggle for the construction of a decent and prosperous life with great enthusiasm. The Indian nation today are successfully pursuing the goal set by Your Excellency and your colleagues in the context of a reasonable and realistic policy and programme and in conformity with the high interests of Indian society. The people of Afghanistan are admiring your untiring efforts for truly serving your people and country and wish the friendly nation of India ever greater success and triumphs under your wise leadership. I am confident that Your Excellency and your distinguished companions in the course of this friendly visit to our country will witness that since the establishment of the Republican regime in Afghanistan the patriotic and hard-working people of Afghanistan, too, are endeavouring to build a new life, ensuring happiness and prosperity for the present and future of the country.

President Daoud informed Prime Minister Indira Gandhi of the steps taken to reform the social and economic structure of his country. He said, 'Developing countries and indeed all countries of the world need peace and stability more than anything else.' He paused and continued:

Madame Prime Minister, I am certain that the warm feelings and friendly sentiments of the Afghans in welcoming you and your distinguished companions show that we receive you in our country as our close and sincere friend and offer you every hospitality. During this short visit we should have the opportunity to discuss and exchange views with you on all questions of mutual interest to both countries. I have great assurance that these talks and exchanges of views will be another significant and useful step on the road to strengthening and expanding friendly ties and wide cooperation between Afghanistan and India.*

Sitting at some distance from the high table decorated with velvety flowers and crystal candelabras, Rustom heard the dignitaries deliver speeches on the international situation and the cooperation both nations sought from one another. Looking at the Indian Prime Minister, he thought of the Indian student who had enchanted and then abandoned him. The next day Rustom, along with a few other officers, accompanied Indira Gandhi to the *Bagh-e Babur* or Garden of Babur where the first Mughal Emperor had been laid to rest among the terraced gardens and streams which the conqueror had missed in the arid landscape of Delhi.

Senior members of the Afghan government walked beside Indira Gandhi, indicating the places of interest until they came to the Ishfahan-style mosque and the exquisitely carved mausoleum where the remains of Emperor Zahiruddin Babur were interred. Indira Gandhi stood there, gazing meditatively at the tomb, reflecting perhaps on conquest, glory, death, and the final destination of the spirit.

One of President Daoud's counsellors beckoned to Rustom, who came forward. The counsellor turned to Indira Gandhi. 'Excellency, this is Rustom Ferghani, whose

---

* President Daoud's actual speech on the occasion.

family came from Ferghana with Badshah Babur. They did not go to Hindustan and stayed here.'

The Indian Prime Minister smiled. 'Then you must complete the mission and visit India.'

Rustom said gravely, 'I had the privilege of visiting India last month—to prepare documents for Your Excellency's visit.'

Indira Gandhi inclined her head with a warm smile. 'I hope you liked my country as I like yours.'

Rustom could only nod. She saw sadness in his blue-grey eyes and wondered why. But prime ministers cannot delve into personal problems of foreign strangers. Instead, she asked, 'Why did Emperor Babur refuse burial in a grand mausoleum in India?'

'Perhaps he did not strike any roots in the land he had conquered, unlike his descendants who loved Hindustan. Perhaps he wanted to lie under the shadow of the Hindu Kush and feel its snowy breath in winter.'

Rustom's reply aroused Indira's curiosity. So, she asked, 'Are you a student of literature and history?'

'No, Excellency. I used to teach International Law at London University and presently I work in our President's office.' Now, Indira heard pain in his voice.

Troubled by the young man's countenance, she frowned, and then slowly moved forward with the Afghan dignitaries.

The visit of the Indian Prime Minister to Afghanistan was a great success. India agreed to provide arms and strategic support against Pakistan's intransigence. Indira Gandhi also encouraged President Daoud to press for forming Pashtunistan that would curb Pakistan's aggression on India's borders. The Indian Prime Minister's visit added bitterness to Rustom's pain; he speculated how it would have been if Minoti and he had married and come to live in Kabul.

While he brooded on these thoughts, his father was summoned by President Daoud. 'Rustom is working well. But I observe a change in him. Perhaps he should settle down with Princess Zubaida.' The President's obsidian eyes had missed nothing. General Ferghani agreed enthusiastically.

Negotiations were resumed with Princess Zubaida's family in Herat. In pursuance of this, she came to Kabul and stayed in the Argh (royal palace) where her aunt, Princess Daoud lived. The First Lady hosted a dinner party where Rustom and Zubaida were intended to renew their acquaintance after two years. General Ferghani keenly watched the proceedings. Aware of her son's angry anguish, Madame Ferghani did not press matters. Zubaida was attracted to Rustom but was annoyed by his courteous reserve.

Princess Daoud told Rustom: 'The President and I would like to see you married to my niece'. General Ferghani endorsed her wish.

Rustom replied sarcastically: 'Perhaps it would be wise to marry Princess Zubaida—as everyone hopes. I will continue our exalted bloodline, and have a privileged life like other well-born young colleagues.'

When General Ferghani pursued the matter, Rustom said, 'Let me think about it, Baba. I need time to settle into my work, make a mark and…'

'And banish memories of the alien young woman!' General Ferghani exclaimed impatiently.

Stung to anger, Rustom replied, 'If you are waiting for that, it may take many years.' He paused, determined to nettle his father. 'Despite the family tradition, I am not polygamous.'

The General flushed a deep crimson at Rustom's reference to his déclassé concubine but he did not argue. 'All right,' he growled. 'Take your time but remember you are 33 and not getting younger…and the princess may not wait indefinitely.'

'The princess,' Rustom replied with a sardonic smile, 'is also showing signs of age. So, we shall deal well together.'

In 1976, a few months after Rustom's visit to Calcutta, Minoti's parents asked her to return to Calcutta so that the two families could discuss wedding plans. She finally told her parents that she was engaged to Rustom Ferghani and could not marry Naveen Sen or anyone else.

'I have thought about this for three years, have pondered over your advice about marriage with a husband of different

nationality and a different religion. I would rather risk unhappiness at a future date rather than make a marriage of convenience. Naveen Sen is a very fine gentleman and deserves a wife who will cherish him.'

After the furore quietened and profuse apologies were offered to the Sen family by the Rays, Naveen Sen wrote to Minoti:

Well, my promised bride, the fictitious betrothal is thankfully over. But if you have a double, I shall marry her. Incidentally, I met your fiancé in New York a few months ago. He is intelligent and refined and spoke of you with evident admiration. I am sure you will find happiness together.

Minoti felt a strange bitter-sweetness at Naveen's letter because he was saying goodbye. Added to that was her anxiety; Rustom had not written to her for two months. Busy with her postgraduate exams she brushed aside these disquieting thoughts and took comfort in Rustom's 'evident admiration'.

After obtaining a postgraduate degree in early 1977, she wrote to Rustom that she could now go to Kabul and have the wedding there since her family had disapproved of her decision to marry him. She was anxious when he did not reply. She wrote again, but there was complete silence.

Minoti thought that Rustom had wearied of waiting for her and had married Princess Zubaida, whom he had mentioned in one of his letters. She could not know that General Ferghani had ensured that her letters never reached Rustom.

Aware of her family's disapproval, Minoti did not return to Calcutta and remained in London. After some job searching she was able to get an appointment as Tutor in the faculty of International Law at University College. At first, she felt lonely but in time became immersed in the new work and resumed connections with old college friends. None of this assuaged the misery of being abandoned by Rustom Ferghani. Every night she kissed the ring given by Rustom and recited these lines,

'A dove's wing clings my heart each night with surging gentleness. The blue stone set in the tryst ring has worn more bright. Love endures, though starving and alone.'

The Darkest Dawn

The last year of peace in Afghanistan—1977—came upon her people. Indira Gandhi, President Daoud's firm ally, was defeated in a general election in March 1977. The Janata Party that came to power had no idea how to rule India, let alone negotiate international relations. The new Rightist Prime Minister was more interested in cultivating the USA, only because his opponent, Indira Gandhi, had signed the Indo–Soviet Treaty during the Bangladesh Liberation War of 1971.

As if sensing turmoil on the horizon, President Daoud established the new National Revolutionary Party. In January 1977, the *Loya Jirga* or National Assembly approved the new Constitution, which established a presidential one-party system of government and which introduced new articles and amended existing ones. He became less enthusiastic about socialist policies. When a rift began brewing with the People's Democratic Party of Afghanistan (PDPA), President Daoud distanced himself from the communist elements within the group. When the socialists in his government advocated cooperation with Russia, President Daoud turned to Muslim states—Saudi Arabia, Iran and Egypt—for economic and military assistance. On their advice he ceased to demand the creation of Pashtunistan and tried to establish amicable relations with the perennial foe, Pakistan. This rapprochement brought USA dangerously close to the Afghan scene.

During a visit to Moscow in April 1977, President Brezhnev advised President Daoud: 'Please maintain your traditional neutrality and do not allow NATO advisers on the Afghanistan–Soviet frontier. Apart from geo-political factors, our nuclear arsenals are there.' Daoud angrily rejected the advice and became closer to the USA, Saudi Arabia, and Iran. He signed a military treaty with President Anwar Sadat of Egypt, who offered to train Afghan military and police forces in Cairo. He began purging Leftist officers in the army and government, and brought back Rightist officers to his government. Soviet leaders watched developments on the Afghan–Soviet frontier with growing concern.

Rustom was posted to the Afghan Foreign Ministry, where he dealt with the pro-Western foreign policy initiated by President Daoud. He travelled to West Asia and North Africa for discussions with his counterparts in those regions. The new horizons and policies diverted his mind from Minoti, whom he was trying to forget.

By the end of 1977 Rustom sensed subterranean tension in Kabul. Young Afghans wanted modernization of their country and favoured closer relations with the Soviet Union, where many Afghan students received medical, scientific and technical education, and where defence personnel were trained. The feudal and conservative groups did not want erosion of their privileges. King Zahir had found a middle path but his cousin and successor was in a Hamletian dilemma.

To gather information for the government, Rustom was instructed to enrol as a member of the Leftist Khalq faction of the People's Democratic Party of Afghanistan. At first, they were suspicious of him; why would a member of the ruling elite make common cause with socialists who wanted to change the political system? Rustom told them: 'I am disillusioned with both Western capitalism and Afghan feudalism. I want to see a modern secular state. That is why I left behind a promising academic career in London.' Thereby, he persuaded the PDPA leaders that he was a socialist sympathiser and a mole in the Afghan government. Rustom's knowledge of the Russian language convinced them that he was, as he stated, a protégé of the Soviet government—a status much valued by the socialist members. The Khalq leaders—Nur Muhammad Taraki and Hafizullah Amin—considered Rustom a useful agent for obtaining information about the government. He supplied innocuous and misleading information.

In April 1978, Mir Akbar Khyber—a prominent member of the Parchami, the moderate faction of the PDPA—was murdered by a Khalq member. Astonishingly, President Daoud did not see the danger posed by the Khalq group and took no steps to neutralize them. More strangely, he regarded the moderate Parchami as a serious challenge because they were connected with the political elite, the senior bureaucracy and the royal family. He had their movements watched. Since the Khalq faction members had connections in the lower bureaucracy, President Daoud did not take them seriously and did not involve them in his government. Most of them were Pashtuns and Ghilzais from the provinces, teachers, intellectuals and students from Kabul University. Their leader was Nur Muhammad Taraki, a minor official with radical beliefs. President Daoud did not know that the Khalqs had penetrated his security police. Learning of this, Rustom immediately informed senior officials that Taraki and Amin were serious threats to the government.

Even clever rulers believe what they want to believe. President Daoud did not want to precipitate a crisis in an already volatile situation. In late 1977 the Iranians revolted openly against their despotic Shah and his American allies. Since USA refused to support liberal Iranians against the Shah, Iranians turned to a dangerous alterative—the powerful Islamic Ulema headed by Ayatollah Khomeini, then in exile in France.

As ballast against the Islamist danger, President Daoud needed the socialist Khalqs as allies. He also needed their support against Pakistani intrusions on Afghan borders. When information of their conspiracies trickled in, President Daoud ordered the arrest of the PDPA leaders. Astonishingly, his orders were implemented a week later. Taraki was arrested, and Babrak Karmal escaped to Czechoslovakia and then to the Soviet Union, while the dangerous Amin was placed merely under house arrest. Though armed guards were posted at his house, Hafizullah Amin contacted party functionaries through family members who acted as messengers. Sitting at home, showing no visible resistance against house arrest, Amin gave instructions on how to organize a coup.

Expecting disturbances, President Daoud placed the Afghan National Army on high alert on 26 April 1978. Fearing that the loyal Afghan army would abort the intended coup, Amin decided to act without further delay. Believing Rustom to be their ally, a Khalq member excitedly informed Rustom about the imminent coup. Rustom immediately reported this to the President's office. Army leaders swiftly sent troops to Kabul International Airport to prevent the PDPA from seizing power. But they met with resistance by security personnel who had already defected to the PDPA. Heavy fighting ensued.

Rustom was astonished at the speed with which the battle began. To fortify the army, the commanders swiftly recalled troops stationed on the Afghan–Pakistani frontier. Rustom rushed to his father's office at military headquarters. 'The troops must come to Kabul at once,' he told the general.

That night, General Ferghani informed his son: 'Pakistan's President Bhutto has ordered his troops to organize skirmishes on the border in order to delay the arrival of the loyal troops to Kabul. The Pakistan-based Haqqani network, Quetta Shura, Hezbi Islami, and other terrorist groups funded by USA and Pakistan's ISI, want chaos in Afghanistan.'

'Didn't our intelligence agencies know what was happening on the frontier?' Rustom asked angrily.

General Ferghani replied: 'We knew of these skirmishes, which have been going on since 1947, but never thought they were part of a bigger game.'

Rustom spoke grimly. 'Baba, a Khalq member informed me just now that they are planning a coup tomorrow. Please leave Kabul tonight with Maman. Fly to Delhi by any available flight or set off on road for Herat. You will be safe with Zubaida's family. From there you can go to India. I will stay behind and do what I can to avert calamity to other family members.'

With a sad smile General Ferghani asked, 'Rustom, have you such a low opinion of me? Do you think I shall leave my country without a fight, without trying to defeat those Khalq scoundrels? Our family has fought invasions for centuries and won!'

'This is not going to be an invasion! It will be seizure of power by a ruthless group! Those associated with President Daoud will be exterminated.'

Listening with a frown, General Ferghani replied, 'I refuse to flee from danger. Let it come. I will fight them.'

The family members heard Rustom with deepening fear. 'I refuse to go without my husband and son,' Madame Ferghani declared. After many arguments, Rustom persuaded his mother and sister to leave by road for Herat on Iran's border. He telephoned Zubaida's father and entreated the old prince to look after his family members. The crafty prince made a bargain. 'If you promise to marry my daughter, I shall welcome your relatives as my own. Otherwise I have no interest in protecting fugitives.'

Desperate, Rustom replied, 'I promise.'

The prince laughed softly. 'When the killings are over, we can have a grand wedding here.'

Putting the phone down, Rustom muttered, 'May that day never come, you old devil.'

As twilight fell over the snow-covered mountains, Rustom drove to the British Embassy to meet his friend Terence Rowland, with whom he spoke frequently on the phone. The Englishman received him with concern. After tea was served, Terence asked, 'Things are bad, aren't they?'

Rustom nodded. 'Worse than we imagine.' He paused before saying, 'Terence, I want you to do me a favour.'

'Of course, anything,' Terence replied.

Rustom took out a letter from his jacket pocket and laid it on the glass-topped table. 'I want you to put this letter in a British Embassy envelope and send it to London through your diplomatic bag at the earliest. Please have it delivered to the addressee. It has no political implications. Please read it.'

Rustom had written:

Dearest Minoti,

I have not heard from you for a year. Therefore, I have no idea where you are. I have now reconciled myself to your marriage to a man of your own creed. In the face of an uncertain future this is no time for bitterness. I expect Goodenough House will forward my letter to you wherever you are. You and the world will soon hear of our fate. If we do not meet again, remember me with kindness because you have been a precious part of my life. I am not the forgetful Rustom of the Shah Nama.

I will always be your Rustom.

Terence Rowland raised his eyes to look at Rustom, who was staring at the flower-filled embassy garden. The British diplomat rose and placed the letter in an envelope and sealed it. 'I will ensure that the letter is sent to the given address in London,' he said. 'If there is anything I can do, Rustom, let me know. If you and your family need political asylum…our embassy is open,' Terence said gently.

A grave Rustom rose and said 'Thank you, Terence. I fear it is too late for that.'

Through an intuition that dark events were gathering momentum in Afghanistan, and perhaps in their very lives, the two young men embraced each other.

'*Khuda hafiz*,' Rustom murmured.

'May the Lord be with you,' Terence said.

Rustom returned home late to find his mother packing and weeping. A distressed General Ferghani paced the marble floor. Other family members also prepared for departure. Three large cars waited in readiness. Though the household retainers asked no questions, they were aware of the danger around them. The mansion, the scene of security and happiness only two days ago, now stood in eerie and ominous silence in contrast to the rustle of spring leaves outside. That dark night Madame Ferghani and other family members left Kabul for Herat.

Father and son watched the family drive away. Suddenly, one car stopped. Madame Ferghani alighted and ran towards the two men; she kissed her husband's hands and held her son in a tight embrace. Then, with tears streaming down her face, she returned to the car and waved to the two men standing at the gate until darkness engulfed them.

General Ferghani, Rustom and others in the beautiful mansion stayed awake that night, waiting for a dawn that would darken Afghanistan for many decades. When dawn broke on the morning of 28 April 1978, Rustom and General Ferghani left home with a bleak premonition. The general went to army headquarters while Rustom went to the Foreign Ministry. An hour later he heard the first bursts of gunfire. Built in the peaceful days of King Aminullah, the walls of the solid Storay Palace trembled. Rustom's terrified secretary came running in to inform him that one Colonel Abdul Khadir had led the coup with a combined armoured and air assault on the Arg, the seat of President Daoud's centralized government. This demoralized the larger loyal forces nearby. Rushing out into the street, Rustom was astonished by the spectacle. Armoured tanks rolled down the streets and MIGs flew over the azure spring sky. He realized that President Daoud's government had been overthrown.

Rustom returned swiftly to his office room. Kabul Radio announced that the PDPA forces had attacked officials at army headquarters. Quick capture of telecommunications, the defence ministry and other strategic centres of authority isolated President Daoud's loyal palace guards, who fought on against the well-trained rebels. As the sun rose higher over the snowy Hindu Kush range, sounds of artillery fire and explosions grew louder. Smoke billowed out from government buildings. People fled from offices, shops, and tea houses to the spurious safety of their homes to avoid the heavy crossfire between the President's forces and those of the PDPA.

Rustom telephoned his father at army headquarters but there was no response. He held the telephone for a few moments, trying to formulate a plan. Then, sensing imminent danger to his father, he put down the telephone and looked around the neat office room, wondering if he would see it again. Quickly, he went into the street to find a tank stationed at the entrance of the Foreign Ministry. Rebel soldiers looked at him; he composed himself to salute them, then got into his car and drove swiftly to the army headquarters. Forces of the PDPA guarded the building, their weaponry on display. Bursts of gunfire alternating with screams of agony emanated from the building. Steeling himself against pain and horror, Rustom entered the building. The spectacle of a clean-shaven young man in western clothes evoked hostile curiosity. But no one tried to stop him. This unintended courtesy allowed Rustom to walk down the bloodstained corridor to the chamber occupied by General Ferghani.

The sight that greeted Rustom haunted him all his life. The proud general was slumped on his chair with a stilled left hand on the telephone. Blood from two bullet holes on his forehead had flowed down to his military tunic and congealed on his medals. Rustom's stunned eyes travelled from his father's body to the photograph the general had pressed to his chest with the right hand—of a laughing Rustom in graduation cloak and cap. The photo had an inscription in Nashtaliq script—'the star of my eyes'. Rustom broke down and knelt at his father's feet, to ask forgiveness, to pay him homage. 'Baba, I am honoured, to be the son of a proud warrior who went defiantly to your death rather than flee or ask for mercy.'

Howling in grief, Rustom did not hear the door open and the entry of three armed men into the once impressive room now splashed with blood.

One man said, 'Take him outside. We have orders to shoot all associates of Daoud.' Rustom rose and shook off the soldier's hand on his shoulder, his streaming eyes now smouldering in fury.

An army officer entered and shouted: 'Take Rustom Ferghani to the interrogation centre—to be questioned and then executed.'

Rustom pulled out a revolver from his trouser pocket and fired at the man. It injured the officer but the others overpowered him and snatched away his revolver. 'Now you can safely kill an unarmed man,' Rustom snapped in Pashto. 'Not quite the Pashtun code but never mind, assassins have no code.'

The soldiers led him away. Gazing tearfully at his father, Rustom murmured, 'Forgive me, Baba. You are a true and noble warrior. You will rest in paradise.'

The Prisoner of Kandahar

It was the beginning of an endless nightmare.

The armed men pushed Rustom into a waiting van and drove him to the PDPA headquarters, where Colonel Khadir gleefully informed him that President Daoud had been shot dead at his palace but not before he was forced to see the murder of family members and loyal adherents.

Nauseated by such savagery, Rustom retorted, 'Prince Daoud assumed power in 1973 without hurting or killing anyone. And look at you! How dare you hoodlums call yourselves socialists!' Rustom spat on the floor.

Colonel Khadir rose, a hairy paw reaching out to his heavy revolver.

Unfazed, Rustom said, 'Go ahead, shoot me, Khadir, who was the shoe-polisher of my father. Amin will reward your chivalry.'

Eyes bloodshot with rage, the mastermind of massacres advanced towards him. 'Save your breath for your last prayers,

Ferghani. I will shortly shoot you as I shot your great father in his room, and bury your bodies together.' He snarled a laugh.

A sudden inspiration came to Rustom. 'Before you shoot me, ask permission from my Kremlin friends. Otherwise they may scalp you afterwards. My friend Commissar Ivan Suvorov is due here shortly to halt your killings.'

The mastermind of massacres paused in his purpose. Now that the fell deed had been done, the PDPA needed Soviet support. So, he prevaricated. 'Be careful, Ferghani. Don't put on your haughty airs. Your sire is dead. If you want to live, become my arse polisher.'

Rustom spat again on the carpet. 'No descendant of Babur would bend before a creature spawned in the sewer.' This time fury overcame the serial murderer. He slapped Rustom hard on both cheeks. A large ruby ring, purloined from the dead Prince Daoud's royal finger and now on the butcher's finger, cut into Rustom's chiselled lips. Smarting with pain, Rustom stifled a cry as blood trickled down his throat.

Colonel Khadir hated General Ferghani's intellectual westernized son. He offered Rustom a sinister smile. 'Lock him up. We will execute him tonight.'

A uniformed man entered and stared at Rustom with the pale sightless eyes of classical statues. He drew Khadir aside and conferred grimly. 'This man has close connections with Russian and British diplomats. We shall need their cooperation in the days ahead. Postpone Ferghani's execution. Keep him as hostage when we bargain with the Russky and Angrezy foxes.'

Colonel Khadir grunted assent and ordered Rustom to be locked in a small room. From there Rustom could hear gunshots, explosions, and blood curdling screams. He waited to be shot and buried with his father. Descendant of conquerors, he had never lacked courage but now he felt terrible fear. As darkness fell, the sounds of firing and screams ceased. Amin's immediate enemies had been eliminated.

The pale-eyed man reappeared, scrutinized Rustom, and murmured commands. His aides nodded, blind-folded, and then thrust Rustom into a jeep. The cold nozzle of a carbine pressed on his neck as the vehicle drove off. Emitting sweaty odour, the men grunted in a rough Pashtu dialect. The journey continued for seven hours to an unnamed destination. It was dawn when they arrived at the intended place. Once again, the butt end of a rifle was pressed on his neck as a man took his arm and guided him to a place. When the smelly cloth was removed from his eyes, he saw that he was in a small, dark prison cell. There were no other prisoners. The jailer was a swarthy, sturdy middle-aged man, who locked the wrought iron cell door. They went outside, where the armed men gave hurried instructions before leaving.

Rustom's mind grappled with the horror of what had transpired in the last 30 hours; his mother's departure for Herat at midnight, the coup d'état at dawn, his father's murder midmorning, his imprisonment at noon, and this prison cell in an unknown place in an unforseen dawn.

Whenever Rustom tried to obliterate images of that terrible day they always appeared before him like fearful phantoms.

A new day came. Exhausted, Rustom rose from the floor where he had slept fitfully and sat on a low stool. His stomach growled in hunger, his throat was clogged with dust. Running a palm over his cheeks he felt the stubble and remembered how his mother used to tell him: 'Grow a beard. You will then look more like a warlord.'

'Maman, where are you now?' he cried out in a hoarse voice. 'I hope you are all safe. Will I ever see you again? At least Baba is safe in paradise.'

A shadow fell across the iron bars of the door. Rustom turned to see the jailor opening the locked door. Entering, he set a plate of tandoor bread and a mug of tea on a wooden table. 'Eat, *Janab*,' the jailer said laconically. 'It is not much of a meal, but it will have to do for now. Later, my son will bring something more.'

Rustom glanced at the freshly-baked bread and then at the jailer. 'Have you poisoned the bread and tea? That would save the hoodlums some bullets.'

Rustom was surprised when the jailer burst into laughter. 'Yes, I can see your arrogance has provoked the revolutionaries. They told me to treat you like dirt...to start with.'

'So, what follows after bread and tea?' Rustom asked, suppressing unease.

'Maybe an old transistor will give you the latest news from Kabul.'

'I want to know nothing more. The world is dead for me,' Rustom replied with a despair that moved the jailer.

'Then rest. My son will bring in a mattress and pillow from my house.'

'In Hindustan there is a tradition to treat a man well before he is executed. Is that what you are doing in my last hours?' Rustom asked.

'This is Afghanistan, *Janab*, a land where debts are repaid.'

After moments of silence Rustom asked, 'What are you trying to tell me?'

The jailer sat on the floor. 'Long ago I worked in the house of your grandfather Iskandar Khan, here in Kandahar.'

Rustom was astounded. 'Kandahar? Is this Kandahar?'

The jailer nodded with a sad smile.

'And you served my maternal grandfather Iskandar Khan?'

The jailer nodded, this time without a smile. 'Orphaned by the many land disputes that plague our land, I was adopted by your noble grandfather and raised as a son—because my father had exchanged his life for that of Khan Saheb's eldest son. So, Iskandar repaid the debt by giving me a home, education, and land where he built a house for me. He got me married to a distant kinswoman of his.' The jailer paused. 'So, Allah has willed that I must repay my great debt by looking after you.'

With bleary, sleep-deprived eyes, Rustom stared at the jailer in silence for sometime. Then he said, 'You are making up a story to disarm me.'

The jailer shook his head. '*Disarm you, Janab*? Why should I disarm you? You are entirely in my power. The soldiers gave me a Kalashnikov rifle to shoot you if you try to escape.'

Rustom shook his head in bewilderment. 'How...why... have I come to be here?' he whispered.

'The will of the merciful Allah has brought you here.'

'I have done with Allah! What I saw yesterday...' Rustom's voice broke.

'Then call it Kismet, *Janab*. Now, have your bread and tea. We will bring bedding, soap, towel, toothpaste.' He paused. 'I will keep you comfortable...and safe... But don't try to escape. Then I have no alternative but to shoot you...for my family's safety.'

The jailer, Hashim Baig, made the cell habitable by sweeping away dust from floor and walls. The primitive toilet was scrubbed clean. A wooden cot and bedding were provided. A trestle table was brought in for placing various articles. Looking around the cell with a heavy heart, Rustom mused, 'That I, Rustom Ferghani, who grew up in a luxurious mansion, have to be grateful for this!'

Several days later Hashim brought a transistor for Rustom. After tuning in to Kabul's news channel and hearing the news, Rustom realized that he had cause to be grateful. Many important Afghans had been arrested and executed. With the passing days, hundreds were killed on the orders of Hafizullah Amin, the bloodthirsty member of the PDPA triumvirate. Even the socialist intellectuals who were the ideologues of the PDPA were killed or jailed for condemning the violence perpetrated by the triumvirate.

From the appalling fabrications doled out on Kabul Radio, Rustom pieced the news together with a sense of impending doom. Gazing at the stained grey walls he wondered, 'Was it like this in medieval times? But they did not have the advanced weaponry or technology to carry out such systematic extermination of rivals.' He wondered how long he would be imprisoned here. Believing the threat he held out—of his powerful Kremlin friends—he knew the pale-eyed officer had postponed his execution. When the Kremlin friends would fail to appear, his execution would be swift. 'I shall try to escape even if I get killed. I have nothing more to live for,' he thought miserably.

The human mind plays tricks with its owner. No sooner had he thought this when he decided: 'I have to find Maman and my sister. I have to reclaim our mansion. Most of all, I have to avenge Baba's murder.' Then he admitted to himself, 'I also want to live for life itself…to see the Hindu Kush rising to the sky, smell unfurling flowers, walk over hard packed snow, feel the cold breath of wind on my face, read books, hear music and…'

He paused in pain and thought, 'Beyond these elementary desires lie the danger of dreams…of love and happiness that I plucked out from my mind even before the violence began.' He would resort to the strategy of conjuring images of days and years prior to the day of carnage. He decided, 'I will sublimate the agony of violence, death, and betrayal by resurrecting a lost arcadia.'

So, he began to write on paper with a nibbed pen that Hashim brought him.

Dearest Minoti,

I will write these messages, knowing full well that you will neither receive nor read them. Yet some irrational part of me— hidden from my own self—believes that by some alchemy your mind will reach out to mine across snow-crested mountains, arid plains and the broad rivers of our lands. Even if you cannot hear my voice you will surely hear its echo in some midnight dream.

I, Rustom Ferghani, was raised as a rational being, studied mathematics, science and law. I never delved into the world of imagination because all dangers spring from that; perils of unwarranted ambitions and unwise passions. But now that enemy—imagination—or phantasm as the ancient Greeks called it—has been summoned to save my sanity.

So, I traverse Time to return to the unclouded days of childhood, of a devoted mother and powerful father, a house of balconies, latticed windows, winding marble stairs and gardens found only in this part of the world, of picnics on the Hindu Kush range, riding a swift horse across swirling mountains streams, of escapades in Grandfather's estate. This world came to an end when my ambitious father sent me to study in a French school, then a British university, so that I may acquire the requirements for a political career in this wild country, where attributes of the mind are despised unless fortified by brute force. So, I devoured knowledge as a starving man swallows food until conflicting thoughts and warring ideas jostled in my mind for space and understanding. I lived in intellectual confusion, and was proud of it. Was this not a renaissance of the spirit?

But a different renaissance came when I saw you, a new student, at the commencement of the Michaelmas term at University College. I never got round to telling you how your tremulous smile touched me, how your softly intoned 'Good morning, Dr Ferghani,' turned a grey London morning into gold. Two years passed with these greetings and academic discussions during tutorials. In that time, you transited from adolescence to womanhood. I watched you bloom, liked hearing you argue and stand stubbornly by your views as you did with

Dr Schwarzenberg, to see your eyes flash indignantly when academics spoke disparagingly about 'under developed countries'. As a member of the teaching faculty, albeit a junior one, I had to assume a neutral position during these debates. The denouement over Chanakya changed things. I no longer concealed my feelings for you, as it was evident to others.

Our path seemed so simple. We would complete our respective studies and then we would marry. We two aliens would stay in imperial London and find happiness there. Then King Zahir Shah's deposing changed the course of my life. Claims were made on my future and demands made on my sense of duty, to return home—claims and demands which, I realize now with the futility of hindsight, should have been declined.

Here I am in this damp cell at the mercy of a man whose professions of loyalty to my grandfather guarantees no security should the villains decide to kill me. How long will I endure this nightmare?

Messenger of the Clouds

While Rustom was composing this letter in a Kandahar prison, Minoti was reading newspapers in faraway London. The day she heard of the PDPA coup in Kabul on BBC radio, she rushed to buy a copy of *Manchester Guardian* on the way to college and was gripped by mounting panic as she read grim reports.

President-Prince Daoud, who did not understand the grim realities of power-politics, had been removed, not by the peaceful coup by which he deposed his cousin, King Zahir, but by a massacre along with his family members. Later on, others who were part of his establishment and entourage were also killed, and their homes plundered. The dailies gave names of some of the victims; General Ferghani was one of them. Minoti trembled; she felt she could not walk further. Hurrying inside a café by the park she sat there with her head in her hands, trying to compose herself. 'If the father has been shot, will they spare his son?' she asked herself. The image of her brave, tousled-haired beloved being executed wrenched a sob from her.

The plump waitress came to her and asked anxiously, 'Dearie, are you all right?'

Minoti shook her head and sobbed.

The motherly waitress brought a cup of tea. 'Drink that, luv,' she murmured. 'Nothing can be as bad as that.'

Minoti took a few sips of tea and then, leaving a few shillings on the table, walked with leaden feet to University College at Gower Street. With great effort she took two tutorials. Her concerned students noted her swollen eyes and pallor. Work finished for the day, a shaken Minoti returned to Goodenough House in a taxi and sat at her desk, rereading newspaper reports. It was as if she was losing Rustom twice over—first by his refusal to respond to her letters and then by the coup which may have taken his life. But stubborn hope banished despair.

Dearest Rustom, she wrote in a note book. *I refuse to believe you have left this world. I would have felt something ominous if that was so. No, you are somewhere in that desolate country. You must stay safe even if I have no hope of happiness with you, even if you have joined your destiny with someone else. Two years have passed since I last heard from you. Perhaps you have found happiness and contentment in your new life. I have not.*

I read of how your family mansion and many others have been ransacked – the home where you promised to take me as your bride, to the windswept room with a balcony that gazed at the Hindu Kush range, where we would find happiness. I had surrendered all hopes of seeing you but now I must summon all my life force, my élan vitale, and pass it onto you. We Hindus believe in this phenomenon—transference of thought and energy to another being.

Minoti went daily to the vast University College library to read journals and newspapers, and listened to BBC news to obtain available information on the events in Afghanistan, of how the country was being ruled by a 'divided, dilettante Marxist clique' whose actions, said an Afghan socialist intellectual, were likely to lead to disintegration of the state. The Khalq faction who seized power called their state the Democratic Republic of Afghanistan or DRA. They dominated the Revolutionary Council, the ruling body of the government, and began purging the Parcham faction. This destroyed Afghanistan's former ruling elite.

When reports on Afghanistan became terrifying Minoti stopped reading newspapers. But her fear for Rustom deepened. April turned to May, which brought apple blossoms and azure skies. Minoti found it increasingly difficult to concentrate on her work, preparing notes for lectures, or discussions for the tutorials assigned to her.

She considered going to Kabul to search for Rustom, then realized it was utterly impractical. Instead, she met a Second Secretary at the Indian High Commission and asked him whether it was possible for the Indian Foreign Ministry to obtain information about a friend who was part of President Daoud's government. The diplomat explained to her the futility of the venture. 'The Indian Government has maintained friendly relations with the new government. We cannot get involved in their internecine politics.' With this magisterial pronouncement her hopes receded.

When summer came to London and the university colleges closed, Minoti wondered what to do over the long vacation. She sat in the adjoining park through balmy afternoons, staring at the sky and remembering the summer of 1973 when her world was splendid, like the July days. One such afternoon she walked wearily back to Goodenough House. The receptionist informed her that an official from the Foreign Office was waiting for her. The man came towards her and asked quietly, 'Miss Minoti Ray?'

Minoti nodded in silence, dreading the news the stranger had brought.

'I have a letter for you from the British Embassy in Kabul,' he said and held out a blue envelope with a red seal of the lion and the unicorn. 'Our apology for the delay—due to certain events in Afghanistan.'

Minoti stared at the envelope. 'What does the letter say?' she asked in a hoarse voice.

The messenger frowned; he realized that there might be ill tidings within that envelope. 'I don't rightly know, Miss. It was sent by the British Embassy in Kabul to our Foreign Office with the instruction to deliver it to you or forward it if you lived elsewhere.'

Minoti held out a trembling hand to receive the letter.

The distressed messenger asked, 'Should I wait, Miss Ray? Will there be a reply?'

'Please wait," she whispered. It was as if the presence of another person would mitigate the misery embossed in the letter. With trembling fingers she opened the envelope. At first, her mind could not grasp what her eyes saw. Then as she re-read the letter, tears of relief streamed down her cheeks. She clasped the messenger's hand and cried, 'Thank you! Bless you for bringing the letter!'

The relieved messenger smiled. 'My pleasure, Miss,' he said and went his way.

It was the letter which Rustom had handed over to Terence Rowland at the British Embassy in Kabul. She noted the date, 27th April, a day before the PDPA's coup d'état. That was three months ago. There was no news of his present state. But he had not banished her from his heart. He had not forgotten nor abandoned her like Rustom of the *Shah Nama*, who had abandoned Tahmina. This Rustom was still hers. Minoti hurried to her room and, sitting by the window, clasped the letter to her breast and wept until exhausted. As the afternoon drifted into a lingering northern twilight, Minoti sat at her desk and continued her message to her invisible beloved.

What joy! Your brief message reached me today. Did I not tell you, dearest Rustom, that I know you are here in this world, that no harm could come to you when my life force is yours, when my very being tells me that you are safe. I am now tempted to go to Kabul and find you wherever you are. The officer at India House made magisterial pronouncement about not getting involved in 'internecine matters'. Perhaps he cannot involve himself in controversies. Take care of yourself, dearest, and don't court danger. Your letter has given me the resolve to make a life with you. Memories of our halcyon days in London and Rome tell me that those days could not have been in vain, could not have been gifted to us only to be snatched away by a capricious fate.

There were others who searched for Rustom Ferghani: his two diplomat friends posted in Kabul—Terence Rowland and Ivan Suvorov. Separately, they made enquiries, first from the few retainers at the Ferghani mansion, and then more discreetly at the Afghan Foreign Ministry, where chaos prevailed. While Terence drew a blank, Ivan—as a member of the Soviet Embassy—was shown more courtesy, but no information was available. The Khalq members who now manned the Foreign Ministry had no idea of Rustom's fate. Assuming he had been executed with his father, they dared not say so. Instead, they told the two foreign diplomats that Rustom Ferghani had fled to the West, as had many members of Afghanistan's elite.

Summer passed and a new university term began. Minoti began to read dispatches of Reuters, Associated Press, and Press Trust of India from Kabul, with the renewed hope that there would be some news of Rustom.

Returning to Goodenough House one autumn evening she found a familiar figure sitting in the foyer. He rose on seeing her. Hesitantly, she went to him and exclaimed, 'Naveen! What a surprise!'

Naveen Sen scrutinized her altered appearance with concern. Her figure seemed attenuated, her eyes loomed large on her thin face. She indicated an armchair and then sat down opposite him.

'I was passing through London and thought I would meet the elusive one,' he said lightly.

Minoti smiled. 'How nice of you to meet remember me… even though…' She stopped, unable to say, 'even though I declined your offer of marriage.'

Naveen divined her thoughts. 'I heard that you had finally written to your father about your engagement to Rustom Ferghani.' Minoti looked away. Naveen continued, 'I respect your honesty and courage to follow a path that might be full of thorns.'

Looking at him sombrely, she replied, 'It is already full of thorns…perhaps bayonets…but that is the only path I can follow.'

After moments of silence, Naveen asked, 'Is there any news of Rustom?'

Minoti nodded. 'One letter—just before the coup,' she replied. 'It was sent by Rustom's friend at the British Embassy through diplomatic bag.'

Naveen gazed at the garden beyond as he formulated his words. Then he said, 'The *New York Times* gives grim reports of the events in Kabul. The Indian press is keeping off controversies.'

'Don't prevaricate, Naveen. Tell me bluntly what you want to say.'

'Rustom is in the most dangerous place in the world,' he said quietly.

'I read newspaper reports, listen to the BBC. I know the dangers.'

Naveen shook his head. 'They will tell you nothing about Rustom Ferghani.' He paused. 'I have asked my American diplomat friend in Islamabad to get information about your fiancé…' Seeing her eyes brimming with tears, he said, 'Until then, be brave and don't give up hope.'

'I will not give up hope.' Blinking back tears, she smiled and asked, 'How is your romance going with the leggy blonde?'

Regarding her gravely, Naveen said, 'I have learned something valuable from you. The things we pursue—wealth, success, status, power—offer no lasting happiness. I live in a world where only these things matter. You don't—you are prepared to suffer in pursuit of a dream—a dream that is superior to what others pursue.'

'What if that dream…does not materialize?' Minoti asked in an unsteady voice.

'That dream itself is precious and ennobling,' Naveen replied gently.

His words had a strange effect on her. 'When I am at the end of waiting, and if you are still free, I shall let you know.'

Naveen composed his words with some pain. 'Don't give up waiting because when Rustom returns, as he surely will, you will regret that you did not wait. That would bring misery to all three of us.'

As Minoti tried to absorb this message of hope and despair, he said, 'Let us deal with events as they happen. Tonight, let me take you out for dinner and try to amuse you with New York society gossip and political scandals.' Over dinner they laughed and chatted but Naveen saw that under her cheerful façade, she was battling dark fears about Rustom. And he, a spectator, could do nothing for the woman he had come to respect and love.

Winter of Despair

Wild autumn winds swept over the rugged terrain of Afghanistan, blowing russet-hued leaves on rooftops and streets. In the Kandahar jail a shivering Rustom yearned for the copper *bukhari*s that once burned fragrant pine-wood logs in their Kabul mansion.

Jailer Hashim Baig brought in a small stove and firewood to the cell. 'Here you are, *Janab*,' he said cheerfully. 'Your grandfather Iskandar Khan had large porcelain stoves in his palace. Your mother, aunts and uncles used to dance around the stoves in the evening.' He smiled, remembering the gaiety of Iskandar Khan's mansion.

Rustom fought against pain. 'My princess of a mother had to flee to Herat with one suitcase on the night of 27th April. I wonder if I shall see her again.'

Nodding, Hashim Baig murmured, 'May Allah keep her safe.'

Rustom fanned the feeble flames licking the dented copper stove. 'What do the rulers have in store for me?' he asked.

'They are too busy establishing their rule to bother about you,' Hashim Baig replied. 'And let it be like that. You don't want to come to their notice. There's danger there. They have probably forgotten you and this remote little prison.'

Hashim's son, Afraz, brought in pine-resin tea and warm walnut bread. As they ate and drank, Hashim informed his prisoner of the events in Kabul. Later, when the electric lights had been turned off, Rustom lit candles and sat at the makeshift table where he kept paper and pen. He wrote:

Dearest Minoti,

Let us make believe that you are soon arriving as my bride in Afghanistan, not the luckless country it is today, but the one which I loved. Do remember that Afghanistan is not alien to you because it has civilizational links with ancient India. Shiva, Creator of the Cosmos, was worshipped here and his image was engraved on the mountains. The Vedas and the Epics mention this land as Gandhara, whose capital became the famous Takshashila, named after Prince Taksha, its first ruler. The Greeks shortened it to Taxila. Indian, Iranian and Sumerian cultures met here. Purushapura (Peshawar) and Gandhara became the centre of Buddhist-Gandhara art. We have these close affinities. I wish I had told my father all this when announcing our betrothal. But he is gone where these distinctions don't matter. But you, my vanished bride, remember this and we will remain close in spirit.

To keep his mind occupied Rustom remembered and wrote random thoughts about ancient Indo-Afghan history, the evolution of a syncretic culture through Scythian-Kushan-Parthian interaction, and the changes brought about by Islam. While he lamented this, news came from the outside world.

Dear Minoti,

Imprisoned in the once great city of Gandhara, now Kandahar, I hear that momentous things are happening in my country. I wish I could see the dramatic changes unfold before me. My jailer-guardian informed me this afternoon that the PDPA government has promulgated many decrees in addition to the ones I mention below and promised many more. These were passed for gaining popular support. The press and radio report that the reform programmes have general approval. The new President, Mohammed Taraki, reported to the Central Committee that '11.5 million landless peasants had been released from the clutches of moneylenders and at least 30 billion Afs. were gained by landless peasants and small farmers.' According to the PDPA government agricultural co-operatives comprising 200,000 participants have been established. The lands of 40,000 rich landowners are being redistributed. Seeds and agricultural machinery have been distributed, new orchards and vineyards have been organized. Veterinary clinics have immunized millions of livestock. President Taraki declared that landless and small farmers have been freed from the oppressive landlords. A peasant declared 'Now no one will flog me to work on his land without a wage'. Students marched and shouted, 'Death to feudalism!', 'Death to imperialism! Long live Nur Muhammad Taraki!'

I had no idea, Minoti, that there was such injustice, poverty, and exploitation of peasants by landlords. I spouted radical humanism in London when Afghanistan is sunk in poverty and ignorance. This inequality has sown the seeds of rebellion. Have we, the elite, lived in a fool's paradise? King Zahir Shah was a good man but he did not transform his realm. The able Prince Daoud allowed the momentum to slip away to the PDPA.

I fully support redistribution of land and opening doors of opportunities to the unprivileged. The ideological challenge of the Russian Revolution frightened Western nations into introducing the welfare state. How did our country on the frontiers of such momentous innovation remain immune? I wonder if we will ever dispel the obscurantism that keeps us chained to a dark past.

When I contemplate on telling the new rulers that I would like to assist in modernizing the country, the image of my murdered father, blood congealed on his medals, makes me an avowed enemy of the rulers even though their policies might modernize this country. Does modernization entail barbarism?

It is at times like this, Minoti, when ideas swirl around me that I miss you most. Time flew on winged feet when we were together. Why didn't the stars warn us of the fate that awaited us?

President Taraki's government soon faced grave problems. The Islamic Revolution in Iran challenged the secular socialist government of the People's Democratic Party. Iran's clergy began inciting Islamic fanaticism in Afghanistan.

Russia first saw the dangers of Islamic fundamentalism. The defeat of secular Afghanistan by Islamist Iran would have grim repercussions on the Soviet Central Asian Republics with their Muslim population. Further, nuclear stations and Soviet arsenals in this region could fall into the hands of irresponsible adversaries. The Soviet Union could not abandon the pro-Russian government because then USA would move in and use Afghanistan as the base of operations against the Soviet Union.

In early 1979, Radio Kabul informed Afghans that the United States was planning to overthrow the pro-Soviet regime in Afghanistan. The US Central Intelligence Services (CIA) poured millions of dollars into the country to organize an uprising against the incumbent pro-Russian regime. The CIA directed its obedient client, the Pakistani ISI, to train and pay unemployed Afghans to sabotage the Afghan government. After closing the US Embassy in Kabul in February 1979, President Carter ordered that *every financial and arms aid was to be given to anti-Soviet factions* in Afghanistan. An anti-government uprising would force Soviet intervention and possibly a war—a war that Robert Gates, Director of the CIA, assured his President would be Russia's Vietnam.

The Jailer's Daughter

Snow covered the Hindu Kush mountains. As the paralyzing Afghan winter set in, agricultural activities stopped. Few people ventured outdoors. They sat in their homes, moulded potteries in courtyards, wove shawls of karakul lamb wool that were highly valued in the West, chiselled jewellery from lapis lazuli and carved tables and vases from slabs of onyx. At dusk, smoke curled out of chimneys on the flat-tiled roofs. On Muslim festival days they emerged in colourful clothes and rode on donkey carts to Kandahar town to buy new clothes and confectionaries of walnut, almond and raisins in the markets, attend prayers at mosques, and return in the late afternoon to celebrate.

Hashim Baig allowed his prisoner to sprint and jog in the wire-fenced yard adjoining his house and the little prison. The jailer's son Afraz stood guard with an assault rifle, watching 'the nobleman', as Rustom jogged around the yard, pausing to gaze wistfully at the sky, yearning for freedom.

Every afternoon the jailer's 17-year-old daughter Dilnaar went to the roof of their house to collect dried clothes, and to gaze at the captive who, despite the shabby clothes lent by her father, looked more like a prince than a dangerous prisoner. Watching him walk or read newspapers, she longed to go to the yard and ask him about the big world outside but dared not because her father had warned her not to go near Rustom, who was considered an enemy of the PDPA regime. 'This learned and dignified prince cannot be dangerous,' Dilnaar mused, and daydreamed of running away with this prince to a safe land where he would make her his princess.

One day, a furious snowstorm ushered in white stillness and emptied the roads of people. Hashim Baig was in Kandahar to collect his salary, and Afraz had fever. Dilnaar took the cell key and went there. She found Rustom writing on a wrinkled sheet of paper. Two candles flickered atop the rough-hewed table. Hearing the iron door open, he looked up and saw Dilnaar wrapped in a shawl, and snowflakes melting on her ruddy cheeks. Breathless with excitement, she said, '*Janab*, I have brought you apricot tea and tandoori *kulcha*s that my mother made. My father has gone into town and my brother, your guard, Afraz, is sick.'

Though Rustom wanted to laugh, he asked her sternly, 'Has your mother allowed you to come? Because if she hasn't, you had better return home at once. I don't want your father to shoot me.'

'Mother won't tell Father. She thinks you have been imprisoned unjustly.'

'Really? And what does your father say?'

Dilnaar grimaced. 'He does not talk in front of Ammi and me. He says women are stupid.'

'Are you good in your studies?' Rustom asked, taking a sip of tea. Dilnaar shook her head. 'Who will allow me to study? I have been taught to clean and cook—to serve the man I marry. That is the nasty fate of Afghan women.'

Rustom asked, 'Would you like to be educated?'

"Oh yes!' She hesitated before continuing, "Our new president, Mohammed Taraki, believes women should be educated. That is why young people support him. The new president wants to abolish the *talaq* custom so that women cannot be easily divorced.'

Rustom pondered over this information. Why did this enlightened president, who enjoyed support among the unprivileged, rule Afghanistan like an autocrat?

Hearing the bells of a donkey cart, Dilnaar whispered, 'That will be my father! I must go! If there is anything special you want to eat, let me know.'

Smiling, Rustom replied, 'If you want me to teach you how to read and write, let me know.'

Dilnaar told her parents that as the new president was encouraging education for women she would like to learn to read and write. Since the prisoner had nothing to do, he could teach her.

Hashim's wife said, 'That is a good idea. And why only Dilnaar? Ferghani Saheb could help Afraz with his school lessons as well.' She paused. 'Imagine, after receiving education, my Afraz may one day join Ferghani Saheb's office and become an important man!'

'If Ferghani Saheb is not executed before that,' Hashim said heavily. This was his way of warning his family not to become close to a man whose days may be numbered. Sobbing, Dilnaar fled the room.

Reluctantly, Hashim Baig requested Rustom to accept Afraz and Dilnaar as his pupils. As Rustom sat with them in the cell illumined by candles and warmed by a *bukhari* stove, he recalled the tutorials when Minoti, along with five others, came to his room in University College, London, to discuss the famous case laws which Dr Schwarzenberg liked quoting. Now those days seemed like phantoms in a dream.

While the teaching hours kept his mind occupied, despair waited at dusk. When one more desolate day ended in captivity, Rustom wrote to Minoti.

Can the Afghan political leaders telescope time and take the country into the modern age. The poorer Afghan people are largely uneducated; they are easily intimidated by threats of punishment and perdition if they support the socialist government. Our mortal foe Pakistan does not want a strong Afghanistan; it is fomenting insurrections along Afghanistan's eastern border. Ironically, both USA and Iran are encouraging Islamic fundamentalism here. This will destroy the secular structure of our countries. Doesn't USA realize that they are igniting a fire that cannot be quenched?

Sadly, I watch the exquisite Afghan spring ripening before me. Snow-covered pines blink in the sunlight; almond blossoms unfurl on highways. I recall my boyhood days when we rode on spirited ponies over mountain tracks and crystal streams. I recall the Buzkashi tournaments at Mazar-i-Sharif where Buzkashi players, Chapendaz, mounted on taut-muscled horses, fought over the headless carcass of a goat and tried to dislodge other riders. Are those days irrevocably lost?

I, who used to stand on our balcony and see the celestial bodies glimmer over the mountains, cannot see the night sky now. I have to sit inside the candle-lit cell. The yearning to see the night sky so overwhelmed me one day that I pleaded with my jailer to let me go out and see the night sky. Handcuffing me, he led me to the wire-fenced yard. I stood gazing at the sapphire sky embroidered by millions of constellations and cluster galaxies. The Milky Way arched over the Hindu Kush range. Against this panorama the fate of men and nations seemed utterly insignificant. I had a strange desire to die so that my disembodied soul could travel in the splendour beyond this world.

Sometimes at dusk Hashim Baig and Rustom discussed the day's events or town gossip. One evening Hashim told Rustom of a mutiny in Herat. 'The Iranian fundamentalists are inciting violence there. It is reported that some 200 Russians have been killed in Herat. They did not spare even the women and children.'

Rustom listened in horror. 'Why did the rebels kill innocent people?'

'They are paid to do so by enemies of the PDPA government,' Hashim Baig replied.

Rustom said grimly, 'There will be reprisals for this. Moscow will not tolerate the massacre of its citizens.'

Hashim Baig told Rustom: 'Some Afghans are being brainwashed by Pakistan's ISI, Saudi Arabia, and the Ayatollahs. They are unaware that the Russians have brought progress with establishment of cottage industries, the construction of the Darunta Dam situated on the Kabul River that supplies electricity, and the Panjshir Valley Project, which brings water for irrigation and electricity generation. This government is curtailing opium cultivation in Nangahar to prevent opium addiction of people to halt various maladies. Landlords who made fortunes by smuggling opium to the West are furious.'

Rustom sensed that there was popular support for the PDPA—who were his enemies. He felt trapped in a painful dilemma: to see his country progress under the PDPA and yet to wish their destruction because they had killed his father.

One afternoon, the jailer's wife, accompanied by Dilnaar, brought almond cakes for Rustom. She described how Major Murad Ferghani came to propose marriage to Rustom's mother. 'Demure, apricot-coloured skin, green eyes, sinuous figure, she seemed like a princess from the Arabian Nights. Being educated, she joined men's conversations. She told an Indian guest that Kandahar, once known as Gandhara, was a city of ancient India. Glaring at his daughter, Iskandar Khan had asked, "We have problems with the Durand Line! You want to create problems on our southern frontier? Suppose Hindustan lays claim to Kandahar?" There was much laughter over this.'

Rustom experienced mixed sensations of joy and pain as he listened to these anecdotes. He wrote to Minoti.

My unseen bride, I am writing to you by candlelight. Today the jailer's wife and daughter came with almond cakes. She narrated how Father was bewitched by Mother's free spirit. When did he cease to be bewitched? When did he turn to another woman? It is a strange sensation to hear of events before one's birth. Was I then in a different life span and space? Or was I in a state of non-being as your Upanishad states. But if the soul is immortal, how can the soul be non-being? I feel I am in a state of non-being, as if my past life has ceased to have meaning. Does Time devour memories, happiness and existence itself?

Storm over Kabul

Reading Indian, British, and American newspapers in the summer of 1979, Minoti realized that the situation in Afghanistan was rapidly deteriorating. One particular report distressed her.

When interviewing President Taraki, a British journalist asked him about proposed reforms. Taraki bitterly complained that he needed the cooperation of the rival factions within the party—the radical Khalq and the moderate Parchams headed by Babrak Karmal. He knew that his ruthless deputy, Hafizullah Amin, was amassing wealth and power. To remove moderate members of the PDPA, Amin was planning to send them abroad as ambassadors—though Afghanistan had only few diplomatic missions abroad.

The British journalist reported:

Caught between a government pushing through equitable distribution of land and social reforms, and the clergy who incite resistance, peasants are uncertain of their future. They have ceased to work in the landlords' fields, causing steep decline in agricultural production, resulting in food shortage and rising prices. Tribal chiefs forbid people to work in the few existing industries. Middle-class entrepreneurs, who were the main support of the PDPA, closed their factories. Unemployment, inflation and food shortage is prelude to an uprising.

The British journalist continued:

The problem in Afghanistan is that the poor people, whom the socialist regime champions, have no idea what the 'revolution' is about. The radical intelligentsia, urban workers and poorer peasants support the regime but not the white-collar employees and clergy. Changing the feudal social structure and improving education is a daunting task. This requires a policy of modernization with reconciliation.

A French journalist based in Kabul, who moonlighted as a PDPA sympathizer, obtained anti-Western information, which was published in a sensational article.

Islamic fundamentalists are gaining ground. Their religiosity is fuelled not by faith but by the shower of some one billion US dollars. Wiser after the Vietnam War, USA will not intervene directly in Afghanistan; instead, it uses Pakistan's Inter Service Intelligence (ISI) to train young men. These so-called mujahidin are being financed and armed by USA, while Pakistan and Iran are inciting them with the banner of Islam. We have information that some 90,000 Afghan guerrillas and another 100,000 reserves are being trained in Pakistan and have been equipped with 122 mm howitzers, AGS-17 grenade launchers, M-4L 82 mm mortars, SA-7 surface to air missiles. Armed bands from Iran and Pakistan have entered Afghanistan to incite insurrection against the new PDPA government.

The Afghan government has to create a new state apparatus, reorganize and strengthen the army and create a new class of administrators, especially in the remote areas where the lawless tribal chiefs dominate. One wonders if Taraki and Amin are capable of doing this.

The once selfless revolutionaries are now corrupt. Afghan army officers and soldiers, who are the main support of the PDPA, are furious at the sudden arrests, summary trials, and disappearance of anyone suspected of deviation. They have fears of their future. Amin controls the secret police, Khademate Ettelate Dowlati (KHAD), to implement his orders.

The journalist did not long survive this exposé. The assassin was never found.

Reading these grim reports, Minoti feared for Rustom's safety. Minoti remembered Naveen's stark words with foreboding. 'Rustom is in the most dangerous place in the world'. She felt guilty living in the security of London, when Rustom's fate was unknown in a land that had descended into chaos. She wrote to her phantom lover.

Dear Rustom, when I fear for you in the turbulence of your country. I console myself that Afghanistan has experienced great turmoil before. Many armies came to your land and plundered your wealth and abducted your women! But now there is an additional complication of a people caught in the dilemma of the twentieth century—progress or regress, and the conflict between rationalism and medievalism. An old game—the Great Game— is being enacted again. How tragic that you—a scholar and lecturer in international law, with no interest in politics—have become trapped in this maelstrom!

If only you had declined your father's command to return to Kabul! How I wish I had pleaded with you not to go! You might have been here then. But you wanted to serve your country and believed Prince Daoud was going to usher in a new era. I have decided to take leave and go to Delhi to find news of you.

Minoti did not go to Delhi. Naveen telephoned her from New York to say: 'I have made enquiries with a Western diplomat in Kabul, whose name I cannot mention. He told me that Rustom Ferghani lives. He has been taken hostage and is imprisoned in a remote place. If I come to know anything more, I shall let you know.'

Minoti burst into tears. 'Dear Naveen! How can I thank you for this? To know that he is alive!'

'Pray that he remains safe,' Naveen replied quietly and ended the call.

Around this time, Hashim Baig told his prisoner that there were speculations about Taraki's visit to Moscow to get assistance to suppress the rebels. President Taraki informed the media that the Soviet government had promised weapons, aircrafts, armoured transports, and training of defence personnel. The Russians were also sending large shipments of wheat for the Afghan people but they refused to send troops to Afghanistan.

In Moscow, when President Taraki pressed for more Soviet military personnel, Premier Alexei Kosygin and President Leonid Brezhnev advised Taraki to address the problems of the peasantry, workers and artisans, because without their support their government would fall.

Through various sources a now uneasy Hashim Baig learnt what was happening. He told Rustom: 'The hasty attempts of the PDPA to introduce radical reforms of land ownership and marriage laws has led to scattered protests in rural Afghanistan. Hafizullah Amin, Taraki's ruthless deputy, has reduced the party apparatus and Revolutionary Council to rubber stamps. Dedicated members of the Council or PDPA or military personnel who oppose him are being executed. Amin's savagery is destroying popular support of the regime.'

After one visit to Kabul, Hashim Baig told his prisoner that Amin was preparing for a US-backed coup d'état. 'Amin has offered USA military bases on our borders with the Soviet Union in return for maintaining him in absolute power. He is also seeking Pakistani assistance and in return is ready to renounce all claims to Pashtunistan.'

Rustom shook his head in misery. 'All the wisdom and diplomacy of King Zahir Shah and Prince Daoud are being nullified by this murderous lunatic.'

The snow on the Hindu Kush range melted; spring gave way to summer.

One evening several adherents of Amin visited Hashim Baig. They were searching for opponents in Kandahar. Dilnaar hid behind a cupboard to eavesdrop. Fearing for Rustom's safety, she then rushed to the prison house, snuffed out candles and closed the wooden shutters. 'Stay inside, *Janab*,' she whispered. 'Men have come from Kabul to ask about the situation here. But they do not know about you.'

'What if they want to inspect this place?' Rustom asked anxiously.

Dilnaar's face tightened. 'I have brought my father's assault rifle. If they enter the cell I will shoot them.'

Moved, Rustom murmured, 'Don't do anything foolish… and endanger all your lives. Now, give me the rifle.'

Dilnaar did as she was told. 'Rustom *Saheb*,' she whispered, adulation in her eyes, 'I will give my life for you.' This declaration only added to Rustom's anxiety.

They sat in the darkness, dreading the advent of the men to the jail cell. As she moved close to him, Rustom toyed with an idea. 'Should I persuade Dilnaar to help me escape with her? One day when Hashim Baig goes to Kandahar we will flee to Termez, board a train for the Uzbek–Soviet frontier and onto my ancestral town of Andijon in Ferghana Valley. I will tell the frontier guards in Russian language that we are Uzbek–Soviet citizens, and fugitives from Amin's rough rule. No one there will harm us. And if history unfolds in my favour I shall return home to Afghanistan.'

He tried to convince himself by thinking, 'I am 34. A man needs a wife, children, home.' But he knew he did not want these possessions. 'My emotions are frozen. Dilnaar is my only hope for freedom.'

Then another thought struck him. 'After I return to my world what will become of Dilnaar? Is this how people at times of ordeals sacrifice others and surrender their humanity for survival? Here am I planning to use and possibly destroy an innocent girl in order to escape. Would freedom be worthwhile after I do this terrible thing?' Though he tried to banish these predicaments, they persisted stubbornly. Turning to her he whispered, 'Dilnaar, return to your room.'

She shook her head. 'I am staying with you.'

In the meantime, at the jailer's house, Hashim assured the visitors of Kandahar's loyalty to the regime. He also plied them with vodka laced with opium; the men swayed and tottered as they walked towards their jeep. After their departure, Hashim

Baig came to the prison cell. Displeased to see Dilnaar sitting beside his prisoner, he ordered her to go home and asked Rustom to return the assault rifle. As if she had heard Rustom's thoughts, Dilnaar offered him a conspiratorial smile and left.

'Something ominous is going on in Kabul,' Hashim told Rustom. 'Those were Hafizullah Amin's men. Since we are near the Pakistani border, they wanted to know the situation in Kandahar and if the people are prepared to cooperate with the Pakistani ISI? As if I know!'

Next day they heard that the jeep carrying Amin's drunken agents had crashed on the way to Kabul.

Several days later on a hot July afternoon in 1979, Hashim Baig told Rustom what he heard in the bazaar. Hafizullah Amin had unexpectedly seized power in a violent coup. Afghans and foreigners alike were horrified when they learnt that Amin's first act after the coup was the murder of his colleague and friend Nur Muhammad Taraki. Amin announced that Taraki had died of a heart attack.

Hashim Baig brought out his transistor and asked Rustom to try to get news channels outside Afghanistan. 'We cannot get genuine news here because Radio Kabul is now under Amin's men. Try Akashvani, New Delhi. We always listen to that channel,' Hashim Baig said.

Rustom shook his head. 'The Indian government will not get involved in Afghan politics. Their news will also be neutral.'

Hashim Baig sighed, 'Then we must rely on our bush telegraph for news.'

There was no need for bush telegraphs. Hafizullah Amin's depredations became swiftly known. From July 1979 the situation became intolerable. Amin's repressive policies compelled thousands of Afghans to flee to Pakistan or India; those who could afford it went to the West. The Afghan intelligentsia which opposed Amin was being eliminated. The loss of a robust professional class damaged Afghan society. Soviet Union sent in more observers and advisers to check the mounting chaos in Afghanistan and check subversion by the mujahidin.

Dilnaar eavesdropped on her father's conversations with visitors and passed on information to Rustom. 'Hafizullah Amin has ordered the execution of the remaining members of President Daoud's government. The butcher, Colonel Khadir, is rounding up people.'

'I will one day kill that murderer,' Rustom muttered.

Looking pleadingly at Rustom, Dilnaar said, 'You must escape, *Janab*! I shall help you to escape but, please, take me with you!'

Rustom was moved. 'What can a fugitive offer you?' he asked.

Tears filled her eyes. 'Happiness—even it is brief—because your world will eventually claim you and I will have no place there.'

Rustom held Dilnaar close and kissed her forehead. 'I cannot do anything that would dishonour you.'

Weeping in his arms, she cried, 'Then go without me!'

Hashim Baig commanded his son to guard Rustom well. 'We may need Rustom Ferghani for bargaining with Amin's men,' he told Afraz.

In London a desperate Minoti read news about Afghanistan. She wrote to her invisible beloved.

Western journalists have portrayed a terrifying picture of Afghanistan, of Hafizullah Amin's reign of terror—what the Jacobins ushered in during the French revolution. When the blood of the aristocrats had dried on the blade of the guillotines, Robespierre killed his confederates. So, Amin is now exterminating the revolutionaries. I have become an insomniac. I shall lose my sanity worrying about you. That would actually be a relief and blessing because when one is mad, the mind registers no pain or grief. But that cannot help you. So, I shall seek information about you at the Embassy of Afghanistan.

In Search of Rustom

Naveen's telephone conversations with Minoti had convinced him that she was heading for a nervous breakdown. Deeply concerned, he took a week's leave from work and went to London. He was not reassured by her appearance or behaviour. Hearing her plan, Naveen said that he would accompany her to the Embassy of Afghanistan in London's stylish Princes Gate, Knightsbridge.

The English bobby guarding the gate asked them sombrely, 'Do you have official business here?'

Naveen replied, 'Officer, I have come to get information about a friend.'

The bobby's kind blue eyes emboldened Minoti to add, 'Not a friend, officer, but my…fiancé.'

The bobby considered the matter, glancing briefly at her sari-clad form. 'I presume he is Indian—like yourself?'

Minoti shook her head and whispered, 'No, he is an Afghan government officer.'

A frown appeared on the policeman's lined forehead. 'Is he…part of the present regime?'

Minoti shook her head. 'He was…in Prince Daoud's government. I have no news of him.'

The police officer took a deep breath. 'My advice is to leave things well alone. If he is a member of the old regime, why alert them about him? For all you know he may be in a safe hiding place.'

Minoti's spoke in a quavering voice. "If he was in a safe hiding place, he would have sent me a line… made a phone call…'

The bobby sighed. 'Well, Miss, meet the bloke at the reception and see what he says. Until then don't mention your gentleman's name.'

Minoti nodded nervously. Naveen asked, 'Can you announce us, officer?'

The bobby accompanied them to the glassed-fronted entrance door. There was an ominous stillness inside. 'Visitors, sir," he said briskly to the man at the reception desk. The gaunt-faced official at the reception nodded. The sari-clad visitor made him careful because India was Afghanistan's friend.

After introducing himself, Naveen asked, 'I have come to enquire about family friends. Do you have any information about the Ferghani family?'

The official regarded them with inscrutable eyes. 'What do you wish to know?' he asked.

Naveen replied: 'I wish to know if the Ferghani family members are safe.'

The official looked down at the reception desk for some moments. Then raising his eyes, he spoke with furtive sympathy. 'I have no information.'

'I suppose even if you know, you won't tell me,' Naveen retorted.

The troubled Afghan official now spoke gently. 'I wish I could help.'

Moving a few steps forward, the bobby said, 'Come now, Sir, Miss. He has no news of your friends.'

Fighting back tears, Minoti went towards the main door. When they were outside, Naveen said, 'Let us try the British Foreign Office. They could help.'

Minoti nodded. 'Yes, I have drawn a blank both here and with our High Commission.'

A few days later, Minoti sought and received an appointment with an officer at the Foreign Office assigned to the Afghanistan Wing. It was with both hope and fear that she, accompanied by Naveen, went to meet the officer. Naveen sat in silence as Minoti explained the reason for meeting him.

The diplomat listened with concern. Frowning, he lit a cigarette, trying to remember something. 'Miss Ray, are you the person to whom we delivered a letter, which was sent by Mr Rowland through diplomatic bag from Kabul?'

Minoti nodded. 'That letter was sent a year ago. I have not heard from my fiancé since then. Would you kindly write to Mr Rowland and ask if he has any information about Dr Ferghani?'

The British diplomat smiled. 'As it happens, Terence is in London for a de-briefing session on Afghanistan. He was here this morning. Let's see if he is still around.'

Minoti waited, tense and breathless. Would she finally hear about Rustom? After several phone calls, Terence Rowland was contacted and told of the matter. He hurried to his colleague's room and stood for a moment looking at Minoti. Rustom had spoken about her many times but after returning from India, he never mentioned her. Now, before Terence was the image of Rustom Ferghani handing him the letter for Minoti on that fateful 27th April 1978, when the terrible events in Afghanistan unfolded. Going to Minoti, he extended his hand. Composing her turmoil, she rose and shook his hand. Then he and Naveen introduced themselves. Terence tried to put her at ease but it was difficult exchanging pleasantries when the shadow of death hovered over them.

Terence began hesitantly. 'Rustom was anxious that you should know about him. I told him to take asylum in our Embassy but he said it was too late for that.'

Minoti bowed her head and said, 'I know…his letter said everything…Do you not know what happened after he came to see you?'

Terence debated the matter inwardly. 'Are you brave enough to hear me?'

Minoti's eyes filled with tears.

Naveen replied gravely. 'I think Minoti wants to know the truth.'

Terence nodded. 'I heard from my sources that Rustom was arrested at the army headquarters where he had gone to warn his father…who had been killed earlier on Amin's orders. He was taken in a jeep but we do not know where. Rustom is not in Kabul.'

As Minoti battled tears, Naveen clasped her hand and said, 'I have reliable information Dr Ferghani lives but not where he is imprisoned.'

Minoti entreated the British diplomat, 'Please find out where he is imprisoned!'

Terence spoke. 'I will try my very best to get news when I return to Kabul in a few days.' He paused. 'Miss Ray, I hope with all my heart that Rustom is safe. You know that hell has descended on Afghanistan. Hundreds are being killed every day.'

Minoti's voice broke as she said, 'I will not give up hope!'

Naveen added gently, 'People of Afghanistan have survived terrible times. So will Rustom.'

Of course, he will! Let us hope that I get good news to give you.' Terence replied. To divert Minoti, Terence said, 'Rustom and I became good friends in Kabul. He used to invite me to his parents' mansion for dinner and discussions. Sometimes we went riding on the hills. He used to talk about you and your university days. During these discussions I got the feeling that he was happier as an academic than in government service. He had no taste for pomp and power.'

'Please don't use the past tense!' Minoti pleaded.

A troubled Terence nodded. 'Right you are, Minoti. Rustom is a fine human being. You should be happy...that he...*loves* you deeply.'

Minoti rose. 'That is why I must find him. Please keep in touch with me. You are my only link with Rustom,' she said.

Moved by her words, Terence said, 'When two people love each other they need no intermediaries. Rustom will somehow communicate with you...'

Naveen rose and said, 'I live in New York. Let me know where I can make enquiries in Washington about Rustom.' He gave Terence his card.

Terence nodded. 'I shall make enquiries and let you know.'

After they left, the senior Foreign Office man said, 'I am confused. It is obvious that Mr Sen is in love with the young lady. Why does he want to find Rustom Ferghani?'

Terence sighed. 'Perhaps Naveen is upholding the highest Hindu ideal—renunciation.'

Lost in sombre thoughts, Minoti and Naveen returned to Goodenough House through sun-dappled Kensington. Red double-decked buses stopped to disgorge passengers before the shops. The tourist season had ended and new autumn fashions were being displayed behind glittering glass windows. There was a time when she stopped to look at new autumn displays, even though she did not wear western clothes unless a cardigan or scarf caught her fancy. Today she walked with unseeing eyes. Her vision went across safe peaceful England and across the seven seas to a land known for its wild grandeur, not far from her homeland. There, in a place unknown, Rustom was awaiting deliverance.

Or was it death? a phantom voice asked.

'No,' she retorted to the dark voice, 'He will be rescued!'

Naveen mused that in such a situation a desolate woman often surrendered to the kindness and love of another man. But he knew that neither of them would enact that drama.

As they sat having dinner at a quiet café in Bloomsbury, Minoti spoke in defiance of a dark fate. 'I will not give up hope of his safe return!' She paused. 'I want to recite a Russian poem of the Second World War—*Wait for me*:

> *Wait for me, and I'll come back!*
> *Wait, when dreary yellow rains*
> *Wait when friends tell you, you should not.*
> *Wait when snow is falling fast.*
> *Wait when summer is hot.*
> *Wait when yesterdays are past*

And others are forgot.
Wait, when from that far-off place
Letters don't arrive.
Wait, when those with whom you wait
Doubt if I am alive.'

Naveen nodded, deeply moved. 'Wait for him, and he will surely return.'

Mindful of Minoti's entreaty, Terence began making discreet enquiries about Rustom after he returned to Kabul. He treaded cautiously because a British diplomat's interest in an Afghan citizen could only create problems for the latter. He wrote in a way so that Minoti would not hope for a miracle.

People say that Afghanistan has ever known such terror. In fact, the Kremlin is deeply concerned about the activities of the party it had supported, now headed by the madman Hafizullah Amin. Moscow wants to replace him by a moderate person but they have yet to act. Meanwhile, a rebellion is brewing in Afghanistan. Amin's ferocity has alienated the people. As a result, the Islamist resurgence that Moscow fears is gaining momentum. Badakshan, the Hazarajat, Nuristan, parts of Paktya and Kunar have broken free of Kabul's control. We hear astounding stories of how the troops sent by Amin to kill Hazara rebels, joined them!

You will appreciate, dear Minoti, that it is becoming increasingly difficult to make enquiries about our Rustom. I went to the Ferghani mansion which has been occupied by one of Amin's favourite officers. General Ferghani's splendid horses have been sequestered. I made a trip to Herat (where I had spent a few enjoyable days with Rustom three years ago), now swarming with Iranian Islamic fundamentalists, to find if Princess Zubaida or any of her family was there. Zubaida told me that Rustom's mother and sister had taken refuge with her family. Then they left for Iran. Nothing more has been heard of them. The Lord grant that they are safe. Rustom had told me on that star-crossed day—27th April 1978—that his mother had sewn her most valuable jewellery inside her heavy coat so that these could be sold for food and shelter in alien lands.

You are right. These events remind one of the insane regime of Robespierre in the France of 1795. Perhaps a Napoleon is looming amidst the Hindu Kush to take charge of this tragic land.

The British diplomat could not reveal to Minoti that the CIA and Pakistan's ISI were planning an Islamist uprising in Afghanistan while trying to suppress an Islamist movement in Iran through the same ISI! Nor could he inform her that Sir Robert Armstrong, the British Cabinet Secretary, had ordered clandestine channelling of funds and weapons to Afghan rebels and Islamists to create chaos in Afghanistan.

Terence remonstrated to the Chargé d'affaires of the British Embassy: 'Why get involved in Afghanistan again? We were defeated in three ruinous wars a century ago. Why not leave the Afghan people to shape their own destinies? Why does

Britannia have to play second fiddle to America, who wants revenge for defeat in Vietnam?'

The Chargé d'affaires glanced at his First Secretary and said, 'I say, Terry, do you want to get the sack? If so, you are going the right royal way.'

After hearing from Terence, Minoti wrote:

Dearest Rustom, your English friend hinted that I should not hope for your return. How easily people give up hope and tell others to renounce hope! It is easier that way. Hoping is a wearying process. It is so much easier to accept loss than to battle against despair. But I will hope and wait! I shall use my willpower for you to return!

There is a Hindu legend—perhaps a true story—where Savitri refuses to accept her husband's death. She engages Yama, the Lord of Death, in a philosophic dialogue to revive Satyavan. Yama refuses to do so because a life taken by him is irretrievable in that incarnation. But Savitri continues to argue. Finally, impressed by her arguments, Yama brings Satyavan back to life. So, I argue with the Fates and tell them I will not renounce hope.

You will return one day when orange blossoms line the hillsides of Costiera Amalfitana. And I will be waiting.

Russia Comes to Afghanistan

By November 1979 the Soviet Union felt it could no longer ignore the dangerous situation in Afghanistan. News came of the siege of the US Embassy in Tehran; Ayatollah Khomeini called for *jihad* against the two 'infidel superpowers USA and USSR'. He had pronounced the USA as 'the great Satan' and Russia as 'the lesser devil'. There was people's unrest in oppressive Saudi Arabia. Rumours were rife of preparations in Pakistan for replacing Amin with a pro-American regime. There was a possibility that the Muslim fundamentalists would foment rebellion in the Soviet Central Asian Republics and fears that USA, with Pakistan's assistance, would occupy Afghanistan and stand on Russia's doorstep.

Now, December snow blanketed the Hindu Kush range. Excitement ran high in diplomatic and press circles in Kabul over rumours of an imminent Soviet intervention. Some journalists tried to bring in merriment for Christmas. But those who knew the imponderables of history saw the grave implications of the situation whose consequences would unfold tragically over the next four decades. The same mujahidin that USA trained to fight Russia would carry the Islamic *jihad* into the heart of America and Europe. But dark events of the future hid behind gaudy slogans of democracy.

Soviet leaders met in the frost-covered Kremlin on 12 December 1979. Reluctantly, they decided to send some 50,000 troops to Afghanistan. Marshal Akhromeyev and his team landed in Termez on the USSR–Afghan border. An operational team arrived at Bagram Air Force base in Kabul on 18 December.

Snow-bound Kabul stood in eerie stillness. When news of these arrivals swept through the city, journalists in Kabul Hotel sent messages on tele-printers, people conversed in offices, markets, and restaurants. The Soviet Embassy was wrapped in silence until Soviet Ambassador Tabayev authorized the official Soviet news agency *Agentstvo Pechati Novosti* to invite press persons to the embassy 'to inform the international media of the dual danger facing Afghanistan and the Soviet Union'.

Terence Rowland sat in his office collecting the news that came through the tele-printer from various news agencies. When he contacted his Soviet counterpart, Ivan Suvorov told him only what he was permitted to divulge.

On Christmas Day 1979, the road to Kabul was clogged with Soviet armoured vehicles flying the hammer and sickle flag. Two divisions of the 40th Army rolled into the north and west over rough snow-covered terrain. An Airborne Division landed at Kabul and Bagram airfields. All operations commenced simultaneously and strategic places were occupied. Afghan authorities informed Afghan troops of the developments so that they did not fire on Soviet troops.

The soldiers looked confident and cheerful; heroism comes easily when the danger is unknown. Only those in the Kremlin who had spent months planning the expedition, debating its necessity, and dreading its possible outcome, knew the peril of the situation.

President Hafizullah Amin had no idea of the outcome of the advent of Soviet troops for which he and his murdered predecessor, Nur Mohammed Taraki, had clamoured for a year. Afghans considered Amin as their real enemy; he arrested, tortured and killed them. He had reneged on socialist promises of a better life, of social and economic justice. He negotiated now with Russia, now with the USA, sometimes with Iran, and again with Pakistan—for one and only one purpose—to remain in absolute power.

To celebrate the arrival of Soviet troops, President Amin held a reception that evening at his heavily-guarded hilltop Tajbeg Palace. What remained of the Afghan Civil and Foreign

Services fearfully attended the reception. Attending foreign diplomatic corps and Soviet military officers were visibly tense.

Tables were laid out in culinary splendour: pilafs, roasted meat, pyramids of caviar on buckets of ice, Polskoi vodka, Crimean wines, Napoleon cognac. But there was no merriment; the guests maintained stoic silence. When one of Amin's deputies was taken away to be shot for insulting him, the guests were stunned.

Terence Rowland had heard family chronicles of his great-grandfather's participation in the Anglo-Afghan wars in the 19th century. But the present scenario seemed more grisly. Seeing his expression, Ivan Suvorov asked, 'Not cricket, is it?'

'No, it is Bushkazi,' Terence replied. 'They drag a goat-carcass around.'

The two young diplomats, who used to meet frequently at the Ferghani mansion, went to a secluded part of the reception hall to discuss the present situation. Both chose their words carefully.

'Is the Soviet government supporting the madman Amin?' Terence asked indignantly.

Since Ivan Suvorov could not divulge what he knew, he tried another tack. 'Terence, Russia wanted the People's Democratic Party of Afghanistan to establish a stable government with the help of officers of President Daoud's government. A society needs administrators to run institutions and maintain continuity for developing the country but Amin dispensed with the services of experienced administrators.'

Terence exclaimed, 'Dispensed with their services? That is a euphemism! Important Afghans have been executed, the educated elite have distanced themselves from this regime and many have fled the country.'

Both diplomats were silent as they pondered over the grim developments.

'Then why support this murderous maniac?' Terence asked again.

'You must be aware that Russia's adversaries are ready to support Amin if he gives them bases on Soviet frontiers. So, we cannot be too fastidious.'

That night Amin went to sleep confident of Soviet support.

Early on the morning of 27 December 1979, Soviet troops carried out Operation Storm 333, the seizure of Tajbeg Palace, where Amin lived in maximum security, guarded by an entire battalion. The citadel-palace was perched on a forest-covered hill. All roads to it, except one, were mined. Amin's handpicked soldiers guarded the palace round the clock. The strong walls were encircled by large calibre machine guns intended to mow down attackers.

Amin was unaware that Soviet commanders had planned this attack under General Drozdov's command while Colonel

Kolesnik was in charge of operations. The assault took everyone by surprise—most of all, Hafizullah Amin.

Two self-propelled anti-aircraft ZSU 23-4 Shilka guns opened fire on the Palace, while automatic grenade launchers began firing on Amin's battalions guarding the palace. Explosions made the rocky ground tremble.

On that bleak morning, people of Kabul were awakened by the first rounds of heavy artillery fire. They saw columns of smoke rising from the direction of Tajbeg palace. There was fierce fighting on every floor, corridor and room. Finally, a spray of bullets hit Amin. The man who had spilled oceans of blood of his compatriots now lay dead on a blood-soaked carpet. The relentless firing continued until the day burned down into darkness.

Babrak Karmal from the moderate Parcham faction was installed as the new President of Afghanistan. People later said that if Babrak Karmal had been installed earlier, the continuing tragedy of Afghanistan would have been averted.

Terence Rowland met Ivan Suvorov again at the New Year's Day reception at the Soviet Embassy. They went to a quiet corner to converse. Suvorov told Rowland that for a year Moscow tried to avoid intervention but Amin's brutalities and his readiness to give USA bases on the Afghan–Soviet frontier had forced their hands.

Terence Rowland shook his head. 'Your country, Ivan, has stepped into a pool of quicksilver. My country learned the lesson in the 19th century in three ruinous wars. My great-grandfather died here in one of them.'

Guests spoke in measured tones. Neither the hosts nor the guests voiced opinions on a situation that was making dramatic headlines worldwide. Toasts were raised, champagne and vodka were drunk, caviar served. When Tchaikovsky's *Marche Slave* played in the reception hall, Ivan Suvorov heard a funeral dirge accompanying it.

Three hundred miles away people of Kandahar were bewildered to hear about Soviet intervention. Hashim Baig rushed home to inform Rustom, who reflected on the implications of Soviet intervention. 'How did this come to pass? For 60 years the Soviet Union and Afghanistan maintained amity and cooperation. King Zahir got assistance from the Soviet Union. Economic and social development projects began under him. A modern professional middle-class emerged. Did Prince Daoud's intransigence lead to the tragic chain of events?'

Hashim Baig frowned, musing over his prisoner's remarks. Then he replied, 'People said that Prince Daoud wanted friendly relations with the West, who gave us nothing and turned against the Russians, who gave us help. So the Russians began supporting the Afghan socialists. But when Amin began a reign of terror, he was removed along with his evil followers.'

A grim-faced Rustom said, 'I am glad the monster Amin has been killed. My father's murder and that of thousands of others has been avenged.' After a long silence Rustom said, 'The people who ordered my imprisonment are gone. It is their turn to be imprisoned. Why are you keeping me here?'

Hashim Baig nodded. 'I knew you would ask this, *Janab*. I am keeping you here for your own safety. Amin ordered your arrest. But Khadir was told to keep you alive as hostage to bargain with the Russians. Many of the Khalq faction of the PDPA are still around. I do not know whether they hold positions in the new regime of Babrak Karmal. Let me find out what is happening and whether you are still in danger as a former member of President Daoud's Khan's government.'

Rustom spoke angrily. 'Release me and let me face the risk of being arrested again. I cannot stand this confinement any longer!' He paused. 'You and your family have looked after me well. Like a good Pashtun I shall repay you one day. But I must go into the real world again. Better to die than to be half-alive in this shadowy world!'

Hashim Baig sighed heavily. 'I agree, *Janab*. Give me some time to find out what is likely to happen here. And then if you are prepared to face danger, I shall open the cell doors.' He paused and smiled wryly. 'Your grandfather

Iskandar Khan liked falconeering. He let them fly freely around his lands because he said falcons should never be caged. He would have said that about you, Rustom Ferghani.'

Filled with nostalgia, Rustom murmured, 'I remember Grandfather sitting me, a little boy, in front of him on his black horse when he went falconeering.'

Babrak Karmal's government brought a semblance of stability. The Soviet and Afghan national army continued fighting Pakistani-backed rebels. Indira Gandhi's new government sent humanitarian aid for wounded and displaced Afghans. Some came to India. Taking advantage of India's cordial relations with Karmal's government, Naveen Sen arrived in Delhi to organize a trip to Afghanistan to get news of Rustom Ferghani. With a letter of introduction from the Ministry of External Affairs to the Afghan Foreign Office, he accompanied one of the teams which carried food and medicines to Kabul.

As the Ariana Airways plane flew over the Hindu Kush, Naveen analysed his reasons for this journey. Was it to end the waiting for Minoti? If Rustom no longer inhabited this world, she would have to accept the tragic truth and not wait for his return. But would truth free her from memories of Rustom?

Arriving in a tense Kabul, Naveen Sen met those in the new Afghan government who could offer information about the Ferghani family. He was told that General Ferghani and his son had been killed by Hafizullah Amin's men. Only the general's wife and daughter had escaped to Iran.

Sitting in the clamorous bar of Hotel Kabul, Naveen tried to formulate his thoughts. In the secret chamber of his heart—where even the Almighty had no access—he had sometimes wondered whether he would be really sad if Rustom died. But now, hearing of Rustom's end, Naveen felt an inexplicable pain. After accepting Rustom's death, Minoti might marry him but she would live in pain. Naveen refused to live in the shadow of Minoti's grief.

Returning to New York, Naveen wrote to Minoti that he had failed to get information about Rustom. He resumed life without hopes of winning Minoti's love. He made brief infrequent telephone calls to Minoti to ascertain how she was and then stopped the calls. She became his beloved phantom.

In the meantime, Afghan rebels began grenade attacks on Kandahar. Situated on the Afghan-Pakistan frontier, Kandahar became a centre of terrorist activities perpetrated by the Pakistani Inter Services Intelligence from 1978. China, Egypt, Saudi Arabia and Pakistan armed the Afghan rebels with only one aim—to overthrow the pro-Soviet PDPA government.

From his cell, Rustom heard sounds of explosions that destroyed hospitals, schools and markets carried out by the murderous mujahidin, followed by retaliatory strikes by the

Afghan National Army who surrounded the city, subjected it to bombardment, and then brought Kandahar under its control.

Dilnaar burst into Rustom's cell one day and announced: '*Janab*! We hear that heavy fighting had broken out in the city! Baba says troops from Herat and Panjshir Valley are landing at Kandahar International Airport!'

Despondently, Rustom had been staring out of the grilled window. After hearing of the arrival of Soviet troops and end of Hafizullah Amin, he had hopes of freedom. But now Kandahar was a battleground. How would he leave? Turning to Dilnaar he said sadly, 'Yes, since last night I have been hearing the jets flying low over this area and heading for the airport.'

Dilnaar did not share his despair. She dared not tell her angry prince she was glad that there was trouble in Kandahar because then Rustom would have to stay in Kandahar and she could continue to see him.

At night when the Ilyushin and Sukhoi jets streaked across the starlit winter sky before landing at Kandahar Airport, Rustom sat down to write another letter to his phantom beloved.

When I heard of the end of the Hafizullah Amin regime and its being replaced by the moderate Babrak Karmal, Hope flew in like a bird with wounded wings. I thought things would improve now. I asked Hashim Baig to end my incarceration. He said he would release me if there was no danger to him or me. Kandahar has now become a battleground between the rebels and government forces.

I hear the symphony of the saddest of all wars—civil war—when Afghan will kill Afghan at the behest of others.

Amidst gunfire and explosions my mind flies to boyhood days when we children came with our mother to visit grandfather Iskandar Khan at his grand estate. There were horses to ride, streams to wade, hills to climb, gargantuan meals to devour, and boisterous tribal dances by firelight at night. Do you remember how we discussed Kandahar while sipping coffee at a Taviton Square café near University College? You told me about a Gandhara princess marrying a Kaurav king. When I told my mother this, she smiled and said, 'Now you can bring a bride from Hindustan to Gandhara-Kandahar'. I remember embracing her when she gave this benediction. It seems the most sacred of all benedictions—by a mother—are unheard in heaven.

I, a prisoner in this silent cell can hear my grandfather speak of how we Pashtuns ruled Kandahar for three millennia. It was a station on the Silk Road where wool, cotton, silk, wheat, barley and exotic fruits were sold to Greece and Rome or were taken by Hindu merchants to their warmer lands. There was covert cultivation of marijuana and hashish, which travelled to Soviet Central Asian republics. So devious were the smugglers that *the Red Army could not intercept them. My mother told me that her indolent brothers received money by smuggling these goods. Hearing of this, Grandfather thrashed them. A powerful Pashtun, he persuaded his friend King Zahir Shah to develop the city. Modernity came with wide roads, housing schemes and construction of the Kandahar and Bagram Airfields by both Soviet and American engineers. Did they envisage that one day this city would become the battleground between two alien superpowers?*

Could I but hope that all this will end quickly and I could flee from this narrow cell, mount a horse and leave my ill-fated country and find you wherever you are. But my hopes have been extinguished. I shall be happy when death claims me. Yet, a stubborn wish persists to see you once more before oblivion comes.

It was as if Rustom's despair was transferred to Minoti. She read all the news that she could get about Afghanistan. Terence Rowland wrote brief letters to her about the situation in Afghanistan but could not help conveying pessimism in his messages. Where in this maelstrom would he go in search of Rustom?

Like many Indians, Minoti hoped that Soviet intervention would bring stability to Afghanistan and put an end to the violence perpetrated by the mujahidin. She knew that a civil war in Afghanistan would tear the country apart. Pakistan's intrusion in Afghanistan caused anxiety in India because the terrorists it trained to disrupt Afghanistan could one day be turned upon India with dire consequences.

Believing him dead, Minoti wrote a farewell message to Rustom.

Dearest Rustom, has the time come to bid farewell to our tenacious dreams and to each other? We are in a new year, 1980, and a new decade. It is six-and-a-half years since we parted, when you held me close at Rome's Fiumicino Airport before boarding the Boeing 707 which was to take to you home. What went wrong with our plans to get married and lead the creative lives we wanted? Your English friend does not hold out hope of finding you. He says people have disappeared or are dead. Does this mean that he has given up his search for you? Does this mean that I can only meet you in Paradise? Dearest Rustom, have you ceased to live in this world? If so, I too am extinguished. Since we have ceased to exist as mortals we are now phantoms. Is there a place for us phantoms where dreams are fulfilled, where the spirit is freed from mortal shackles?

Chains Unbound

The battle for Kandahar between the Afghan National Army and the rebels continued for many weeks. The ferocity of the fighting took a heavy toll on civilian lives. Throughout those months and the years that followed, the Afghan National Army controlled the city. Rustom told Hashim Baig that the battle could continue indefinitely.

'Nobody has enquired about me in Kabul, have they?' Rustom asked his jailer.

'No, *Janab*,' Hashim Baig assented.

'Perhaps they have forgotten me. Or those who held me as hostage or planned to execute me, no longer exist.'

Hashim Baig said, 'That is possible.'

'Let me leave then, with your blessings. In the Pashtun tradition, repay my grandfather's kindness to you by setting me free.'

Hashim Baig saw in his prisoner's eyes a steely determination to leave—now that those who had ordered his incarceration had been jailed or killed.

That evening Dilnaar came to Rustom's cell. 'Baba says you are going away now that President Amin is dead and his hoods are in jail.'

Rustom nodded. 'Yes, I am planning to leave shortly.'

'Take me with you, *Janab*!' she entreated tearfully. 'Marry me! I will be an obedient wife!'

Rustom wondered, briefly, would it not be simple to have a naïve, obedient wife instead of women like Zubaida and Minoti, who wanted to marry eligible bachelors. Then the bitter thought was replaced by good sense. He shook his head. 'Dilnaar, dear child,' he said, deliberately using words that would place a distance between them. 'The road I am going to take will be a rough and dangerous one. I cannot take anyone with me, least of all a pretty, innocent girl like you.'

Defying rules of propriety, Dilnaar flung her arms around his chest and sobbed. He held her close because it was this simple maiden who had lightened the misery of imprisonment. He had felt a growing tenderness for her when she used to bring in candles, fresh warm bread, and spiced tea, and then sat across the table to learn grammar and history.

He kissed her forehead and murmured, 'Dear Dilnaar, do you think I have not been tempted to erase my desolation in your arms? Or take your help and escape together beyond our frontiers? But to dishonour an innocent girl would be a crime. I will always remember your kindness. So, wish me well on my dangerous journey.' Gently, he released himself from her embrace.

Weeping, she asked, 'Will you really remember me, *Janab*, even when you return to your own world?'

Rustom nodded. 'I will remember you all my life.'

Looking at him with tear-filled eyes, Dilnaar left the cell. For her Rustom became a phantom dream.

A strange silence surrounded the house and the adjoining small prison. Hashim Baig's wife baked walnut bread, wrapped it in paper, along with apples and apricots, and put them in a wicker basket. Dilnaar washed and ironed the clothes that Hashim Baig had given to Rustom. Afraz cleaned and oiled a Colt revolver that Hashim Baig gave to Rustom.

One cold morning the jailer, his family and the prisoner stood at the high iron gate of the compound. Rustom profusely thanked the family for their care. He embraced Hashim Baig and his son Afraz, and bowed to the jailer's wife. He held Dilnaar close for a long moment. But he did not make false promises of meeting again. Then, murmuring *Khuda hafiz*, he set off for Kandahar with Hashim Baig.

The picturesque city of his boyhood was different now as two armed groups tore down buildings with explosions. Market stalls shifted, shops were relocated, and Kandaharis fearfully went about their business and daily routine. They were afraid of the mujahidin, who they knew were mercenaries and not the warriors of god that they professed to be. They were relieved that the Afghan national army had taken control of Kandahar, but this did not reduce the ordeal of being caught in rival crossfires in which many were being killed.

'Do you wish to see your grandfather's mansion?' Hashim Baig asked Rustom.

'No,' Rustom replied. 'Let me remember my bright boyhood days in Iskandar Khan's house. If I see its ruins, my resolve to think of a new life might be weakened. So, get me into a bus bound for Kabul.'

The Kandahar–Kabul Highway has seen exchange of culture and commerce as well as battles for five millennia.. As the bus raced past fields, Rustom felt he was transported back in time. The parched landscape merged into the rugged barren hills. River beds and terraced fields intervened between walled villages of rust-brick houses that stood in the shelter of ancient trees. Amidst this, children tended Bactrian camels and karakul sheep. Smoking on hookahs, men sat on frayed carpets, and looked at the passing parade. Inside their huts, women baked bread and emerged only to serve food to the menfolk and children. The bus passed crowded bazaars where farmers, artisans and traders brought their products to be displayed and sold. The bus stopped now and then so that passengers could drink tea at roadside *chaikhonas*. Rustom glanced at the desolate landscape—as desolate as his own mood. 'I am alive and free,' he kept repeating to fortify himself but the mantra was ineffective against the rage within him.

Rustom arrived in Kabul as dusk set in. Images of twilight in the Kabul of another lifetime overwhelmed him…of riding back from the hills, of mother and sisters waiting to have tea with him, of a stern father presiding at dinner over a splendid onyx table while guests discussed political gossip…of the plan to bring Minoti here as his bride. Stubborn memories of the last day in Kabul two years ago surfaced; Amin's and Khadir's bloody coup d'état and the murder of his father. It was incredible that General Murad Ferghani, who ruled his soldiers, wives and progeny, should be killed, while making a phone call, by a former subordinate.

Rustom composed himself before alighting from the bus with a small suitcase containing borrowed clothes. Before initiating moves for a new life he knew he had to say farewell to the old. Taking one of the few available taxis he guided the driver to the park-enclosed Ferghani mansion in Wazir Akbar Khan area. Expecting a wrecked building, he was astonished to see the large house lit up; armed guards stood at the entrance. Uniformed men came in and out, battered limousines and army jeeps were parked outside.

'Who is staying here?' Rustom asked the turbaned taxi driver.

'It is the residence and office of a high official of the Defence Ministry.' The driver paused. 'You know him, *Janab*?'

Rustom shook his head. He took deep breaths as he felt his chest tighten, alighted from the taxi, and stood before the high iron gates. Armed Afghan Army guards stood in the compound of the mansion. They watched him enter through the gate. One of them came forward and asked curtly, 'Whom do you wish to see?'

With blazing eyes, Rustom replied, 'The thief who has stolen my house.'

The guards stared at him. They were so astonished that they did not try to stop Rustom. There was something forbidding about him as he strode past them and ascended the wide granite steps that led to the marble-terraced floors. Then, recovering from their surprise, the guards followed with guns pointed at him and tried to bar his way to the main door of the house.

Trembling with rage, Rustom shouted, 'This is the home of my father General Murad Ferghani. He was killed by Hafizullah Amin's goons. How dare you stop me!'

Hearing the commotion, an army officer opened the main door and came to the terrace. He stood there for a brief moment, looking at the gaunt faced, shabbily dressed man with dignified bearing. The Afghan army officer asked, 'Who are you?'

'I am Rustom Ferghani, son of the murdered General Murad Ferghani, grandson of Nawab Iskandar Khan of Kandahar, and descendent of those who came with Emperor Babur.' Rustom paused before asking, 'Do you wish to see my birth certificate? You will find it in Somerset House in London. I was born there when my parents were with King Zahir Shah.'

The angry certitude of his words made the army officer come forward hesitantly and stretch his hand. 'I can hardly welcome you to your own house, *Janab*,' he said. 'But welcome, nevertheless.' He paused. 'I offer you my deepest sympathy for the death of your esteemed father.'

'Cold-blooded murder would be an accurate description,' Rustom retorted.

'Hafizulla Amin's men committed many such crimes,' the officer replied. 'I am Colonel Nasir Brezhna, of the Afghan National Army. Please come and meet those who can be your friends.'

'Friends!' Rustom spat out the word. "No one is a friend unless they want something."

The two men walked into the large room which had been the reception hall where the General and his Begum had hosted parties and dances, where music was played, where laughter had resounded in the chandeliered hall, and images of uniformed men and bejewelled ladies had been reflected in the tall Belgian mirrors lining the walls. Now, as the two men entered, uniformed officers of both the Soviet and Afghan armies seated at the large onyx table stared at the duo, aware that something strange was happening.

'Gentlemen,' Colonel Brezhna said quietly, "this is Dr Rustom Ferghani, son of the late General Ferghani who built this mansion. The General was killed on the day of the coup—on Amin's order.'

There were moments of silence. The assembled men remembered that horrific day and Amin's regime. They rose and murmured words of sympathy and muffled words of surprise. A Russian in civilian clothes came forward and stretched out his arms.

'Rustom Ferghani! I had relinquished all hope of seeing you again!'

There was a ghost of a smile on Rustom's gaunt face as he murmured, 'The ubiquitous Ivan Suvorov!'

Briefly embracing Rustom, Ivan Suvorov asked, 'Where have you been? After deposing Amin, we looked all over for you! We heard so many rumours…that you had also been killed with your father, that you had escaped to India…or that you were in England…but despite our efforts, we could not trace you.'

Rustom's eyes clouded. Sighing, he said grimly, 'It is a long story.'

A senior Russian officer who was chairing the meeting murmured, 'We shall adjourn for the day. I would like to speak to Dr Ferghani…when he is able to do so.' He turned to Colonel Brezhna. 'Please make arrangements for Dr Ferghani to stay here.' He came forward and took Rustom's hand. 'Dr Ferghani, you must forgive us for occupying your home. We were under the impression that you…were…'

'…Dead,' Rustom said. The Russian officer nodded grimly.

'It is a kind of death. Everyone from my life has vanished.'

A Russian officer nodded. 'We Russians know how you feel. We were devastated during the Second World War. We have seen carnage and chaos.'

Colonel Brezhna spoke. 'After your father's death, Amin's goons occupied your home for a while. Then the Afghan defence personnel moved in here and made it our office. Your old retainers returned to tell us that many treasures of the house had been removed, furniture destroyed. We have repaired what we could. But we could not retrieve your father's horses.'

Rustom Ferghani glanced around the hall; tears came unbidden to his burning eyes. Seeing this, Colonel Brezhna said, 'We shall return your home to you as soon as we can move to another place, Dr Ferghani.'

Rustom shook his head. 'No, Colonel, I do not wish to live here. All those who lived here are gone. I will see only their phantoms here. My dreams of living here with my parents and…' he stopped abruptly. The last thing he wanted was to remember Minoti. 'I want to leave Afghanistan,' he concluded quietly.

Ivan Suvorov had been listening sadly to the conversation. 'Where do you wish to go?' he asked.

Rustom replied, 'I plan to go to London. I was teaching there at the university. Perhaps I can resume that life…if they are willing to have me after seven years.'

'We can offer you safe haven and work in Moscow or Leningrad University. You speak Russian,' Ivan Suvorov said gently.

'No, thank you. I want to go to a place where I have known peace…where shadows of death do not hover over me.' Rustom's voice broke.

Ivan Suvorov nodded. 'Until then…let us know how we can be of service to you. It is your class of professional educated people who were our allies in the days of Zahir Shah and Prince Daoud. Afghanistan was progressing then.'

'Russians should have supported President Daoud instead of those socialist hooligans,' Rustom retorted angrily. 'President Daoud was fiercely independent, sometimes pro-Western, but he would have maintained stability in his realm and been a reliable and wise ally.'

Ivan Suvorov sighed. 'I agree. And now we are paying for backing the wrong horse. Hopefully, Babrak Karmal will bring stability.' Suvorov paused. 'What you need now is a hot bath and hot food and a stiff drink. Come, let me take you upstairs. Your mansion has many rooms where you can stay.'

Rustom went slowly up the wide winding staircase. The dark blue and white Shiraz carpet had frayed but he could still see the rectangular designs. The crystal lamps on the walls emitted light through dust and grime. The broad landing where he used to stand and gaze out of the bay windows to the mountains beyond was empty of the settees where his mother and her companions used to sit to drink tea and play cards. Walking down the corridor, he opened the door of his room. Rustom stood motionless as his eyes swept over it. It was largely untouched since the marauders had found nothing of value.

Following him, Ivan said, 'Entering this room, I knew this was yours. The photos, the books, records of western classical music, and French Impressionist paintings …could only be your possessions.'

Going over to the tall windows he saw the mountains glistening with melting snow. Briefly, he recalled of how he planned to bring Minoti to this windswept room on their wedding day. He turned away abruptly and looked at Suvorov.

'Thank you, Ivan. I shall stay here for a while until I make my plans.'

Ivan nodded. 'Come down for dinner after you have a bath. I have asked an orderly to bring up your suitcase.'

Rustom laughed bitterly. 'The pauper's suitcase brought to the palace! It is like a fairy tale from Baghdad.'

Ivan sadly shook his head. 'Such things have happened in my country too.'

'Yes, I remember the scene from Pasternak's *Dr Zhivago* where Yuri returns to the Gromyko mansion after the revolution when the plebs had taken over the house. Tonya was so ecstatic at his return that she did not mind plebeian insolence.' Rustom became sombre again and sighed. 'But my story is different, isn't it?'

Both young men sat on winged armchairs. Hesitantly, Ivan asked, 'Where is your fiancée?'

Rustom's face tightened. With anger in his voice, he said, 'I can no longer call her my fiancée. How can I call a woman my fiancée when she is married to another man?'

'I am sorry to hear that. How did that happen? Was it when you…disappeared after Amin's coup?'

'Oh, no. Her betrayal occurred before that. When I was free and had many plans.' Seeing Ivan's surprise, he said, 'She chose to marry an eligible man of her own tribe. Finally, it is all about tribes. We Afghans swear by it.'

'Then forget her. You will find many women to take her place.'

'One can find women to take the place of a beloved in bed, at one's table, even to bear one's progeny…but it is difficult to find someone to fill the empty place in one's heart.' Frowning,

Rustom continued, 'Who knows? It might be for the best. If we were married she might have been killed or violated after Amin's coup. So many Afghan women suffered. And she was a foreigner as well. Yes, destiny removed her from bloodshed.' Rustom rose. 'I had better freshen up and join you downstairs for dinner.'

Ivan nodded. 'And after dinner let us discuss how we can help you to start a new life…wherever you choose.'

Rustom stayed for a few days at his once beautiful home. Both Afghan and Soviet officials made arrangements for his travel to England. They gave him money, saying that this was in lieu of the rent for the Ferghani mansion.

Rustom drove away, reluctant to gaze upon the house from where all his beloveds had vanished. Yet, he could not but help turning to bestow a last glance on the home where he had known security and happiness and where he had dreamt of paradise.

Sweet Thames, Flow on Till I End My Song

Rustom Ferghani set out on the long journey from Kabul to London with neither hope nor pain. He had tried to forget his idyllic youth in that city.

Five thousand miles away in New York, Naveen accepted that Minoti would grieve a long time for Rustom. For two years he had tried to find the whereabouts of Rustom through acquaintances in the State Department and had visited Kabul, only to be told that Rustom may have been killed. Reluctant to tell this to Minoti and hesitant to intrude on her stubborn sorrow, he retreated from her life and tried to make a new one for himself.

Rustom arrived in London a week later and checked into a small hotel in Kensington. A sunburst woke him and beams of morning light peeped through the lacy curtains of the room. It reminded him of spring mornings in Kabul. He once told Terence that though different in many ways, imperial London and indomitable Kabul had the same hauteur and resilience.

Going over to the tall glass windows he peered below at Kensington Street. Early commuters were heading for tube stations; double-decker buses moved slowly, waiting for passengers. He knew he must shake off the despair and lethargy that had taken possession of him and 'get on' with life—or whatever remained of it, he thought angrily.

Rustom had spent some of the funds given by his Kabul friends on clothes—not the elegant ones he had once purchased from Saville Row but from Burton's. He could not resist buying a pair of brogues from Saxone's on Kingsway. Thus attired, Rustom went to the Foreign Office to meet his old friend from Kabul—Terence Rowland. He had made the appointment through Terence's secretary but had given a different name because he was not certain if his diplomat friend would meet a fugitive from a vanished world with neither power nor influence.

Rustom stood looking below at the courtyard where well-dressed men and women drove up in smart sedans, where police guards saluted important officials. This scene reminded him of the terrible scene outside the Afghan Defence Ministry on the day of the coup, when he had rushed to meet his father—only to find General Ferghani shot through the head. Terence's chirpy secretary brought him back to the present and announced that Mr Rowland would see him now.

Terence Rowland's eyes widened in astonishment when he saw Rustom. He rose unsteadily, unable to summon appropriate words to greet his long-lost friend. After long moments of shocked silence, he asked, 'Is it really you, Rustom?'

Rustom nodded and said, 'Unless you think I am a Ferghani *doppelganger*?'

Terence murmured, 'We had given you up for...'

Giving him a bitter smile, Rustom completed the sentence. 'Dead? So many people have said they thought I was dead that I think maybe I am dead.'

Recovering from the shock, Terence indicated a chair and murmured, 'Come, sit down, dear friend.'

When they were seated, Terence asked questions and listened intently as Rustom narrated his adventures and events in his unfortunate country for four years. Tea and biscuits were brought in but remained untouched. Visitors were sent away and telephone calls were not answered. After Rustom completed the chronicle, a visibly shaken Terence asked, 'What can we do for you?'

Rustom shook his head. 'Nothing. Thought I would let you know that I exist.'

Terence Rowland was silent again, pondering over a matter. 'Would you like to work for us? Would you return to Kabul on an assignment and inform us about what is happening there?'

Rustom's blue-grey eyes darkened with anger. 'You want me to be your espionage agent? After what I have endured?'

'The Soviets have occupied your country. The West is very anxious. The next Soviet move will be in the Middle East— where our oil interests are.'

'Terence, I give a damn what will be the next Soviet or US move. USA armed jihadi rebels to the teeth. Now those illiterate goons are wreaking violence on our people. This war is between the Soviet Union and USA–UK. It is not my war…I have had my share of violence and tragedies.'

A chastened Terence was silent. Then he said, 'I apologize. You have indeed returned from hell. What do you intend to do now?'

'I met my former senior colleagues at University College. They have offered me the post of Senior Lecturer. I am returning to academic life.' He rose and smiled. 'Let us meet for dinner when you are not recruiting espionage agents for Afghanistan.'

A contrite Terence said, 'Yes, I look forward to meeting you soon.'

Rustom frowned, debating something inwardly. 'As a matter of information…did the letter I gave you on 27th April 1978…reach Miss Ray?'

Terence nodded. 'Yes, the letter was delivered to Miss Ray.'

'To which address was it delivered?' Rustom asked inaudibly.

'To the address you gave—Goodenough House. Did she not reply?'

Rustom stared at his English friend. 'I…assumed she had left for India…'

'No, Miss Ray is very much here in London.'

Rustom felt a hammering inside his chest. Breathless, he asked, 'Alone?'

Terence nodded.

Rustom was furious. 'Why did you not tell me at once? Why did you ask me to return to Kabul?'

'I do not know how things are between you and Miss Ray.'

Struggling with a chaos of emotions, Rustom murmured, 'Then I must find out how things stand between us.'

In their halcyon days it was Rustom's and Minoti's habit to sit under a crab apple tree in Tavistock Gardens on Wednesday afternoons, where they conversed on diverse matters. Even seven years after their separation, Minoti continued to sit on the same bench as if the empty ritual would keep alive a long-ended relationship. As always, she closed her eyes for some moments to retrieve mirages of the past.

'Soon,' she thought, 'the bleak winds of autumn will blow around me. Then all dreams will be buried in winter snow. That will be a relief. Waiting for happiness can only bring misery.'

That Wednesday Minoti sat on the bench with her notebooks. These were an essential part of the ritual, so that passers-by did not mistake her for an idle vagrant. Gazing at the flowers swaying in the summer breeze, she sensed a presence that emanated inexplicable warmth.

'I knew I would find you here,' the presence murmured.

Afraid that her eyes were deceiving her, Minoti looked up slowly and saw Rustom standing before her. He looked thinner and his once bright eyes were dark with grim memories. His tawny hair was now woven with grey strands. He noted the changes Time had also gifted to Minoti.

'You are a phantom. You are not real, are you?' Minoti whispered hoarsely.

Rustom sat beside her. 'Decide for yourself. Take my hand and see if this is the hand that caressed you. Touch my lips and see if they are the same which kissed you. Feel my breath on your cheek to verify if I am alive.'

She clasped his hand tightly, then traced his features with trembling fingers, and gazed at him with tear-brimmed eyes.

'From where have you come?' Minoti asked inaudibly.

'From where I thought I would never return.'

Minoti cried out: 'Tell me everything…why you never wrote, why you never telephoned…why you vanished! What crime did I commit that you abandoned me, Rustom Ferghani!'

Rustom halted her words by saying, 'Calm down, my love. It is a long story but I have some questions of my own.' He paused, trying to assemble the sequence of events that had changed their lives. He told her of how he had written to her to say that he would be visiting Delhi in April 1977 to prepare for Prime Minister Indira Gandhi's visit to Kabul, and asked her to meet him in Delhi so that they could announce their engagement.

'I never received the letter!' Minoti cried. 'How did it miss me?' Then she frowned and nodded. 'I was in Devon that month, preparing for my final exams...'

"Could the letter have gone astray?" Rustom asked.

'Possibly. But letters for students are usually kept safely at the reception desk.'

'So, I went to your home in Calcutta in the hope of finding you there. Instead...I met your brother, who informed me that the family was making preparations for your wedding to his New York-based friend.' Rustom closed his eyes to forget the bitterness of his Calcutta visit.

Minoti listened in rising bewilderment. 'But I never agreed to marry Naveen!'

Rustom frowned. There was anger in his voice when he asked, 'Then how could your brother make such a statement?"

Minoti stared at the swaying daffodils before replying. 'Forgive me. To prevent a furore, I played along with my family regarding marriage to Naveen. I thought when you arrive in London, we would announce our intentions to both families.'

Rustom admonished her. 'I always told you to tell our parents our intentions. Were you so afraid of your father that you could not face his opposition? Think of the misery we would have avoided if we had told them the truth, got married, and faced the consequences.'

Minoti began to weep brokenly. 'I have gone through these seven years like a somnambulist! Now, tell me what happened to you.'

Minoti listened in anguish as Rustom narrated the events after his return from India in June 1976 to his arrival in London in autumn 1980. When he finished, they sat in silence, their hands clasped together to assure themselves that they were not phantom lovers.

Rome, the City Eternal

Since Minoti's parents were unable to make the journey in a hurry and the whereabouts of Rustom's mother was unknown, both decided to be married in a civil ceremony in London. Minoti telephoned Naveen to tell him of Rustom's return and their wedding day.

'It will be sad without our families present,' Minoti said sadly. She hesitated before asking, 'Will you come, Naveen? You have helped me to endure the bleak years.'

There was a furtive pain in his voice as he said, 'It is not every day that a man gives away his promised bride to another man.'

'Only a man with your honour and nobility could do it,' Minoti said unsteadily. 'I hope destiny will gift you a splendid wife.'

'I hope the dream woman appears soon because I am tired of waiting.'

Naveen flew in to London for the wedding. Minoti met Naveen at Heathrow Airport where she kissed him for the first and last time. In those few moments in his arms, Minoti felt inexplicable pain for the loss of something strangely precious.

The two men met that evening at Goodenough House. Neither discussed the sad tumult of the past, the confusion and the bitterness that had followed. Though Naveen assumed a cheerful air, his eyes told a different tale. Understanding the message with a sapient gaze, Rustom could only admire the nobility of his rival. Naveen saw the courage in his rival that had enchanted Minoti.

On the morning of the austere wedding, Rustom said, 'It is appropriate that you, Naveen, who has been a witness to the dark events in our lives, should be the witness to a happy one.' He paused. 'I doubt if Minoti could have survived without your strength.'

Naveen shook his head. 'The hope of seeing you again kept her going.'

The shared ordeals of the two men who could have been adversaries made them friends.

In the years that followed Naveen began a new life. He tried to banish memories of his unrequited love for Minoti. He married a gentle and sensible woman and together raised a family who brought him happiness. But the springtime spell of Minoti stayed forever in the secret chamber of his heart where no one had access.

Informed of Rustom and Minoti's marriage, King Zahir Shah of Afghanistan invited them to Rome to celebrate the event.

King Zahir Shah's villa at Olgiata, a stylish Roman suburb of Rome, was festooned with flowers and streamers on an amber dusk in 1980. Tables covered by damask lace and chairs twined with vines were laid out in the gardens. Waiters placed candles encased by Murano glasses on the tables. Crystal glasses, and gleaming crockery and silver were laid out in splendour. The master of ceremonies scrutinized the arrangements.

There was a sudden rush of activity as a Fiat 1100 drove up to the ornate gate. Dressed in Afghan costume, Dr Rustom Ferghani stepped out of the car and then helped his Benarasi-sari-clad bride to alight. Both stood for a few moments, gazing at the grand villa, remembering their idyll here seven years ago. During their odyssey of despair, they had never imagined, even less hoped, that they would be standing here as husband and wife.

Members of the royal Afghan retinue now rushed to receive them, bowed and shook their hands. Then they were escorted up the wide marble staircase and through the corridor to the room where King Zahir Shah awaited them.

Seeing them, the king rose from his gilded arm-chair and held out both arms. Rustom bowed deeply before his liege lord and then kissed both his hands. The Afghan king embraced him tightly. 'Welcome back, my son,' he murmured. Then Minoti bent down and touched the royal feet in the Hindu custom. King Zahir Shah touched her head in benediction and said, 'Brave, good girl to have waited for the elusive Rustom!'

They sat together and discussed the events in Afghanistan. The exiled King Zahir Shah had lived in the Via Cassia mansion since his deposition. He had watched the macabre drama in his country; the coup by the PDPA that overthrew and assassinated his cousin, Prince Daoud, the well-intentioned but star-crossed reforms of President Taraki, the brutal excesses of President Amin, and the machinations of the CIA, ISI, Saudi Arabia, and Iranian Islamic fundamentalists that compelled Soviet intervention, and the ensuing civil war between the Soviet-backed socialist government and the American-backed jihadists which was tearing his country apart. He could do nothing; he had been forbidden to return to Afghanistan.

King Zahir informed Rustom: 'Some Western countries asked me to form a government in exile in Italy. But I did not think this a good idea. There is enough in-fighting without a former king adding to the strife.'

'It was not a bad idea,' Rustom replied. 'With you here, heading a government in exile, there would have been a check on the PDPA's excesses. And the people—even the jihadists—would have rallied around you.'

The king shrugged off the idea. 'I was educated in the West and liked the ideas of the 18th-century Enlightenment. Naturally, I hate jihadists.'

'How do you occupy yourself, Your Majesty?' Minoti asked.

The king smiled. 'I while away my time playing golf and chess, tending my beautiful garden and occasionally—to the dismay of my security guards—I amble along to a nearby bookstore, where I purchase books and then go to a café to drink caffe macchiato. Then after I have feasted my eyes on Italian sirens, I return home to read and be chastised by my queen and flattered by my hangers-on.'

Minoti laughed, hearing this account of how the king passed his days.

Rustom addressed his king. 'I learn that the governments of the Soviet Union, India and Afghanistan have tried to persuade Your Majesty to return as chief of a neutral, possibly interim, administration in Kabul. Why did Your Majesty not accept that offer?'

The king shook his head. 'Let the civil war end. I cannot be neutral when my children are fighting each other. I must take sides and that would have to be against the Pakistanis and jihadists.' He sighed and was silent for awhile. Then, rousing himself from sombre thoughts about Afghanistan, he said, 'And now, let us forget the strife in our land for one evening and celebrate your marriage. The guests will be arriving soon. But before that I have to give you a wedding present.' He beckoned to an Afghan retainer and said, 'Please ask Her Majesty and her friend to come and meet Dr and Mrs Ferghani.'

Afghan retainers threw open the gilt doors with a flourish. Queen Hamira entered, wearing an embroidered gown, jewels and a tiara. Rustom stood transfixed, unable to make his obeisance to the queen. Behind her stood a woman whose face he had visualized in the dark prison cell and—believing her to be dead—to whom he had prayed for his salvation. Like a somnambulist he stumbled forward, arms stretched towards his mother.

Embracing her, he whispered hoarsely, 'Maman, tell me I am not dreaming! I have so yearned, so prayed, that I might see you—not in heaven—but in this world!' The thin grey-haired lady touched his head in benediction and wept on his shoulder for lost beloveds and wasted years. Then, he turned to Queen Hamira, and made his belated obeisance.

Brushing aside grief, Madame Ferghani turned to Minoti, standing in bridal splendour. Minoti bent to do *pranam* to Madame Ferghani, who embraced and kissed her. Then Minoti paid her respects to Queen Hamira. King Zahir watched the reunion, deeply moved.

Madame Ferghani told her son how she and her daughter had fled from Herat to Tehran after they heard of General Ferghani's murder. There they stayed for several months until they could flee to England in the hope that Rustom may have escaped and gone to London. Rustom's university colleagues told her that they had no news of him. When her daughter married an Afghan émigré based in France, Madame Ferghani moved to Rome to be with her old friend, Queen Hamira.

Rustom and Minoti listened in anguished silence as the desolation of wasted years blew over them.

Turning to Rustom, King Zahir said, 'The high-powered Italian officials and diplomat guests are arriving shortly. I suggest that you, Dr Ferghani, escort the two majestic ladies downstairs while I come down with the wise bride.'

As the king descended the marble staircase with Minoti, he said, 'My child, do you remember me telling you seven years ago when you came to see me before returning to London, that I have little experience in matters of the heart because we princes marry where we are told to marry. I could not advise you about Rustom.'

'I remember, Your Majesty,' Minoti replied.

'But the wisdom of the heart is another matter. Those who follow it are rewarded as you and Rustom have been.'

There was a hushed silence as the king entered the reception hall. Guests bowed. Then the band broke into strains of the Italian national anthem followed by the Afghan anthem. After that the sound of spurting champagne competed with the melody of Puccini arias. Guests toasted the couple. While some conversed, others danced to the music of Viennese waltzes. Rustom led his bride to the terrace outside from where they could see the jewelled silhouette of St Peter's Basilica.

'There is something eternal and universal about this city,' Rustom murmured. 'It is the only city in the world where Empire and Church, power and faith, cruelty and compassion coexist dramatically. He paused, 'Here, in the citadel of Christianity, you a Hindu and I a Muslim, planned our destinies and dreamt of happiness.'

Minoti nodded. 'Yes, some benign force has brought us here. When tomorrow dawns, we shall begin to reclaim our dreams.'

The Tempest of Time

Rustom and Minoti lived in London for many years, raising their son and daughter. They pursued their academic careers with many plans of the future. Despite the happiness of being together in their comfortable apartment in Bloomsbury, enjoying London's cultural and social life, Rustom longed to see his native land.

They were deeply saddened by the raging civil war in Afghanistan. A grim-faced Rustom read the newspapers, saw scenes of carnage and explosions on television, and told himself he had escaped from hell. Another part of him told him to return to his native land.

In 1983 the Government of Afghanistan, prodded by Russian President Yuri Andropov, signed a truce with the charismatic Northern warlord, Ahmed Shah Masood who was engaging the Soviet and Afghan national army under the command of General Sokolov in the Panjsheer Valley. President Andropov wanted hostilities to end. Ahmed Shah

Masood gave promise of a truce but used the interregnum of peace to train fighters in his domain. When ready they swooped down on the Afghan and Soviet forces.

Meanwhile, the CIA and the Pakistani ISI provided funds to another warlord Gulbuddin Hekmatyar, who became known for his brutality and involvement in drug trafficking. Hekmatyar was closely associated with Osama bin Laden, who founded Al-Qaeda in 1988. Simultaneously the CIA and MI6 continued to back the mujahidin to attack the Soviet and Afghan national army in southern Afghanistan. Some years later the intrepid Masood was assassinated by two Al-Qaeda terrorists, sent by Osama bin Laden.

Rustom followed events in Afghanistan, where Soviet and Afghan leaders tried to defeat the mujahidin through military action. The mujahidin carried out ambushes on Soviet and Afghan troops and supplies. Thousands died in this tragic conflict, on both sides. He frequently thought of Hashim Beg and his family, especially Dilnaar, and wondered if they were safe amidst the maelstrom.

In February 1989 snow lay deep in Kabul and on the mountains ringing the capital when the last of the Soviet army divisions withdrew from Afghanistan. The Soviet troops were jubilant; they were returning home from Afghanistan, a country that their government had tried to bring into a modern age. It was a star-crossed venture. The departure of

Soviet troops did not bring peace; it brought Afghanistan one of its darkest ages.

Watching the retreating armoured vehicles on television, Rustom wondered if the lives of nations were as futile as the lives of men. Or was this the unravelling of another historical drama?

The attack on New York brought US-led NATO forces to Afghanistan in 2001, to fight the very jihadis they had weaponized to fight the Soviet army. History had come round in a violent and tragic circle.

Another civil war was unleashed on the hapless land. This one was between USA's new protégés and their former protégés—the Taliban. The districts which were peaceful and prosperous became scenes of chaos and carnage. As the opposing armies perpetrated violence, the 'war on terror' brought terror only to innocent Afghans.

In 2002, the new government of Afghanistan under President Karzai invited King Zahir Shah to return to Afghanistan, to open the tribal *Loya Jirga* or parliament. Zahir Shah, the last scion of the Durrani dynasty that had unified and ruled Afghanistan from 1747 to 1978, declined to be king and was content to be called Baba or Father of the Nation.

As an Italian military aircraft flew over Afghanistan's frontier, King Zahir Shah looked out of the oval windows to gaze at his native land which he had left 30 years ago. When the plane landed at Kabul's bullet-scarred airport, a long red carpet was rolled across the tarmac. The old king came down the steps and walked slowly, while the new Afghan leaders walked at his side. He stood erect when a military band played to honour and welcome him. Many memories must have assailed him; memories of power, glory, betrayal and pain. Living in Italy, he knew the Roman phrase *sic gloria transit mundi*—so passes the glory of the world.

Rustom and Minoti visited Afghanistan several times with their son and daughter during the years of American occupation. Rustom met old friends and surviving colleagues to explore possibilities of helping his suffering compatriots. He donated large sums of money to various organizations in the hope that those in distress would benefit.

It was during one such visit that Rustom Ferghani was astonished to see a woman walking down the street before the hotel where he stayed. Neither the long blue dress nor blue shawl covering her head could hide the face that had remained in his memory for 30 years. He strode swiftly to her and exclaimed 'Dilnaar! Is it really you?'

The middle-aged woman halted abruptly and looked at him in amazement. It took her some moments to recover. '*Janab* Rustom! Is it you or your ghost?'

Rustom laughed and then seeing the pain in her face, he nodded. 'It is I, your prisoner in Kandahar.'

She paused and asked, 'Have you finally returned to our wretched homeland?'

'I have been coming here now and then. When in Kandahar I enquired about you and your family. I was told you had all left. Are they well and safe?'

'My parents passed away. My brother Afraz joined the American forces and then left in disgust.' She hesitated. 'He is now in the Panjsheer Valley with a group that is preparing to evict the NATO armies.'

Rustom looked around him. 'Be careful what you say. They now rule Afghanistan.'

'Didn't they—Americans and British—always want that? Are they not the people who created the mujahidin to overthrow a socialist government friendly to Russia?'

Rustom looked at Dilnaar with concern. Looking at his anxious face she gave him the merry smile of her girlhood when they shared harmless secrets. '*Janab*, would you be our prisoner again and share bread with us?'

Rustom had an impulse to draw her close and erase her sudued anguish. Instead he said, 'I would be honoured, Dilnaar.'

'Then please come to our humble home this evening. My army officer husband was wounded in battle. He is now a school teacher. He and my children will be delighted to meet you. Afraz and I used to tell them about you—son of General Ferghani, grandson of Iskandar Khan.'

That evening Rustom Ferghani went to Dilnaar's home where the family welcomed him. The husband Karim showed a courteous reserve but the daughters were cheerful like the young Dilnaar. The teenage son scrutinized him before saying, 'I am named Rustom after you, *Janab*.'

Dilnaar blushed and avoided Karim's eyes. Rustom Ferghani was moved. "Your family has been kind to me. This too is an honour.'

As banks in Kabul were not functioning, Rustom Ferghani had previously taken off the heavy gold chain of his father, which he wore around his neck, and his Rolex wrist watch and wrapped them securely in a packet. He addressed it to Dilnaar Khan with a note; 'This may help the education of your children. May you all stay safe.' It was signed 'The Prisoner of Kandahar'. He handed this package to young Rustom, saying 'This is for you and your sisters. Give it to your parents. I'm sure they will find a good use for it.'

Dilnaar and Karim thanked him and they shared a simple meal enlivened by the chatter of the children. After their meal, Karim and Dilnaar told Rustom of the events that bloodied their land.

As the civil war raged into the second decade, bomb blasts and explosions by the Taliban and terrible retaliation by the Western forces tore the country apart. They narrated how British and US Special Operation Forces had murdered thousands of innocent Afghans during the occupation. Even after Afghan citizens surrendered, the Special Operation Forces executed these unarmed people.

Afghan civilians were dragged out and shot at random to instill fear. Bullet holes at floor level indicated that the victims were shot while lying down. Special Forces Death Squads of the UK and US were reported (by British journalists) to have taken the law into their own hands by going on a killing spree. Even after British investigative journalists brough these cold-blooded war crimes to the notice of their government, no enquiries were made. When evidences were brought to their notice, the head of the Special Forces responded that 'men of the Special Forces maintained the highest standards and served with courage and professionalism' and questioned the 'factual accuracy' of the allegations. No member of the Special Forces were questioned or charged. Further, they actively withheld information about the war crimes; enquiries which began were terminated by General Mark Carlton-Smith, former head of the Special Forces, who became head of the British Army—to ensure suppression of all facts.

Karim Khan said, 'We heard that a BBC television group unearthed details after they were given access to leaked documents of the Ministry of Defence, which reveal the truth of the allegations. We Afghans saw the 'Western rule-based order' on display. We deeply rued the day they had collaborated with UK–US backed mujahidin to evict Russians from Afghanistan. The number of Afghans killed during the US–UK occupation was four times more than during the Soviet occupation.' (This report was later screened in BBC's 'Panaroma' programme.)

As with other invaders, the powerful Western armies also left Afghanistan in defeat in 2021—leaving behind a shameful spectacle of chaos and callous ineptitude. Fearing Taliban vendetta, thousands rushed to Kabul airport, trying to board waiting US-NATO aircrafts. Some clung to the flying planes and crashed to their deaths below. Those who had collaborated with US–NATO invading forces were hunted down by the Taliban, while US drones massacred innocent citizens on suspicion they were Taliban sympathisers. Apologies were belatedly offered for 'negative information' and 'collateral damage'. But no one was held responsible for the annihilation of entire Afghan families and their homes. Afghan lives were expendable.

As the Afghan economy crashed, with horrifying food shortages due to crushing sanctions inflicted by democratic nations, children were seen foraging in dustbins for food. They plucked out fungus-encrusted bread and fell ill. Hospitals had no medicine to treat them. The wounded died quietly in hospital corridors. Then winter snow came and buried everything—even grief.

In the midst of this West-induced catastrophe Rustom and Minoti came to Kabul. They were now in their autumnal years. The events in Afghanistan had saddened Rustom beyond words. Not even in the dark days of Hafizullah Amin's rule had he seen such misery and injustice. After hearing of the grim episodes perpetrated by the foreign Special Forces, Rustom no longer wanted to live in the West. It seemed a betrayal of his country and compatriots. He remembered his grandfather Iskandar Khan exulting over Afghan victories over the imperial British army in 1834 and 1841. He wondered 'Are the brutalities of the British Special Forces a bizarre vendetta for their past defeats. Afghanistan was the only nation which halted the imperial progress of the West in Asia. 'And now the West had returned to wreak havoc in the name of democracy.'

USA and other 'civilized' nations of the West inflicted crushing sanctions on Taliban-ruled Afghanistan. The vicims were not the Taliban but the already suffering people of Afghanistan. Rustom and Minoti witnessed the huge humanitarian crisis. Mass starvation stared at the people. Parents told them how they drugged their little children to put them to sleep because the childrens' cries of hunger was unbearable.

Parents openly declared that they were selling little girls and boys (for $200) to affluent people who would feed them. 'You open an Afghan home and will see disaster and desolation,' one Afghan journalist told Rustom and Minoti. 'Our once proud people have no dignity left. Hunger has taken away all hope and pride.'

Minoti and Rustom decided to stay in Kabul and use their financial resources to organize food relief, rebuild hospitals and schools. He brushed aside disquieting thoughts of dealing with the Taliban, whom USA-led NATO forces had not been able to defeat even after 20 years of armed occupation.

Rustom took Minoti to his old office, where on a beautiful spring morning in 1978 the tragedy of Afghanistan had commenced, when tanks rolled over roads and gunfire drowned the twitter of birds. Four decades on, this autumn, the turmoil and suffering had not ceased. Then they went to his once and forever home.

As the Ferghani mansion was now a government office he took permission to visit the place. They went to the room which once had been Rustom's and gazed at the starlit sky, the snow-capped Hindu Kush range, and the flower-filled gardens. Standing together, Rustom said, 'We have all been caught in the tempest of time. Let us hope that eventually peace and order will come to my native land. Until then let us stay here and try to bring that day closer.'

Minoti replied, 'Sometime people have to wait a long time for their dreams and hopes to materialize.' She glanced at Rustom and smiled. 'We waited and found our happiness. So too will your beloved land. A time will come when tempests have calmed, when people are safe and can pursue their dreams.

Rustom nodded, gazing upwards at the dazzling stars. 'Perhaps you and I will see a happy Afghanistan from the legions of splendour above.'

Acknowledgements

I would like to thank those friends—Indian, Afghan, English, Russian, Italian—who have contributed to these two novellas by sharing with me their memories and thoughts.